For nearly a minute neither man spoke

"Whatever's going on between you two is none of my concern," Bolan growled. "Will you help me or not?"

Subaharam nodded and Neshbi began to speak. "I do not know who might want to rekindle the hatred between my people and the government. But we are certain it was started by an outside influence."

"Any idea who that influence might be?" Bolan asked.

"At first I thought it might be your CIA," Neshbi replied. "Now I am uncertain who is behind it, but I think they are trying to threaten the alliance."

"What alliance?" Bolan queried.

"You did not know? The MEK has formed an accord with the Armed Islamic Group."

"For what purpose?" Subaharam demanded.

"What else? The utter destruction of the West."

Don Pendleton's Mack Bolan.

Hellfire Code

A GOLD EAGLE BOOK FROM

W🌐RLDWIDE.

TORONTO • NEW YORK • LONDON
AMSTERDAM • PARIS • SYDNEY • HAMBURG
STOCKHOLM • ATHENS • TOKYO • MILAN
MADRID • WARSAW • BUDAPEST • AUCKLAND

First edition May 2007

ISBN-13: 978-0-373-61517-9
ISBN-10: 0-373-61517-5

Special thanks and acknowledgment to
Jon Guenther for his contribution to this work.

HELLFIRE CODE

Printed in U.S.A.

Goodness without wisdom always accomplishes evil.

—Robert Anson Heinlein

I have no fight with others who walk a like path to mine. But they make my cause inhumane and despicable when they kill without cause. I will hold them responsible for that.

—Mack Bolan

Hellfire Code

PROLOGUE

A torrential downpour had slammed into the six men for the past hour, soaking them to the bone, not to mention reducing visibility to such a point they could hardly make out their target.

Alek Stezhnya had spent the better part of his career in the worst hellholes the world had to offer, but those spots had yet to beat May in Atlanta, Georgia. He wiggled his toes. The pressure squished water into the spaces between his wool socks and leather combat boots. Okay, so his employer paid him enough to stand here drenched, but that still didn't excuse this sorry mess. The sooner he could get out of here and back to the comfort of shelter and warm, dry clothes the better his temperament.

Stezhnya lowered the infrared night-vision device, flipped a switch to kill the power and then handed it to his aide for storage. Fortunately, that particular make of NVD was waterproof. Not that it mattered, since the rain washing across the lenses smeared any hope of a clear image. Stezhnya made a conscious effort not to let it bother him. Instead, he checked his watch.

They could still do this thing by the numbers.

Stezhnya held up two fingers, and the signal was passed along the line of men spread across the rooftop every ten meters. Their target, a three-story apartment complex in one of Atlanta's seedier neighborhoods, stood directly across from them. According to Stezhnya's intelligence, the New Corsican Front, a French Islamic terrorist group operating an underground smuggling operation inside the U.S., kept their human cargo in twin apartments on the top floor. And Stezhnya knew he could trust that intelligence since it had come from the former deputy director of the NSA, Garrett Downing.

Stezhnya lost his position with an elite commando unit in the Russian army following the dissolution of the USSR. He immigrated to the U.S. with relative ease, since his American mother returned a few years prior after her husband succumbed to alcoholism. Downing's connections inside the NSA led him to Stezhnya. When Downing offered him the chance to head up a new elite antiterrorist unit known as the Apparatus, Stezhnya immediately accepted. After many months of training and preparation, the Apparatus had its first assignment.

"Take them down," Downing had ordered. "All of them. Understood?"

Stezhnya understood perfectly. He owed the terrorists payback for the lives of a few men with whom he'd served in Russia, not to mention for the loss of his home. Now a mere fragment of what had once been a glorious nation, the Soviet Union owed some of its demise to terrorism. The KGB had fought nearly every known terrorist organization over the past two decades. Only corruption, misery and death resulted, and now someone had to pay. Terrorist groups like the New Corsican Front seemed the logical choice.

Stezhnya gave the signal as soon as the two minutes elapsed.

One of the men stepped forward and raised a crossbow to his shoulder. He sighted through an IR scope that ran the length of the weapon, then squeezed the trigger. The lightweight grappling hook attached to the crossbow bolt sailed across the opening between his position and the opposing roof. The man waited for a few moments, then yanked up and back on the crossbow at a critical moment. The sudden change in direction caused the rope to loop around a thick, steel ventilation pipe emerging from the rooftop. Eventually it became entangled in the grappling hook. The bowman quickly tied off to a roof stanchion on their end and then nodded "all-clear" to Stezhnya.

Stezhnya pointed at his aide, Lyle Prichard, and a man named Barry Galeton. He gestured for them to begin the perilous journey across the rope to the apartments. They were young, not as experienced as some of the other men in the Apparatus, but Stezhnya couldn't afford to be selective right now. If the trip proved too treacherous, it was better to lose those with less talent than to risk the veterans.

Prichard seemed intense, focused. The lanky black

man swung his legs into position and proceeded across the rope with undaunted enthusiasm. Stezhnya had first met him when Prichard worked as a cop in L.A.

Every man in the Apparatus had been hand-picked by Downing because their profiles matched the kind of men he sought: young, idealistic, impressionable. These were the key traits of revolutionaries. Downing trusted Stezhnya to lead them to victory, and there was no way he'd betray that trust. The Russian knew he would persevere even if it meant his life. They had to succeed simply because they couldn't afford not to. America was under siege, and it was up to the Apparatus to do something about it. Downing would have enough trouble gaining support for his cause, and Stezhnya wanted to make sure the Apparatus was part of the solution, not the problem.

Galeton waited until Prichard was about halfway across before following him. The rope was a twisted-fiber blend with a polymer sheath, rated to one thousand pounds. It would easily have held twice the weight presently testing it.

Once both men were safely across, Stezhnya went next. He crossed the gap with the speed and efficiency of a practiced expert. The pair on point had a perimeter established by the time Stezhnya reached them.

Stezhnya ordered Galeton to take point. They had left one man behind to cover their exit. Once they completed the operation, there wouldn't be time to go back the same way they'd come. That meant a more conventional means of exiting the target area to facilitate rapid extraction, which in this case happened to be the back door. The getaway driver sat waiting in a panel van parked on the next block.

It took less than two minutes for their Italian demo expert, Mick Tufino, to burn through the rooftop door lock with a high-temperature minitorch. The group descended the stairs, now producing the weapons they had stowed in waterproof bags. The old stairwell stunk faintly of urine mixed with industrial cleaners. It was pungent combined with the odors of sweaty men in wet clothes.

They traversed the steps from the rooftop door to the third-floor landing without a sound. Galeton reached the door, waited for Stezhnya's approval to open it and then stepped into the hallway. He tracked both sides with the muzzle of his weapon, a Spectre M-4, and then indicated the rest of the group could follow. At this point, they would split into two teams. Stezhnya would accompany Prichard to one apartment, Galeton and Tufino to the other. The last man on the team, a former Somali peacekeeper named Kofi Jamo, would provide rear guard action if required, and ensure no stragglers escaped. Of course, the idea was to make sure the terrorists never left their apartments.

The two teams took out the flimsy apartment doors with well-placed kicks. Stezhnya tracked the room and quickly realized his eight targets ranged around a large table. The room smelled faintly of spices, a smell that wasn't unfamiliar to Stezhnya. He'd fought and killed enough of this kind in the past to know their culinary preferences. That alone fueled the rage he felt as he and Prichard simultaneously triggered their weapons.

Their enemy never stood a chance.

The Spectre M-4s chattered their messages of death, spraying the hapless targets with 9 mm Parabellum bullets. The sound of autofire was thunderous inside the confines of the small apartment. Plaster dust and woodchips were whipped into the stale air from rounds that went either wide and dug into walls, or ate into furniture. The Spectre M-4s were ingenious inventions, sporting special 50-round capacity magazines that looked like they held the typical thirty rounds. In less than fifteen seconds, Stezhnya and Prichard pumped one hundred rounds of high-velocity ammo into their targets.

They changed out magazines before the last body hit the ground. Blood and smoke commingled with the stench of spent gunpowder. Stezhnya whirled on his heel and headed for the hallway, Prichard in tow. They met with the others outside.

"It's done?" Stezhnya asked Galeton and Tufino.

The pair nodded and Stezhnya grunted with satisfaction.

Jamo took point and started for the stairwell exit when noises attracted their attention. Stezhnya turned and noticed an old woman had entered the hallway from the apartment next to the one he and Prichard had stormed.

"What's all this racket?" the woman demanded. Obviously she was hard of hearing.

Stezhnya turned and continued for the exit, instructing his men to follow and ignore her, but then they heard a shout. Several more of the terrorists emerged from the apartment and toted hardware of various makes.

The Apparatus reacted just as their repetitive training mandated. They fanned out, brought their weapons into play and opened up on the newcomers with sustained bursts. Stezhnya tried to warn them to utilize discretion, but at that range chances were abysmal the old woman wouldn't be hit. Fate wasn't on her side, and a moment later she toppled with the terrorists under the onslaught of automatic weapons fire.

"Damn!" Stezhnya barked at his men. "Damn it to hell, you just killed her for nothing! Now shag your asses! Move!"

There wouldn't be a second chance, because now the hallway was filled with onlookers—some of them big and armed with an array of implements—and murderous intent raged in their faces. Stezhnya continued sounding retreat. Obviously some people in the crowd seemed determined that Stezhnya and his group were not leaving. After all, they had just gunned down a helpless old woman.

"You all brought your shit into the wrong place, whitey!" shouted one hulking black man with a baseball bat.

The man started toward them, and a few exchanged glances among the rest in the crowd was enough evidence for Stezhnya that they weren't going to get out of this easily. The crowd rushed them and as Stezhnya backpedaled for the exit, he roared at his men to retreat. They tried, but the hallway proved too narrow for any type of orderly departure. Tufino and Jamo opted at the same moment to open fire with their weapons, probably more in the desire to drive back the crowd than to kill anyone. It didn't have the desired effect, and even though the team rushed for the exit, they continued a covering barrage that proved lethal.

Stezhnya pushed through the exit door and descended the steps, the ghostly images of more bystanders falling on the firestorm of 9 mm stingers etched into his conscience. He could now hear the shouts of excitement mixed with fear from his men as they quickly followed. It was anything but a calculated retreat, but they managed to reach the back of the small apartment building without further incident and immediately made haste for the waiting van.

Stezhnya reached down and withdrew a tactical radio clipped to his belt. It took him a moment to notice it had stopped raining.

"Alpha One to Bravo Six."

"Bravo Six, sir."

"We're out. Make for your rendezvous point."

"Understood."

Stezhnya replaced the radio and continued along the escape route, his men now in position around him. He couldn't feel anything in his legs. In fact, he couldn't feel much throughout his body. Stezhnya couldn't say he was proud of everything he'd done in life, but he could affirm he'd never engaged in atrocities as a soldier. Tonight had been nothing short of murder. In all likelihood, Garrett Downing would be furious with him. One simple mission and they'd blown it all to shit. Without question, he'd impose some form of punishment.

His men had committed an atrocity, but Stezhnya would be held responsible as their leader.

Yes, there would be hell to pay.

CHAPTER ONE

Mack Bolan breathed deeply, appreciating the fresh, mountain breeze that whistled through a stand of trees. He enjoyed the solitude but was ever watchful for some change in the current climate. He knew blacksuits were patrolling the grounds, perhaps even a couple observing him at that moment. But Bolan rarely let his guard down, no matter how safe the environment. Even here at Stony Man Farm.

Bolan's week-long vacation to Stony Man Farm drew nearer the end, and it had proven his only safe haven. Just about anywhere else in the world he could think of would have been too dangerous. Bolan could hardly expect to enjoy some down time if he had to spend it looking over his shoulder, and the Blue Ridge Mountains of Virginia proved as good a rest spot as any. Sometimes Bolan took only the bare basics in a day pack and headed into the mountains for a couple of days. Those were times where he could reflect on the past, charge his mental batteries before rejoining his War Everlasting.

For the moment, though, Bolan would enjoy his R and R in Virginia. He knew it wouldn't last much longer.

Recent intelligence revealed a group calling itself the New Corsican Front had established an underground for getting French-Islamic terrorists into the country. He didn't have much to go on, but Bolan knew enough to believe the operation existed beyond speculation. Actually, he'd been waiting for additional intelligence, but his contact had missed their rendezvous in Atlanta. The Executioner wouldn't typically have worried about something like that; it might not have meant anything. But the fact ex-NSA analyst Roger Neely hadn't followed standard procedure bothered Bolan. It had never happened before, and he couldn't think of any reason for it to change now.

A pager clipped to his belt signaled it was time for his meeting.

Bolan emerged from the trees and headed for the farmhouse. The Farm had gone through some renovations in the recent past, adding a new dimension to its layout. The addition—simply referred to as the Annex—boasted some of the most advanced electronic surveillance and counterintelligence equipment in the world. The modern subterranean facilities were camouflaged on the surface by a wood chipping mill. Call it pure nostalgia, but Bolan preferred the warm, charming surroundings of the old operations center secreted beneath the farmhouse to those of the modern, sanitary Annex. Meetings in the old War Room seemed cozier and somewhat less impersonal. Able Team and Phoenix Force espoused similar sentiments, so to keep the peace Brognola deferred to majority rule.

The Executioner entered the farmhouse and descended the stairs two at a time. He reached the basement and entered the War Room, expecting to find Brognola, Barbara Price and Aaron "The Bear" Kurtzman waiting. He wasn't disappointed.

"Striker," Brognola said. He got to his feet and shook Bolan's hand. "It's good to see you."

"Likewise, Hal," Bolan said. As they took their seats he added, "I assume you have something for me."

"Indeed." Brognola looked at Price.

Price nodded and then turned to Bolan. "At your request, we started a full inquiry into Roger Neely. You aren't going to like what we found."

"Is he dead?"

"No, he's hiding. Or at least he thinks he is. He's taken up residence in a small apartment in Manila with a native woman."

Bolan's eyebrows rose. "The Philippines? Well, if I didn't have reason to be concerned before, I do now. That doesn't sound at all like the man I know."

"You would think a man with Neely's training and experience could do better than that," Brognola said. "Maybe he wants to be found."

"Or he knows I can find him there and no one else can," Bolan replied.

"We think we might know why he's there," Price continued. "It seems to have everything to do with the New Corsican Front. You said before he was working on getting some more intelligence for you?"

"Yeah," Bolan replied. "Neely got word their underground was smuggling French-Islamists into the country. He was supposed to get back to me with something more solid but he blew the meet. That's why I called you."

"Well, that was the angle we worked from. There's been a buzz in certain circles within the CIA and NSA. In fact, the American intelligence community suspects the NCF is actually a cover for this smuggling operation. You see, officially the NCF exists as a special interest to protest the treatment of French-Arab citizens and American involvement in Muslim countries. They get financial support from a number of sister organizations. They don't deny their actions in saving victims from persecution, particularly if they can make it look as if America is behind its perpetration."

"What you don't hear in the papers is many of the people they've pipelined into America have a history of violence and known affiliations with terrorist groups," Brognola added.

"Fine, so let's assume Neely's telling the truth. The million-dollar question is, why did he run?"

Price nodded at Kurtzman who dimmed the lights and projected a photograph on the screen. "That very distinguished-looking gentleman is Garrett Downing, age sixty-two, born in North Carolina. We think he's the chief reason Neely's hiding."

Bolan did a double take at Price. "You're talking about the Downing who's former deputy director of the NSA?"

"The same."

Bolan knew the name well, as did most anyone involved in covert operations for the U.S. government. Downing had spearheaded most of the projects dealing with electronic surveillance and countersurveillance following establishment of the Department of Homeland Security. His guidance and direction had tipped the scales to America's advantage and put her well ahead of the game in technical sciences to achieve a superior intelligence community. His passion had saved countless lives, and significantly reduced not only the casualties of terrorist attacks in America but the chances of a repeat attack on American soil.

"How does Downing fit into this?" Bolan asked.

"Less than twelve hours ago, we received a report of a slaying of twenty persons in Atlanta," Kurtzman said. "I wouldn't have thought much more of it until our systems flagged it for probability scenarios on various algorithms I use to scan all data throughput."

Bolan nodded. "Neely believed Atlanta was one of the major areas of operation for the NCF."

"What Bear discovered is almost incomprehensible," Brognola said. "Reports are still coming in, but I got wind as soon as it went down and we sent a team to investigate. It fell into the Justice Department's jurisdiction when we discovered automatic weapons were used and thirteen of the victims were of French-Arab descent."

"Looks like maybe someone beat you to the punch on this underground operation, Striker," Price remarked.

Bolan nodded. "So how does Downing fit into this?"

"He's taking credit," Price said.

"Come again?"

"Downing claims the people who executed this operation were a special team of commandos operating under his orders. He also said this was the first official act of what he's calling the Organization for Strategic Initiative."

"Great," Bolan said.

Brognola cleared his throat. "He issued a very heartfelt apology through all the major networks, as well as the press, for the families of the innocent people who died. He said while tragic, the losses were acceptable when we consider the costs of battling terrorists. He promised the next operation would be on a much larger scale, which signals there may be more, and I quote, 'casualties of war' before it's over."

"Sounds like a real lunatic," Kurtzman remarked.

"Hardly," Bolan replied.

"Mack's right," Price agreed. "Downing might sound fanatical but he's not crazy. He views himself as a patriot."

"An idealist," Bolan added. "That makes him more dangerous."

"Whatever his reasons, we obviously can't let him continue," Brognola said, "The President had suggested we use one of the teams to handle it, but I told him since you were here and already pursuing a lead we should ask for your intervention. He agreed."

"Fine," Bolan said with a nod. He looked at Price. "You mentioned Downing was the reason you thought Neely split the States. What's the connection there?"

"Everything we have on Roger Neely says he's a

straight shooter all the way," Price replied. "There's no middle-of-the-road with this guy. His psychological profiles suggest he's fiercely loyal, and his past performance reviews indicate he does everything strictly by the book. For a guy like that to suddenly give it all up and run tells us he's afraid."

"And with good reason," Kurtzman interjected. "Barb, may I?"

Price inclined her head and Kurtzman keyed the projector to project a new photograph. "This man is Peter Hagen, fifty-nine years of age, born in Sarasota, Florida. He's an MIT graduate who served as senior technology officer during Downing's tenure at the NSA. He resigned the same year Downing did, but at the time he was working on a secret project to develop a comprehensive assault platform with Multi-Geo Transversal capabilities.

"MGT is a relatively new concept the U.S. military has only been inclined to pursue over the past six years or so. In essence, the concept is centered on small-scale assault mobility operations, like those conducted by elite military teams or antiterrorist units. Multi-Geo Transversal is actually the shorter version of Multiplied Geographical Transportation Universality."

"Sounds like something out of a science-fiction novel," Bolan said.

Kurtzman chuckled. "Simply put, MGT theory theorizes effective first-strike scenarios by small, specialized teams mobilized through some mechanism capable of traveling by sea, air or land."

"A multiterrain vehicle, then," Bolan said. "Is that all we're talking about here?"

"MGT is a wee bit more than that. A core group of military scientists first toyed with this idea toward the end of the 1990s. The thought was that if they could create a transport with MGT abilities, it would allow them to cross-train smaller units more effectively. This, in turn, would reduce the cost of special operations, and by eliminating the coordination of multiple branches during insertion and extraction operations, secrecy stood severely reduced chances of compromise."

"You see, we think Downing diverted enough funds from government surplus and project remainders to actually come up with a prototype," Price said. "Peter Hagen was the brainchild of the operation at the time, but he's now supposedly working in the civilian sector with a government contractor."

"And guess where he's currently residing?" Brognola asked.

"Atlanta," Bolan said with a nod. "Okay, that's enough evidence for me. What's the plan?"

"We're inserting you as a last minute add-on with the federal task force Justice sent to investigate the slayings down there," Price said. "You're cover will be Matt Cooper, a weapons specialist with the ATF. We have the full credentials ready."

"You should have no trouble fitting in there," Brognola added.

"Right," Bolan agreed. "I'll have to find some way of getting in touch with this Hagen. What do we know about him?"

Price handed him a personal digital assistant and

smiled. "That contains all the information we have on Hagen and Downing."

"It also has the ability to access our mainframe data systems through a cable network or wireless connection," Kurtzman added. "You can even plug it into a phone line and get to us by dial-up."

"Understand, the information on that device is encoded and will only unlock if you place your thumbs simultaneously on the back of it," Price said. "If anyone other than you attempts to access the information or tampers with it in any way, the thing will instantly melt its circuits."

"A little extra fail-safe we added at Hunt's suggestion," Kurtzman said with a grin.

Bolan could believe it. Some of the greatest minds on Earth comprised Kurtzman's technical team. Huntington "Hunt" Wethers, the black former cybernetics professor from Berkeley with a near genius IQ; Carmen Delahunt, former FBI agent turned assistant extraordinaire; Akira Tokaido, a young computer hacker with an intellect as profound as his punk rock attire.

"I'll find this Hagen," Bolan assured them. "What has me more concerned, though, is Neely. I've known Roger quite a number of years now, and he's always been dependable. Something must have really scared him that he would run."

"We believe it's possible Downing found out about Neely's involvement from a mole inside the NSA," Brognola replied. "It's proving it that might be a bit more painful."

"We'll keep an eye on Neely," Price said. "I promise if anything happens we'll let you know right away."

"I just don't want things to go sideways before I can get to him, Barb," the Executioner said. "I'm sure this is his way of calling for help."

Price nodded, and Bolan could see from her expression that she empathized with his concerns. Since he had severed official ties with his government, Stony Man had never interfered with his right to pursue private missions. If anything they had supported him more times than he could recall. He'd tried to return the favor whenever possible. Sure, he could have walked away right now from this thing and chosen to go after Neely instead, but he knew that wouldn't do any good.

Bolan believed Neely was on the run because of Downing. The only way he could clear Neely's name was to get the heart of the issue as soon as possible. Barb and Hal were right. This mission had to start at the source, and the soldier knew if he could get to the source of Downing's operation he could get to Downing. By removing the threat posed by Downing's OSI group and whatever project this Hagen was working on, the threat to Neely would probably go away, as well.

"We've arranged for a commercial flight out of Dulles," Brognola said. "Tonight. I wish we could have sent Jack with you, but he's currently on assignment in Turkey with Phoenix Force."

"Cowboy's arranged to have all your special friends waiting for you in Atlanta," Price said with a knowing wink.

That was good news. John "Cowboy" Kissinger was Stony Man's chief armorer and a first-rate operative. Cowboy had a unique talent for assessing the needs of the

Stony Man crew before they even knew what they needed. Rarely did a weapon jam or fail when serviced under Kissinger's practiced eye and meticulous craftsmanship.

So Garrett Downing was calling out the terrorists. Unfortunately, he'd chosen to ignore the rules of the game and he'd called out the Executioner, as well. Even in war the purposeful taking of innocent lives was unacceptable. Bolan knew that creed well, and he'd lived by it. It had earned him the respect of his comrades and the moniker of Sergeant Mercy. The Executioner would have to teach Garrett Downing this lesson the hard way.

And he planned to hold the first session of class in Atlanta.

CHAPTER TWO

Bolan's flight touched down short of midnight.

Toting only a carry-on with two days' change of clothes, Bolan bypassed baggage claim and headed straight to the underground parking garage where his car waited. Scrutinizing the garage a moment, he retrieved a special key from his pocket and used it to access the trunk. He traded his carry-on for a satchel there and the keys to the door and ignition, then climbed behind the wheel and exited the garage.

A light mist coated the windshield. Bolan maneuvered into the departure lanes with signs pointing the way to Interstate 85. Even at that hour, Hartsfield-Jackson Atlanta International wore its proud distinction as the busiest passenger airport in the world. Bolan took advantage of the logjam to open the satchel and retrieve a leather shoulder holster. At a red light, he slipped into the rigging and retrieved his Beretta 93-R, which had been wrapped in a thick silicon-coated cloth. After loading the Beretta with a 20-round clip of 135-grain Hi-Master rounds, Bolan nestled the pistol in the holster beneath his left arm.

Another ten minutes passed before he reached the highway and headed northeast. According to the dossier provided by Stony Man, Peter Hagen lived in the affluent suburb of Brookhaven. The Executioner wasn't sure what to expect. Hagen might not have a clue about Downing's current whereabouts, or even if Downing had continued to pursue the idea of his multiterrain vehicle.

Kurtzman had managed to pull some very basic schematics from data fragments within an obsolete NSA mainframe. The information proved fascinating and simultaneously puzzling. Bolan had never touted vast technical savvy, but one thing he did understand was the frightening prospect of a vehicle like that. In the hands of personnel trained to utilize it properly, such a dreadnought could prove a formidable opponent he wouldn't be able to neutralize with mere small arms. The schematics alluded to twenty-six-inch homogenous armor, which belied a significant ability to withstand even heavier munitions.

Bolan could believe Downing would have credible reasons to pursue the construction of this vehicle. If Stony Man's intelligence proved correct—and Bolan had learned long ago to trust it—Hagen was the kind of guy who could build it. Still, the lead wasn't as solid as Bolan preferred.

Then again, he had other things to worry about. Like the twin set of headlights quickly moving up on his back end as he slowed to make the exit at Brookhaven. As the vehicle got within a few feet of his rear bumper, the driver switched to his high beams. The Executioner knew that trick, and he closed one eye so as not to be blinded by the bright-white glare in his rearview mirror.

Bolan would have chalked up the whole thing to an impatient motorist had it not been for the second vehicle that raced up the shoulder of the exit ramp into a parallel position. Unfortunately for this crew, the Executioner knew that trick. The driver would get his car just far enough past him and then veer into his path. An untrained driver would jam on the brakes, and the rear vehicle would contact the bumper and spin the target so that it left the ramp and crashed onto the highway below. Then the assailants would finish the job before the driver could recover.

The Executioner beat them to it.

Bolan increased speed, then turned the wheel hard right. The driver of the parallel vehicle stomped on his brakes and went the only place he could without ending up scrap metal below—to his left and directly into the path of his colleague's vehicle. The second driver couldn't stop his car in time and smashed into the swerving car's rear driver's-side door. The car spun as the one that struck it started to fishtail. Force of impact sent the first car skidding through the intersection at the top of the ramp. Its tires struck the sidewalk hard enough to flip the car onto its side. It slid into a telephone pole and ground to a halt.

The second vehicle, a late-model Buick, faired a little better. The driver managed to get it under control and bring it to a stop. For all the good it did him. Bolan was now EVA. He converged on the Buick with his Beretta 93-R in play. The driver saw him approaching and tried to open his door, but the impact had apparently wedged it shut. Three passengers bailed from the vehicle and reached for hardware, but Bolan already had them marked. He thumbed the fire selector switch to 3-shot mode as he targeted the closest enemy gunner and squeezed the trigger. The reports from the Beretta cracked sharply in the damp open air as all three rounds struck the man midtorso. The impact drove him backward into the rear seat.

Bolan grabbed what cover he could behind a metal light pole. The other pair returned fire, as eager to take him out. The Executioner had played the game more often, though, which proved unfortunate for his opposition. He waited for a lull in the fire, then sprinted directly toward the enemy gunners while they reloaded.

When the pair popped into view Bolan saw their eyes register surprise. He was now virtually on top of them. The Executioner squeezed the trigger once more, blowing off the better part of one man's face. The remaining enemy gunman tried to draw a bead on Bolan, but his fumbling move was almost comical. The man's shots went wide of Bolan's left shoulder. The soldier dropped him with two rounds to the chest and a third to the throat. The man's head bobbed to and fro awkwardly before his knees gave out and he collapsed to the ground.

The entire exchange had taken less than a minute, and the driver was just now coming to the realization he wasn't getting out through his door. He slid over to the passenger side and made his exit in time to get disentangled with the toppling corpse of his cohort. He shoved the body aside and managed to get both feet on the ground. He stood and found himself facing the smoking muzzle of the Executioner's pistol.

"Stand still," Bolan ordered him.

He did.

"Who sent you?"

The guy didn't answer at first, but a hard tap on the forehead with the Baretta changed his mind. "I'm n-not sure. We just took some money from this guy who told us to watch for you."

"What guy?"

"Don't know," he replied. He nodded at the dead man lying between their feet. "Eddie took the money. I didn't even get my cut yet."

Bolan never took his ice-blue eyes from the man. He just gazed at him, trying to decide if he was hearing the truth or not. The four men hadn't behaved like professionals. They were obviously just young thugs who had taken some money to rub out a target, and clueless they'd been pitted against a veteran operator. That meant whoever hired them either didn't really know what to expect, or knew exactly what was coming and simply decided not to pass it on to the hired help.

Bolan's eyes flicked once to the upended vehicle, but he saw no movement. He returned his attention to the lone survivor. "Take a message to your boss. Tell him next time he wants a crack at me he'd better send men to do the job, not punks."

"But it's like I said, man—"

"I'm not finished," Bolan cut in. "Even if you don't know who sent you, they'll be in touch to make sure the job got done. Tell them it didn't and then give them my message."

The wailing of sirens in the distance signaled it was time to get moving. Bolan ordered the young hood to his stomach and made him interlock his fingers behind his head. Then he sprinted for his car and sped from the scene. He had absolutely no desire to meet up with the police this early in the game, even if he could explain it away using the ATF credentials supplied by Stony Man. He didn't have that kind of time. He still had business to do with Peter Hagen.

But first he had to make a phone call.

BOLAN FOUND A PHONE BOOTH on a deserted street a few blocks from Peter Hagen's palatial Brookhaven estate. He called a worldwide access number from memory that connected him directly to Harold Brognola. The Stony Man chief answered on the first ring.

"We have a problem," Bolan told him.

"What kind of problem?"

"My cover may be compromised."

"For the love of—" Brognola began, but he ended it with, "How?"

"Not sure. I had a run-in with a couple of wagons crewed by local hoods."

"I take it you mean nonprofessionals," Brognola replied with a sigh.

"Right," Bolan said. "One of them loved life enough

to talk, although he didn't say much. Claims he and his crew were paid by some faceless wonder to make sure I wasn't long for this life."

"You think Downing's on to you?"

"For lack of a better candidate, yeah," Bolan said. "Let's face it. The guy's former NSA, which means he has eyes and ears all over the world."

"That's true."

"And as much as I hate to say it, we know where the leak is if Downing's people are on to me already."

"Neely?" Brognola guessed.

"Right."

"Okay, I'll put Neely under round-the-clock surveillance immediately," Brognola said. "Bear can freeze his assets until we get a better picture on this. At least he won't go anywhere. What about your end?"

"For now, I'll stay on mission," Bolan replied. "If you're right about Downing's plan to build this new MGT transport, we're going to have bigger problems than a few hired punks."

"Agreed. Hagen will definitely be your best source of information."

"He may be my only source."

"Good luck, Striker."

"Thanks. Out, here."

Bolan hung up and returned to his car. The mist had grown into a light rain, and the wet streets reflected the light from overhead lamps. Brookhaven boasted some of the most expensive homes in the area. Bolan had never been to this part of Atlanta, but from where he sat not a single house looked worth less than a half million.

While Hagen's choice to transfer to the corporate sector probably proved more lucrative, it seemed like a pricey neighborhood on a scientist's salary.

Bolan took a moment to study Hagen's dossier in the dim blue-green cast of the handheld's LCD screen. Hagen had studied at MIT followed by a fellowship at CERN and USC, Berkeley. He then took a job with the Defense Advanced Research Projects Agency. His work caught Downing's eye—who at the time had just been appointed to the NSA—and Downing immediately hired him. Through that relationship they produced a number of significant technological advances. Senate investigators at one point accused Downing of shelling funds to unauthorized research, a charge he vehemently denied. Most of the upper echelon in Wonderland forgot it when Downing tendered his resignation. Maybe Hagen had been into Downing's work for the friendship or money, and maybe he'd just done it to elevate his position with the NSA. Bolan didn't really give a damn either way unless Hagen had stepped over the line. That's where the Executioner would draw his.

Bolan started his car and circled the block twice to verify nobody had followed him. He parked half a block from the residence, killed the engine and watched the entrance. Two lights were on, he saw one in a downstairs room and a second upstairs window where the light existed only as a thin seam around the window blinds. Okay, so Hagen was divorced, had no kids, with little social life to speak of, so he was probably home alone. Good, that would make things a bit easier.

Bolan had opted to forego his blacksuit for the operation. First, this was a soft probe. He only wanted to ask Hagen some questions. Second, he would probably get farther dressed in his casual slacks, polo shirt and unmarked black windbreaker than as the Angel of Death. Money or patriotism most likely motivated a man like Hagen over violence and treachery, even if he was in Downing's employ. The guy was a scientist, not a thug.

The soldier reached the door and perfunctorily rang the doorbell. Nearly two minutes passed before a young, petite woman in a traditional maid's uniform opened the door. She was young but quite beautiful— Bolan guessed her at around nineteen or twenty—and appeared to be of Hispanic heritage. Her dark eyes studied Bolan, and although she smiled the Executioner could read just a hint of suspicion behind them.

"Hi," he said, doing his best to be charming.

"Good evening," she replied.

Bolan held up his badge. "My name's Cooper, I'm with the ATF."

"You're with what?"

"Bureau of Alcohol, Tobacco, Firearms and Explosives. Is Dr. Hagen in?"

"Yes, but he has retired for the evening."

"You'll have to wake him," Bolan replied. "It's an urgent matter and I need to ask him some questions."

"It's almost two o'clock in the morning," she protested. "You can't ask me to—"

"Lupe, who is that?" a voice called from what sounded like the top of the stairs.

Bolan prepared for any treachery, but Lupe only directed her voice over her shoulder and replied, "It is the police, Mr. Pete! They wish to talk with you."

"The police?" Bolan could hear the stomping of feet as they descended the steps and, a moment later, a man appeared at the door.

Peter Hagen wasn't as tall as he looked in the pictures, and he'd certainly gained a few pounds since leaving the NSA. In all the photographs Bolan had, the man normally wore large glasses with gold-plated wire frames. Now he stood and squinted at Bolan with unaided eyes. Tufts of gray hair pushed outward in every direction. He was unkempt with one side of his face flushed, and the red eyes were an indication he'd been yanked from a sound sleep by Bolan's intrusion. That, and the crimson bathrobe he'd obviously donned with haste.

"Mister, you'd better have a damn good explanation for waking me up at this hour," Hagen said.

Bolan flashed the badge again. "ATF, and I do. Are you Dr. Peter Hagen?"

"Humph," was the scientist's answer.

"My name is Cooper. I'd like to ask you some questions about work you did at the NSA," Bolan said. "May I come in?"

"I suppose so," Hagen said, opening the door some and stepping aside to allow Bolan to enter. "Lupe, make some coffee, will you? Agent Cooper, would you like anything?"

"No, thanks," Bolan said.

Hagen showed the Executioner into a massive den. The walls were covered with trophies from bowling to golf, not to mention a decent taxonomical collection that included a goat, bear, elk and deer. One wall sported a very old Lee-Enfield rifle that Bolan dated from about a 1946, and twin stainless M1911-A1 trophy pistols mounted on a burnished wooden plaque. The room couldn't have been more sporty and masculine.

"Have a seat," Hagen said, waving toward a leather armchair as he took a seat in a recliner directly across from it. He yawned as he asked, "Now what do you need to know, Agent Cooper? I had a very long day, I'm very tired, and unfortunately for you I'm short on patience for night-owl visits from the Feds."

"As I said, this won't take long," Bolan replied. "You were a lead scientist with the NSA throughout most of the 1990s, is that right?"

"You obviously know the answer to that already. So why ask?"

Okay, so Hagen wanted to be a hard-ass. Bolan couldn't say he blamed the guy in one respect. After all, he'd dragged Hagen out of bed at a late hour and then started off the conversation by asking an obvious question. So now he had an idea of Hagen's personality. The guy was no idiot, and he certainly didn't mince words.

"Fair enough," Bolan replied. "I'll get right to the point."

"Please," Hagen interjected.

"Last night, twenty people were gunned down in an apartment complex in one of the poorest sections of Atlanta," Bolan said.

"I saw it on the news." Hagen yawned again.

"The perpetrators used automatic firearms. Thirteen

of the targets were French Arabs. The other seven were innocent bystanders."

"Again, I saw that on the news. I already know about it."

"Then you also know the man who claimed responsibility for it is Garrett Downing."

"What?"

Bolan scrutinized Hagen's reaction. It was hokey.

"That's preposterous!" Hagen said, jumping to his feet. "I've known Garrett Downing for more than twenty years. He'd never hurt a fly."

"Yes, he would, and you know it," Bolan said, jabbing a finger at Hagen. "Now sit down, Doctor. I'm not finished."

"I think you are," Hagen snapped. "You come in here, wake me up, start accusing a close friend of murdering innocent people, and then—"

The windows of Hagen's den suddenly exploded. Fragments of glass and wood framing shrieked through the room, followed by the reports of automatic weapons fire. Hagen's body danced and twitched under the impact of dozens of rounds. Angry slugs punched through his back and blew large holes up and down his front torso. Flesh and entrails splashed across Bolan's face and shirt before the Executioner hit the floor with a speed that only came with years of experience. Bolan landed and turned to find Peter Hagen's lifeless eyes staring at him.

CHAPTER THREE

A hot, humid gust of wind swept across the nearly barren streets of south Manila.

Late afternoon was the hottest part of the day this time of year, hot enough that not even the monsoon rains had any effect. These were the same times where Warren Levine wondered how he ended up with a thirty-six-month assignment in this godforsaken hellhole. The fact he'd spent the better part of his teenage years here—a bit of an occupational hazard for the child of a widowed Navy father—had apparently left the higher ups with the impression he actually liked the Philippines.

A crazy notion on their part. Almost as crazy as standing on a corner near a market, chain-smoking cigarettes and drinking Gatorade by the bucketfuls. Why he couldn't have simply paid the houseman of his air-conditioned office to keep up this vigil and notify him of any changes he'd never understand. But the call earlier that day had come directly from the deputy director for Foreign Operations.

"What's so important about this Neely anyway, sir?" Levine asked the DDFO after his brief.

"It's not my place to ask why, Warren, and it's not yours, either," was the reply. "I don't like it any more than you, but those are our orders and so we follow them. We can't screw this up. Understand? You keep on this Neely and don't let him out of your sight."

"But, sir, I have a lot of work—"

"Your other duties are rescinded. You just keep this guy under surveillance until you hear otherwise. Got it?"

The next thing Levine heard was a dial tone.

So he'd packed up his stuff, changed into the lightest and most comfortable clothes he had and then set out for the address the DDFO had given him. Six hours later, he was still hanging around and this Neely character hadn't made a move. Levine tried to remain inconspicuous, but after hanging around so long he figured it was about time to hang a sign around his neck and shoot off fireworks.

What he knew about Neely wouldn't have fit written in the palm of his hand. The guy was ex-NSA and "of special interest to certain members on Pennsylvania Avenue." Or at least that's how the DDFO had painted the picture. Okay, so either Neely was dirty or so important that Levine could shirk all of his other ridiculously important tasks to baby-sit. Not to mention he wouldn't fool someone with Neely's training.

The door to Neely's apartment building swung open

and Levine would be damned if it wasn't Roger Neely who stepped into the afternoon sunlight. Levine turned so he could keep the guy in his peripheral vision, but not so as to pretend he had any interest in the man. He counted fifteen seconds before risking a fresh glance in time to see Neely making distance with a vigorous stride.

Levine cursed the insanity of it all. On an almost deserted street this time of day he'd most likely draw Neely's attention if he followed him, and that would blow his cover, as if he really had any to start with. If he lost this guy he'd attract attention from the boss, and that led down a path of career destruction. Of course, maybe unemployment would get him home.

Levine considered this a moment longer but finally opted to pursue his quarry.

ROGER NEELY SPOTTED the observer almost immediately when he stepped out the front door of his Manila apartment. He'd seen the guy earlier, watched him while sitting in the window ledge smoking a cigarette after a two-hour romp with Malaya. The man had Agency written all over him, which of course didn't surprise Neely in the least. Well, as long as he didn't have to face that big bastard with the cold, blue eyes one more time. Especially not now, after he found himself at the mercy of Garrett Downing.

There had been a time when Neely felt good about what he was doing for his country. He didn't know exactly who Matt Cooper worked for—and obviously he knew that wasn't the guy's real name—but he did believe Cooper was on America's side. Neely was on America's side, too, but he couldn't risk Malaya and his baby. How Downing had ever managed to find out about his wife and child, secreted in Manila to protect them from exposure to danger, he couldn't be sure. Then again, what did it matter? Downing had connections everywhere and could get to just about anyone; at least, that's what Neely believed and that's what mattered.

Neely had hoped once he did what Downing asked, the guy would leave him alone. After all, he'd arranged to get Neely secretly out of the country and back to Manila, and to protect him. Of course it didn't seem he was doing a very good job of that now. Once Neely gave him the information on the location of the New Corsican Front's underground headquarters, he figured that would square things.

Apparently not.

Downing's representative, a muscular and intense man with a brush cut and Russian accent, had first made contact. Neely had never met Downing in person and had only spoken to him once by phone. The Russian-American, who Neely later discovered was named Alek Stezhnya, apparently headed "the Apparatus," a group of highly specialized commandos hailing from nearly every continent, and they served to enforce the goals of Downing's Organization of Strategic Initiative. Somehow, Neely had become a full-fledged member of the OSI and he'd never had any interest to start. But the threat against Malaya and Corinne, whether direct or implied, was more than enough to keep Neely interested. He would have joined the AARP if Downing had told him to.

Neely cursed himself for allowing this kind of manipulation. How many times had he been taught not to develop any strong bonds to anyone with whom he'd had a professional affiliation? It made innocent people a target, and the agent a test bench for blackmail. But his love for Malaya and his daughter went well above any of the NSA's regulations, and he would do anything to protect them. Even swear allegiance to a man like Downing.

Neely slowed his pace, listened carefully to ensure the man followed, and then set his eyes upon the goal. He considered this a defining moment since the Russian-American had called to say Downing wanted to meet personally. He had a plan in place, and once he heard what Downing had to say he planned to tell the guy where to get off, then take Malaya and Corinne and beat it out of here.

Neely took comfort in the weight of the 9 mm SIG-Sauer pistol concealed at the small of his back beneath the loose flower-print shirt he wore. His clothing would have seemed absurd most anywhere else, but it fit the part of a gaudy, wide-eyed tourist perfectly. The short haircut would have most pegging him as a career military, probably Navy, on shore leave and looking for a bit of action. And that was exactly what he wanted them to think.

Neely rounded the corner and found the first cab in a group lined along the sidewalk. As the afternoon turned toward evening, people would start leaving the cool interiors and enjoying the ocean breezes that blew off the Pacific. The cabbies waited for them like vultures circling desert carrion, hopeful for an easy fare to the uptown area of Manila crammed with clubs and local watering holes.

Neely leaned through the window and handed the cabdriver a twenty-dollar bill. "This is yours if you agree to leave here now, drive to the downtown area and then circle back."

The cabbie expressed suspicion as he pulled an unlit cigarette from his mouth. "What's the catch?"

"No catch," Neely said. "Another cab might follow you, but don't worry about that. Now I'm out of time, so do it or don't."

"Done," the cabbie said as he snatched the twenty.

While the cabbie started his engine, Neely turned and found shelter in the vestibule of an apartment complex. The follower rounded the corner a moment later as the cab sped from the area. The man obviously figured Neely was in the cab, because he jumped into the back of the next available car and gestured for the driver to follow. Neely watched through the long, narrow window of the apartment building as they pulled away. After about a minute lapsed, Neely stepped onto the street and continued toward the address the Russian-American had given him for the meet.

Neely took personal satisfaction at the thought of surprise on the man's face once he realized he'd been duped.

GARRETT DOWNING SAT with Alek Stezhnya and awaited Neely's arrival. Stezhnya had seemed impatient during the vigil, and Downing couldn't resist a smile. Despite the fact Stezhnya was a professional soldier, his youth and inexperience in some matters made him a bit impetuous. Not that Downing minded all that much. Downing had a special interest in games like chess, where only his intellect and savvy would see him through. He'd excelled at these things at the War College in Bethesda and later in the NSA.

If there was one thing people couldn't have said about Downing, though, it was that he was self-serving. He believed in America—cherished the Constitutional concepts of freedom and security—but he thought enough time had gone by that the government should be doing a better job of protecting the country. Sure, the President and his predecessors had talked up a great game about pursuing the terrorists abroad, not giving them a chance to attack the country once more, but Downing didn't see much accomplishment. If anything, the American taxpayers had shelled out billions of dollars to bring down the dictators and political radicals of the world, and really very little to combat true terrorism.

Well, Downing believed they had reached a point where enough was enough. The people were sick of paying the high price of freedom, and seeing nothing in the results to make it seem as if the investment were paying off. In the next forty-eight hours, Downing planned to change all that.

Downing stood and went to the portable bar of his makeshift office. These weren't ideal surroundings, but it worked for this kind of meeting.

"Would you like a drink?" Downing asked Stezhnya.

"No, sir," Stezhnya replied. "You know I don't drink."

Downing shrugged, poured a double malt Scotch whiskey over rocks and then turned and smiled at Stezhnya as he studied him over the rim of his glass. "That's right. Dulls the senses, clouds the mind, and all that rot. Right?"

Stezhnya's smile looked forced. "Something like that, sir."

"Do you think I'm crazy?"

"Sir?"

"Don't be surly, Alek," Downing said as he took another sip of his drink and returned to his seat. "I asked you if you think I'm crazy."

Stezhnya shrugged. "I suppose some people might think of you as crazy, sir."

"I didn't ask you what other people think, I asked what you think." Downing didn't make it a habit to let people off the hook so easily.

"No, sir. I don't think you're crazy. I think you're eccentric."

"Good," Downing said. He slapped the thigh of one leg crossed over the other and leaned back in the chair. "I'd hate to think you see yourself as working for some crazy. I'm not a nutcase, you know."

"I never thought you were, sir," Stezhnya replied evenly.

Downing considered his glass for a time, and finally said, "I love my country, is all. Perhaps too much. And I'm sorry about the loss of innocent people. Very sorry."

"As am I," Stezhnya interjected in a quiet voice.

"Bah, I don't blame you, Alek," Downing said. "You were responsible for the mission, sure, and it didn't go as planned. Still, you got the job done. That's the important thing. What I am trying to say, and not very well, is I'd trade the lives of a few countrymen over an entire country. Including my own."

Stezhnya nodded and then looked at his watch. "Neely's late."

"He'll be here," Downing said.

A rap at the door caused the Russian-American commando to jump to his feet and reach beneath his jacket. Downing raised a hand to signal he should relax and then gestured toward the door. Stezhnya padded across the room and opened the door a crack, one hand inside his jacket. He opened it a little more to admit a somewhat haggard-looking Roger Neely.

"Ah, Mr. Neely," Downing greeted. He rose from his chair and extended a hand. Neely looked behind him and noted Stezhnya had closed and locked the door before he shook Downing's hand. "We were just talking about you. Please, have a seat."

Neely took the seat Stezhnya had occupied. The Russian chose to stand over his shoulder, a move Downing noticed made Neely nervous. Well, that was fine because he needed Neely's cooperation. Downing hated having to put Neely in a situation like this—forcing him to betray trusts and leak sensitive information—but it was for a much greater cause. Downing would not, of course, have brought any real harm to Neely's family but he couldn't let Neely onto that secret. Downing knew Neely would eventually attempt to escape with his wife and daughter, but he hoped it wouldn't come to that before he'd finished with the man.

"So, we finally meet face-to-face," Downing said with a deep sigh. "What a moment, yes?"

"I'm thrilled to be here for it," Neely said drolly. He cast another suspicious glance over his shoulder.

"You've been a great service to us, Mr. Neely," Downing said. "I do hope we can count on your continued cooperation."

"Do I have a choice?"

"Oh, come now. Your NSA file suggests you're quite the patriot. I'm positive you would want to further show your support if you better understood our mission and goals."

"What I understand is thirteen dead people who should still be alive," Neely said. "Somehow, I don't think much else matters when you go around wasting kids and grandmothers."

Downing shook his head with sadness. "We were just speaking of this. It was not my desire that innocent people suffer. It was an unfortunate accident. But in war we must accept the fact that innocent lives can and often are lost, that casualties are a consequence to both sides, and we must come to terms with that fact."

Neely's smile lacked warmth. "We're not at war, Downing."

"Oh, but we are," Downing replied. He rose and went to the small window overlooking the street below the three-story building. "In fact, we've been at war for some time now. We declared that war when the terrorists chose to attack us on our own soil. Even before that, I'm afraid."

He turned to look at Neely, folded his arms. "You see, we'd been battling terrorism for years. You know the history of our secret societies. Of course, we'd done a good part of it behind the backs of our fellow citizens, but that was only so we could protect them from the horrors of our war. And yet after all this time, how far have we really come? I ask you, Mr. Neely, how much closer are we to victory? So we've overthrown a dictator here and there, kept one or two network cell leaders on the run. But what real benefit has this reaped for us? Nothing.

"Our people continue to live in fear, and we still issue regular high-level alerts for terrorist threats. We scan air and sea alike for any danger, search our people at airports and train stations and bus depots without evidence of wrongdoing. We detain citizens at border checkpoints, thereby restricting freedom of movement. And what I find most detestable is that we permit our government, under the guise of that ridiculous and unconstitutional *Patriot Act,* to impose any sort of order it sees. Washington bureaucrats continue to operate unchallenged and unchecked, Mr. Neely, and good Americans continue to die. So while we do what we think needs to be done to stop terrorism, groups like the New Corsican Front are smuggling in an army of devils right under our very noses. And what do we do about it? Again nothing!"

"And you plan to change that?"

"We've already changed it," Stezhnya barked.

Downing nodded with a smug and satisfactory expression. "Alek is correct. The New Corsican Front lost thirteen of their men in our operation in Atlanta. That's thirteen who won't threaten our country with suicide bombs. Thirteen who won't shoot or blow up any American children tonight. Thirteen who won't hijack any planes or kill any service people in defense of some outdated religious ideology."

Neely's sneered. "That's also seven people who won't watch their sons and daughters graduate high school, or spend Christmas with their families. Seven people who won't kiss their children good-night. Seven people who won't attend church this Sunday. Doesn't sound like much to be proud of."

"So, you're not going to let go of that," Downing said. "I see. That's too bad, Mr. Neely, because I had big plans for you."

"Really."

"Indeed. You're well respected in the intelligence community, with many good connections. You could probably provide me with significant information. At best, you could identify the individual who keeps meddling into these affairs."

"I've already told you, I don't know who he is," Neely protested. "He uses the name Matt Cooper, but it's an alias and not one I can find in any of our systems. He's probably some kind of black ops. We were friends…sort of. But I'm sure by now he knows I betrayed him. Plus, I don't know how much more use I could be to you. Somebody was following me."

Downing could see Stezhnya become immediately alert. "Who followed you?"

"Don't worry," Neely said. He waved it away. "I

made sure to lose him well before I got here. But I don't know who he is. I'm assuming he's either with the NSA or a Company man."

Downing looked at Stezhnya and frowned. "You need to take care of that."

"Yes, sir," Stezhnya replied.

"Now just wait a goddamned minute," Neely cut in. "Don't start going around killing our spooks, or you're going to bring a whole shitload of people down on your operations here, and I'm sure you're anxious to avoid that kind of attention. Besides, this guy isn't important enough to worry about."

"What makes you think so?" Stezhnya asked.

Neely looked at the man and expressed incredulity. "What are you, some sort of ignoramus? If he knew anything about you two, he wouldn't have been assigned to watch me. You go and off the guy, you're just proving to whoever he's working for that there's something to have them concerned. That'll just send a message they need to come down and look at things more closely."

Neely looked at Downing and pleaded, "That's why you should forget about me. I'm no more good to you, because I don't know anything else. I just want to be left alone. If I don't do anything to arouse this guy's suspicions, then that should be enough to throw him off your trail."

Downing studied Neely for nearly a minute, looked for deception. He had to admit Neely was right. Their work sat at a critical juncture, and he didn't want to call unnecessary attention to this area. The Philippines were his central base of operations. He couldn't afford to have soldiers of the same side scrutinizing this part of the country too closely. Up until now he had the luxury of operating in secret, and when he was so close to the goal he needed to maintain the status quo.

"Okay, Mr. Neely, what you say makes sense," Downing said. "For now, you're free to go. But don't make any attempt to contact this man or do anything foolish."

"Fine," Neely replied. As he rose from his chair and headed for the door, he added, "Just try not to kill any more noncombatants. Okay? I don't like being a participant to murder."

Something turned cold in Downing's otherwise impassive expression. "I don't like to brag, Mr. Neely, but we're just getting started. Part of this operation was a way of raising support for the OSI, to be sure, but we've only scratched the surface. Before all is said and done we're going to show the world we take care of our own, and in so doing will send the terrorists a message."

"Oh, yeah?" Neely scoffed. "And what kind of a message is that? Your wanton disregard for human life?"

"Not at all," Downing replied. "We're going to demonstrate what kind of trouble they've bought themselves for threatening the peace and stability of America. In just a short time, we're going to bring hell itself to them."

CHAPTER FOUR

Mack Bolan couldn't be sure if he or Peter Hagen had been the target, although it hardly mattered at this point. Rain and plaster chips rained on him from the fractured ceiling. The soldier choked back a cough. He couldn't allow himself to succumb to the dust-thickened air as long as the threat remained.

Bolan watched bullets dance across a nearby wall. China inside a cedar cabinet burst under their impact. The rounds shattered the glass in the doors and ripped massive gouges in the antique wood. A bullet trail stitched the wall and headed directly for Lupe, who now stood in the entryway of the den and screamed in horror at the sight of Hagen's torn and broken body. Bolan leaped to his feet and threw his body toward Lupe, tackling the maid as a continuous stream of autofire buzzed the air where she'd stood a millisecond earlier. They hit the ground hard and the impact knocked the wind from the woman.

Bolan ordered her to keep her head down, drew and primed the Beretta, then crawled to the front door. He reached up, yanked on the latch-style handle, and opened the door wide enough to crawl onto the porch. The soldier rolled into the L-shaped hedge for cover, then risked a glance over the top.

A dark sedan sat parked at the curb and three men dressed in black stood in a line just outside its open doors. Bolan watched as they ceased firing their Uzi submachine guns and took a moment to reload. The Executioner seized the advantage in the lull. He pushed his body beneath the base of the hedge and came out the opposite side with a perfect field of fire on the enemy. He aligned his sights on the nearest target and squeezed the trigger. The single 9 mm Parabellum round took the man in the face. The impact spun the gunner and slammed him into the open door.

The other pair was still trying to reload while frantically searching for Bolan. One man reached down to grab his deceased comrade and drag him inside the sedan while the second guy fumbled with a fresh magazine. Bolan decided to change tactics, to prevent the enemy's escape. He realigned his pistol sights on the driver's side of the front windshield and pumped two slugs into it. The driver's skull exploded into a gory mess under the Executioner's skilled marksmanship.

Bolan returned his attention to the more immediate threat, which had now identified his position and was swinging an Uzi in his direction. The soldier thumbed the selector switch to 3-shot mode, snap-aimed and squeezed the trigger. The trio of 9 mm stingers struck groin, stomach and chest. The man dropped his weapon and grabbed at his stomach. His body pitched forward a moment later and landed prone on the wet lawn.

The remaining gunner had the body of one of his cohorts halfway inside the sedan when he saw the second man fall. Obviously he realized self-preservation was his only remaining option, so he quickly dived into the front seat and crawled to the driver's side. Bolan climbed to his feet and sprinted toward the sedan as the surviving gunner fought with the deadweight of the body behind the wheel. The engine suddenly roared to life. Tires spun on the slick pavement as the sedan rocketed away from the curb.

Bolan changed direction and headed for his own car. He figured if he played his cards right, the guy would try to return to the safety of his own kind, and that meant he'd lead the Executioner right to the answers.

Bolan jumped behind the wheel, started the engine and gave chase to the fleeing sedan. He didn't know exactly where it would all lead him, but he was desperate for answers. The enemy had been onto him since his arrival in Atlanta, and perhaps even before that. He didn't like the thought that Roger Neely had betrayed him, but there was no other reasonable explanation. Few people outside of Stony Man should have known of any connection between what had happened in Atlanta and Dr. Peter Hagen. The only other people who would have that kind of information were Downing and any people he had on the inside.

What Bolan couldn't help but wonder was if he had been the one to lead them to Hagen. He had made damn sure nobody followed him before he contacted the scientist, but it was possible he could have missed them. And if he hadn't led them to Hagen, then why did they wait until Bolan was there before making the hit? Had they hoped to kill them both and somehow sow a disinformation campaign that would tie things up and leave Downing smelling rosy clean? That didn't make much sense, since Downing had already claimed full responsibility for the operation in that slum neighborhood.

Well, he could figure it out later. For the moment the Executioner knew he had to keep his focus on the mission at hand. He stayed back far enough not to spook his quarry. Bolan had felt uneasy about leaving Lupe behind to contend with the mess there, but he didn't think she was in any further danger. Whoever was behind this hit had probably accomplished what they went there to accomplish: the assassination of Peter Hagen. Bolan wasn't buying the hit team had been there for him. There was something else going on here, something deeper and more insidious.

The sedan left Brookhaven city limits and merged onto the highway, heading toward Atlanta. It was possible the driver had a ruse in mind, but somehow Bolan didn't think so. Unless the hit team had observed him park his vehicle, they wouldn't know he had transportation close by. In all probability, the driver would think he'd gotten away clean. At most, he'd be looking for marked police units that might have a description of his car. That would have him a little paranoid and thus less watchful of civilian vehicles.

They continued along the highway until they entered

the city, and soon the sedan took a north side exit. Bolan continued to follow at a relatively neutral distance. He reached into the bag sitting next to him and pulled out a Fabrique Nationale Herstal FNC compact assault rifle. The FN-FNC was as versatile and dependable as the acclaimed FAL. However it chambered the 5.56 mm round, the most popular high-velocity slug in use by military units around the world. At a cyclic rate of 800 rounds per minute, the weapon had become a trusted ally in Bolan's war and he often included it in his basic mission arsenal.

Bolan was checking the weapon to ensure he was ready for action when the sedan's brake lights caught his attention. The vehicle made a sharp turn onto a side street between a pair of large, abandoned buildings. He noticed they had entered a rundown industrial area, and most of the businesses were either closed or abandoned. It seemed like a strange place to set up shop, but Bolan could see where it might prove the perfect place to hide something—something like an elite hit team.

The Executioner increased speed and prepared for action.

THE SOUND OF TIRES crunching gravel and skidding to a halt brought Lyle Prichard to the steel hopper window of the old warehouse. This whole deal had him a bit jumpy. He hadn't been very keen on the idea of maintaining this ridiculous vigil from the moment Alek Stezhnya had ordered it, and now they had company. He checked his watch and hoped it was Galeton and the crew returning from Hagen's place. They were already an hour overdue.

Prichard looked through the slightly open window to stare at the alleyway below and confirmed it was the sedan. It was about damn time. Now maybe they could get the hell out of here. After their operation in Atlanta, Stezhnya had insisted on returning to headquarters in the Philippines and leaving him in charge to complete their operations. Hagen had remained the one loose end in their business here in the States, and apparently Garrett Downing didn't like loose ends. Assuming Galeton and the crew had done their job, they could now report the mission completed and return to the temporary training grounds south of Milan.

Prichard turned from the window and looked at Mick Tufino. The Italian's feet were propped on a plain, metal table. A half-smoked cigarette dangled from his mouth while he flipped through a *Hustler* magazine.

"They're back," Prichard said.

"That's nice." Tufino grunted.

"For chrissake, put that down and start getting our gear together, Mick," Prichard said. He flipped open his cellular phone with a snap of his wrist. "I'll call the boss and let him know we're ready to extract."

Tufino sent Prichard a flat look before tossing the magazine aside and getting to his feet. He went to the bags stacked nearby and began to inventory their equipment. Two of the bags contained an assorted cache of automatic weapons, including four M-16 A-3 carbines, four MP-5 subguns, and a pair of HK 33Es. Another bag held most of Tufino's demolitions. He'd packed twenty-five, one-pound sticks of C-4 plastique, an equivalent number of detonators, plus some standard GI-issue

M-1 fuse igniters. They hadn't needed any of it for these missions, but Tufino didn't like to be shorthanded and Prichard could appreciate that. It was good to have such supplies in a pinch.

Prichard heard the door on the first floor roll open, and then a set of footsteps rapidly ascend the stairs. He furrowed his eyebrows at that. There should have been four men coming up the steps, and to hear one set of footfalls seemed a bit odd. Maybe the rest had waited in the sedan, but that didn't make much sense. He and Tufino sure as hell weren't going to carry all this equipment down the steps themselves.

A moment later Galeton's head popped into view followed by the rest of his lanky form. The color of his skin was visible from across the room even in the dim light afforded by the two of at least a dozen overhead lights, the only ones actually working. Prichard had never seen Galeton look so ghastly and haggard.

"What—?" Prichard began.

"We've got problems!" Galeton called.

"That's not what I want to hear right now," Prichard said as he looked in Tufino's direction with a measure of panic.

"What kind of problems?" Tufino asked.

"Somebody beat us to Hagen," Galeton replied.

"Okay, so where's the rest of the crew?" Prichard asked.

"Dead," Galeton said.

As Galeton came close Prichard could see his comrade was visibly shaken.

"What?" Tufino rasped.

"I'm serious," Galeton said with a nod. "I think it was that Cooper guy Stezhnya said we should watch for."

"Stezhnya also told us he'd be taken care of," Tufino said, the anger evident in his voice.

"Well, obviously he was wrong," Galeton replied harshly.

Before Prichard could comment further, the sound of another vehicle approaching echoed through the deserted factory building. Prichard spun on his heel and dashed to the window. A plain, unmarked car slowed to a halt behind their rented sedan. Prichard watched a moment longer and saw a lone, tall driver in casual dress exit the vehicle. He held the thin, unmistakable silhouette of an assault weapon tightly against his muscular form.

Prichard stepped from the window and gestured for Tufino to pull weapons from their stash. Galeton tossed the Uzi at Tufino who traded it for one of the MP-5s. Tufino then withdrew a pair of the M-16 A-3s. Prichard yanked the .45-caliber Detonics from his shoulder holster, jacked the slide, then holstered it and took one of the M-16s from Tufino. The three men fanned out, each toward a point of cover that would also facilitate interlocking fields of fire.

According to the intelligence Stezhnya had given them, Cooper was some type of secret operative. They didn't know much more about him than that, and apparently even all of Downing's connections had come up with zilch on the guy. This Cooper apparently had no registered face, no identity, not even a set of fingerprints. Evidence suggested he'd probably engaged in other special operations, but where or when those operations had taken place, and what authority had sanctioned them, remained a mystery.

Prichard only hoped he wasn't a cop. He didn't care for killing cops if there was some way out of it.

"We take him alive if we can," Prichard whispered to the others. "Shoot to wound."

The men grunted their assent, then fell silent to wait.

WHEN BOLAN EXITED the vehicle, he studied the massive sliding door that stood open just wide enough to squeeze through. He then looked up and saw dim lighting through the third-story hopper windows, one of which was ajar, and human shadows on the ceiling that moved with frenetic pace. Obviously the occupants had seen him and were now scrambling to set up an ambush.

The optimal plan at this point was to find another way into the rundown factory. If all else failed, then he'd have to try for a frontal assault, but Bolan wasn't feeling particularly suicidal at the moment.

Bolan sprinted the length of the factory and rounded the far corner. He stopped and looked up to find a fire escape. It was rusted with age but appeared more than adequate to hold his weight. He searched the area and quickly spotted a large garbage bin nearby. He trotted to it, pushed his weight against it and smiled with satisfaction when it gave under a test push. The wheels groaned and squeaked under protest as Bolan shoved it into position beneath the fire escape. He slung his FNC, then leaped nimbly onto the lip of the bin. He jumped up and reached the bottom rung of the fire escape. Muscles tensed as he pulled his weight up through the narrow opening and into a seated position on the grated walkway.

Bolan catfooted up the steps until he reached the third story. He found the door ajar, which didn't surprise him. The building was abandoned, a number of its windows broken. It was little more than a shell that its owners had left to its own fate long ago, which meant nobody would care who entered.

The soldier slipped through the door and crouched. No sounds greeted him, and he wondered for a moment if he'd been duped into a well-laid trap. Then he heard the slightest movement, just a shuffle of feet, and it told him he was close. One of the ambushers was becoming impatient. That was good. It would give Bolan a point of reference; determine the location of his enemy and perhaps their numbers.

The Executioner felt his way through the pitch-black hallway and carefully placed each step. It wouldn't do to let them hear him before he was in a position where he felt he held the advantage. Bolan continued his slow, agonizing journey but eventually the sight of two men crouched behind large wooden crates rewarded him. He couldn't see their faces, but a cursory inspection was enough to tell him neither was the man driving the luxury sedan he'd followed here. The closer gunner was black and the other, swarthy and dark-haired. Bolan made the latter for Greek, maybe Italian. Since neither matched the description of the sedan driver, he knew at least three lay in wait for him.

Bolan stepped from the shadows and leveled his

weapon at the black man. "Don't move," he commanded in an icy tone. The other man started to shift and he added, "Either of you. You're not that fast."

"Looks like you got the drop on us, my friend," the black man said.

"I'm not your friend," Bolan said. He directed his voice toward the general direction of the loft and called, "Whoever else is waiting, you might as well show yourself!"

The hesitant sound of quickened breathing, the creaks in the floor as someone shifted weight on his feet, and the enemy appeared to Bolan's left in a swift and sudden blaze of autofire. It was the sedan driver, and he made a beeline for another piece of cover, tried to flank Bolan with a suppressing volley. The Executioner swung the muzzle of his weapon with practiced ease and held back the trigger on a long burst as he led the target just slightly. The man stepped right into the path of Bolan's fire, and the 5.56 mm slugs ripped an ugly pattern in his chest. He spun from the impact and skidded along the dusty floor.

The other pair seized the attempted distraction of their cohort's sacrifice, but as Bolan had previous alluded, they weren't that fast. The soldier hit the floor, and twin bursts of slugs from the M-16 carbines zinged well over his head. He answered the assault with a blinding one of his own, the slugs hammering away at the targets. The first shots took the black man full-force in the gut and slammed him into the crate he'd been using for cover. Bolan's second burst caught the survivor in the thigh and grazed his right midriff. He shouted in pain, released his weapon and sat back on his haunches as the carbine clattered to the floor.

Bolan crossed the expanse in seconds and kicked the weapon well out of reach. He then moved close enough to see that the man was badly wounded, perhaps fatally if they didn't do something to stop the spurting blood from his leg wound.

"You got a medical kit?" Bolan asked.

The man still seemed in shock as he nodded and pointed in the direction of several large bags. Bolan dug through the weapons and found a large red case that contained bulky field dressings. He moved quickly with the entire pack, knelt at the wounded man's side and expertly stripped one of the dressings and applied it. He then tore a long strip from a roll of gauze wrapping, folded it in two and quickly applied it to the bandage. That accomplished, he tore a second strip and after thumbing rounds from one of the clips for the Beretta, used it to twist the bandage tightly enough to provide a makeshift tourniquet.

"That should hold," Bolan said. He looked into the man's eyes, which were rapidly going dim. A second glance revealed blood seeping to the surface of the thick bandage.

The man looked at him and grimaced with pain. "Maybe not."

They both knew it at that point.

"You know," the guy continued, "we had you figured all wrong, Cooper. They led us to believe you were one of the bad guys. I'm thinking now maybe we were the bad guys."

"Yeah," Bolan replied quietly. "Maybe so."

"You won this round," the guy said, the tone in his voice even weaker. The light began to leave his eyes.

"The innocents killed last night. Your men did it?"

"Yeah," he replied. "But they ain't my men."

"Who gave the orders?" Bolan pressed. "Downing?"

The man seemed to have only enough strength now to nod. He coughed—although to Bolan it seemed more like a ragged exhalation—but then said, "You're a decent man, Cooper. For patching me...up...I mean..."

"Do something decent in return," Bolan said. "Tell me where I can find him. Where can I find Downing?"

Before he died, the guy managed to rasp, "Manila."

CHAPTER FIVE

The Executioner contacted Stony Man once clear of the warehouse in Atlanta.

"I'll need the first bird that can get me to the Philippines," Bolan said.

"You're in luck," Price told him after keying an inquiry into Stony Man's information supernetwork. "There's a flight leaving for Andrews inside of two hours. From there it looks like you might have a pretty long wait. It's been more difficult to get military flights into and out of the Philippines since the loss of our bases there."

"I'd like to get Jack," Bolan said. "Any chance of that?"

"David called less than an hour ago with an update. They should be here by morning."

"You think Jack can cut and run straight for Andrews?"

"I think it'd take an army to hold him back," Price replied.

Bolan would have bet on it. He and Jack Grimaldi, Stony Man's ace pilot, were longtime allies and friends. In fact, Bolan had known the man longer than any other Stony Man operative. Grimaldi, tough and tireless, had taken Bolan out of an incalculable number of scrapes.

"Good. Tell him I'll meet him at our private hangar." The wait in Washington would give Bolan a chance to catch some shuteye. "Is Hal there?"

"No, I finally ordered him to bed."

Bolan grinned. "Now that's an order from you I'd have no trouble following."

"Watch it," Price replied in a soft, teasing voice. "Anyway, what's the news?"

"Very little," Bolan said. "Hagen didn't live long enough to tell me about anything he might have been working on for Downing. In fact, he gave me the whole righteous indignation act. Then Downing's murder crew killed him before I could extract any real information."

"What about this crew?"

"Same ones who did the job on that NCF house," Bolan replied. "I managed to get one of them to talk before he died. I was surprised to find ID on all three of them. I'll send you the names via up-link once I reach the airport."

"We'll be waiting," Price said. "Anything else?"

"Downing's behind this whole deal, no doubt there. But I don't get the feeling he had direct control on this hit team."

"Why not?"

"These guys were professionals, well-trained. Black ops all the way. Definitely a military man headed this crew."

"Well, Downing does have a lot of connections from his NSA days," Price said. "Maybe he's got ex-military training his special teams."

"Possible," Bolan said. "There was something especially familiar about these teams, though. I can't quite put a finger on it. Maybe it'll come to me with time. For now, you can assume I'm going to push this all out."

"What support do you need?"

"Have Cowboy send additional munitions reserves with Jack. In the meantime, I'll try to stay out of trouble."

"You do that," Barbara Price replied.

A LARGE PART of the Filipino population would have said the Ninoy Aquino International Airport stood as the iconic symbol of the country's poor economy. The few who would have disagreed with that view numbered those with questionable standards on what was "clean and modern."

In any case, Bolan wasn't here on a sightseeing tour so it didn't matter to him. The heat and humidity assaulted him like a wet, wool cloak, and Bolan could understand why Grimaldi had chosen to stay behind in the comparatively cool interior of the jet. Not that he didn't deserve the rest. Bolan would have preferred to bring the pilot along for backup, but he figured the guy deserved a respite after the long flight.

Bolan had changed into lighter wear for his arrival, and didn't prompt a second look as he moved past the baggage claim and headed for the exit. He had learned long ago the value of role camouflage. He'd used it since nearly the start of his war with the Mafia. The soldier based it on the concept that careful study of an environment would reveal telltale clues of what others accepted as normal. It was then a simple matter of exploiting those details and appearing just as everyone would expect, thus blending into the setting and attracting as much or as little attention as required. Bolan had effectively applied the technique to penetrate everything from Mob Families to the narcotics underworld, even terrorist groups on occasion.

Bolan left the terminal and stepped onto the sidewalk bordering twin lanes jammed with cars of various makes, models and colors. Noxious fumes spewed from tailpipes throughout the long, covered port that made Bolan want to choke when mixed with the sweltering heat. One of the most popular vehicles in the country was the Jeepney. Bolan hailed a brightly colored one covered with bumper stickers and sporting a red-orange paint finish. It took him nearly a minute of broken conversation before he was satisfied the driver knew where he wanted to go.

As they left the hectic scene, Bolan reflected on the mission ahead. All leads pointed to Manila, and the natural place to start would be the downtown apartment where the CIA surveillance had located Roger Neely. According to official reports, Neely was on a scheduled two-week vacation. Bolan had no reason to think Neely's choice to come here was anything other than it appeared. It didn't seem an unusual choice for a vacation spot, since Neely's career-Navy father had spent a long tour of service here. The woman and child he was reportedly spending time with was another matter entirely. Stony Man's intelligence had dug up very little on the native woman, Malaya, or the mysterious child. Bolan suspected the most obvious: she was Neely's mistress and the little girl was their daughter.

Bolan recalled his conversation with Barbara Price on the trip overseas.

"The apartment is rented in Malaya's name," Price said, "but from everything we can determine she doesn't have a cent to her name. She doesn't work, and she doesn't collect any form of public assistance from the Filipino government."

"So she has no income but somehow she survives," Bolan replied.

"Exactly. I think it's obvious where she gets her money, though."

"Neely."

"Well, we've determined over one-third of his salary is unaccounted for. He doesn't live high off the hog, has only a modest balance in a savings account, and no real investments to speak of outside of his government pension fund. A name search shows he regularly uses a charge card to purchase international traveler's checks, balance paid in full every month without fail. Those check purchases stopped three weeks ago."

"Are the checks traceable?"

"Bear's on it now, but he says it'll take time."

"Well, either his money's going to this woman or he's socking it away for a rainy day."

"If he's on Downing's payroll, taking care of this Malaya might be part of the deal."

"Possibly," Bolan replied. "I'm still skeptical about that."

"Why?"

"Seems to me a man as fanatical about duty and honor as Downing is would probably use this woman more as leverage to keep Neely in line. I've known Roger Neely for some time, and he never struck as me the kind seduced by greed or power. But do something to threaten his family, I think he might cooperate."

"That's assuming a lot," Price replied.

"Like what?"

"Like this Malaya and her kid are Neely's family."

"Okay, maybe they are and maybe they aren't," Bolan said. "Just do me a favor and have Hal get the CIA to back off on the surveillance."

"Sounds like you have a plan."

"In a way," Bolan said. "I'd rather handle it myself. Neely knows me and he trusts me, and right now that may be the only thing going for us. I don't want to spook him."

Yeah, Bolan had Neely figured. The NSA agent was a straight-lace guy all the way according to his performance reviews. Smart, educated and born into a family of old money, Neely joined the NSA as a junior analyst following six years with a U.S. Army Signal unit where he'd specialized in cryptography and domestic intelligence. He met the challenge with acclaimed success, making analyst in an unprecedented three years and senior analyst on the eve of his fortieth birthday.

Downing had some leverage on Neely and he was using it to his maximum benefit.

When they reached Neely's apartment building, Bolan passed the cabbie twenty U.S. dollars and then exited the Jeepney without waiting for change. He pushed through the cheap front door and ascended a flight of rickety wooden steps. They creaked with every footfall, and Bolan figured if Neely hadn't been expecting him he was now. The lack of security held no surprises for the Executioner, especially not in this part of town. There was little crime, mostly because the residents in this section of Manila had little if anything of value to steal.

Bolan located Neely's apartment and knocked. A minute elapsed before he knocked again and waited patiently in silence. He pulled a lock-pick set from his pocket and expertly overcame the cheap door handle. The apartments here didn't even have dead bolts. Bolan opened the door wide enough to slip through, and then quickly swept the apartment only to find it empty.

The Executioner took a position in the darkened recess of a doorway and waited.

ALMOST TWO HOURS ELAPSED in Bolan's vigil before he hit pay dirt. It started with the sound of keys jingling outside the apartment, then the click of the lock. Bolan peered out of his shadowy position to watch as the door handle turned and the door swung inward. He recognized his mark the moment Neely entered, and waited until the door closed before he stepped from the shadows and raised the Beretta. He aligned his sights on the back of Neely's neck as the NSA agent closed the door and locked it.

"Don't move," Bolan ordered. Neely started to turn and Bolan drew back the hammer on the Beretta. "I said 'don't.'"

Neely froze.

Bolan walked over to Neely, pistol unwavering, and quickly frisked him. He found a 9 mm SIG-Sauer pistol tucked in Neely's front pocket and relieved him of it. Bolan then grabbed Neely by the collar and pulled him backward into an overstuffed chair. He studied Neely for a moment, watched his eyes, but saw only surprise there.

"I can see from that look you weren't expecting me," Bolan said.

"Actually I was," Neely replied. "I just didn't think it would be this soon. It took you long enough."

"Don't try it," Bolan said in a clipped fashion.

"Try what?"

"Try to make it sound as if this was all part of your plan. You skip on our meet without so much as getting a message to me. Then you show up in the Philippines, chumming it up with terrorists."

"What terrorists? You mean, Downing?" Neely let out a snort. "That guy's no terrorist."

"I think ordering the wholesale slaughter of innocent people and then calling them 'casualties of war' qualifies him for the title," Bolan replied.

"Downing didn't order any such thing, Cooper," Neely shot back. "His little hit team did all that on their own. It wasn't intentional."

"Doesn't explain why you're running," Bolan said.

"Because Downing's a crazy son of a bitch, and so is Stezhnya."

"Who's Stezhnya?"

"Alek Stezhnya." Neely waved his hand with irritation. "He's some type of gun-for-hire, ex-Russian military I think. The guy creeps me out. Both of them creep me out."

Bolan expressed frostiness. "Most fanatics do."

"They're not fanatics, they're— I don't know…fatalists." Neely paused to take a deep breath. "Look, Cooper, I didn't mean for anyone to get hurt. I'm sick about it."

"So do the right thing and tell me how I can get to Downing and his mercenaries."

"I don't know for sure."

Bolan didn't hide his skepticism.

"Look, I swear I don't," Neely said, throwing up his hands. "I know Downing has a base of operations somewhere south of here."

"How far?"

"Can't be sure, but I'm positive he's operating out there."

"The woman and child living here," Bolan said quickly. "How do you figure in with them?"

"My wife and little girl."

"Why aren't they living with you in the States?"

"Because I had some difficulty with her immigration status," Neely replied in a tone Bolan read as truthful. "It's been hell trying to get her over there since the crackdown on terrorism. Lots of bureaucracy and red tape."

"You shouldn't have trouble given your connections," Bolan challenged.

"I decided not to use them," Neely said. "I was trying to keep it quiet."

"Why?"

Neely gestured in a nondescript fashion. "Because I wanted to avoid Downing finding out about them. Somehow he got on to Malaya and Corinne before I could do anything about it."

"So you came here to make sure they were okay," Bolan finished.

"Yeah," Neely said with a sigh of relief. "I had some vacation time coming and I thought I could beat him to it. First he contacted me and asked for my help. When I turned him down flat, he threatened my family."

"Why you?"

"Who knows, but I'm sure it's because he didn't know who else might have the information he needed. Nobody has intelligence on the terrorists like the NSA. Hell, you probably know that better than most. There were times I figured you knew more than I did and I was just confirming your facts."

"Maybe so," Bolan interjected. "Keep talking."

"Word on the inside is that Downing's horned off a few important people. In NSA-speak that means he's out of any favor with most of our internal bunch, and what few friends he has he either alienated with the Atlanta stunt or just plain murdered."

"Where's your family now?"

"I've moved them, hopefully where Downing and his goons can't get their hands on them."

Bolan shook his head. "Not likely, buddy. They managed to find out about them just like they managed to track you here. That tells me he has eyes and ears in town. The score's zero and two in the other team's favor. He'll find them again. You can't protect them and still do your job."

"What job's that?"

"Helping me get inside Downing's operation here."

"But I don't even know where that is," Neely protested.

"No, but you can contact him and set up a meet," Bolan said. "That's a step closer than I am right now."

"Okay, so you get a step closer. Then what?"

"Leave that to me," Bolan replied, boring through Neely with ice-blue eyes.

"What, are you some kind of one-man army?" Neely asked in a joking tone.

Bolan's smile lacked warmth, and with good reason. "Maybe Downing thinks he's invincible and maybe he thinks he's out of reach from the American government. But he's not out of my reach. Let's leave it there."

"Okay, I'll set up the meet, but then I want out."

"Fine. So let's get back to this deal with your wife and daughter. You've told me the truth?"

"Nothing but, Cooper. On my mother's grave. You have to believe me."

"Maybe I do," Bolan said. "When did you last see Downing?"

"Last evening," he said without hesitation.

That seemed to match up with what Price had told him, so Bolan decided for the moment Neely was shooting straight. He still didn't completely trust the guy, but he could see how it might have gone down like this. The thing he had to do now was get to Downing before any-thing else happened. Simultaneously, he'd have to con-tact Stony Man to see if they could arrange safe passage out of the country for Neely and his family.

Bolan decided to play his wild card.

"You know a scientist by the name of Peter Hagen?"

Neely appeared to search his memory, nodded slowly. "Yeah, I think so. If I remember right, he was some kind of big-wig with the special projects division at the Agency. In fact, now that you mention it, I think he worked under Downing's tenure."

"That's him," Bolan said. "You know of any reason why Downing would want him dead?"

"Not off hand, but I'm sure it has something to do with these big plans he keeps bragging about."

"What big plans?"

"I didn't get details. Downing doesn't like to give out details. He's the kind to hold on to what little pathetic power he has. All I know is what I've told you. Sounds like he has something up his sleeve, something he plans to use to spearhead his operations against the terrorists."

"You don't think he'll stop with the NCF." It wasn't a question.

Neely produced something between a laugh and a snort. "Hell no! Downing's just getting started, my friend. Whatever he's planning, you can be sure it'll be big and spectacular."

Okay, so Downing obviously felt he had what he needed to make a move, which meant he was probably going to act soon. He'd eliminated Hagen—who in all likelihood had produced the technical goods Downing needed—and he thought he probably had Neely under control. Soon, very soon, he'd receive the word that his killing team in the States was no more. That would most likely put him in a rage, and he'd lean on this Alek Stezhnya to act. When Downing broke out whatever he thought was big and spectacular, the Executioner would have something big and spectacular of his own waiting. And he'd shove it right down the enemy's throat.

CHAPTER SIX

Mack Bolan peered through the rangefinder scope mounted to his Heckler & Koch PSG-1 sniper rifle.

Neely had agreed to contact Downing with the excuse he'd changed his mind and was willing to cooperate. Bolan counseled Neely to sweeten the pot by relating he had new information on the mysterious interloper who'd taken down Stezhnya's crew in Atlanta. Downing had seemed hesitant at first, but finally agreed to meet Neely at the same location later that afternoon. The timing was perfect, as Bolan had used the delay to get Neely's family safely out of the country, just as he promised.

"You kept your word, Cooper," Neely had told him. "I owe you, so now I'm going to keep mine."

Bolan could appreciate Neely's sense of duty, and he could also understand why this would have torn the emotional seams of even the strongest men. The soldier had learned the hard way it was suicide to build such ties in his line of work. Bolan had dared to love too much in the past, which caused people to suffer and die. From the very beginning he'd lost many good people, allies and friends alike. He'd learned to distance himself over time. Solitude was a soldier's lot, except when it came to other soldiers who had taken a similar oath.

From his vantage point on the rooftop across the street, Bolan observed a Jeepney cab, this one standard yellow, stop at the curb. Two men climbed out and Bolan checked his watch. Right on time. The Executioner didn't recognize the first man to exit, a dark-haired muscular type, but there was no mistaking the tall, distinguished frame of the man who followed: Garrett Downing.

Bolan put his eye to the scope once more and leaned his shoulder against the rubberized buttplate of the rifle stock. He had no plan at this point to gun down his enemy. Downing's death wouldn't necessarily secure an end to OSI's plans. Downing was too smart for that. He'd have a backup scenario in the works. His time in the NSA would have taught Downing to prepare alternatives. The guy was a tried-and-true strategist whose background would have taught him to prepare more than one battle plan.

Bolan watched as an unmarked sedan bearing four men parked at the curb behind the Jeepney. Then four men exited the vehicle, he pegged them as a security team when they fanned out to surround Downing. The Executioner hadn't planned for an encounter here and now, but the civilian traffic was light.

The soldier watched through the scope as Neely's

cab arrived and the NSA agent stepped onto the sidewalk. Neely waved to Downing, the prearranged signal that all could proceed as planned.

Bolan sighted carefully on Neely's chest. The first chambered round was a subsonic cartridge the Executioner had modified to yield half the normal impact. He took a breath, let half out. His finger wrapped around the trigger, the pad resting naturally against its curvature, and gave a steady squeeze. Neely's chest exploded in a crimson spray that washed over Downing and his escort.

Bolan sighted next on one of the security men. He squeezed the trigger again and this time a high-velocity 7.62 mm bullet traveled to the target in milliseconds. The man's head burst open like a melon under a sledgehammer, and his corpse slammed against the adobe facade of the building. Pandemonium erupted as Bolan sighted on a third target to deliver a similar fate.

The Executioner swung the scope toward the front door and watched as the escort pushed Downing through the doorway. Bolan sighted on the target, and through the scope magnification he noticed the man matched Neely's description of Alek Stezhnya. Bolan squeezed off a shot, but the man moved inside at the last moment and evaded the deadly projectile intended for his chest.

The other pair on the security team grabbed cover and wildly searched the area around them, apparently oblivious to the fact the assault had come from above. Bolan left the scope and yanked on the PSG-1 to pull it from view. Quickly and efficiently, he folded the mounted bipod against the weapon, took to his feet and headed for the rooftop entrance.

Bolan descended the stairs two at a time, careful to keep the rifle balanced as he moved. He'd arranged the entire operation with Neely, and he could only hope the ruse worked. The fact Neely had kept his word confirmed Bolan's intuition the guy was on the side of his country.

Downing would know it was a setup, but that didn't much matter now since he thought Neely was dead. He'd have to go to revert to his backup plan, and that would reduce his options. Bolan had wrenched the offensive from Downing. That would leave the guy feeling cornered and thereby more prone to mistakes.

And that was exactly where Bolan wanted him.

GARRETT DOWNING STRUGGLED to get his shaking hands under control.

When the shooting started, the rented Jeepney cab that had delivered them—driven by one of his men and not a local—tore from the scene and circled the block. Stezhnya had already put an evacuation plan in the works for just such an event. The Russian-American's quick thinking had saved their lives, and Downing wasn't sure it was a debt he could repay. Not that Stezhnya would have bothered to mention it.

Stezhnya guided him into the back seat of the Jeepney. He turned to scan the rear and verify nobody followed, then stepped in and slammed the door shut. He ordered the driver to get them out of there, and then turned his attention to Downing.

"Are you all right, sir?"

"Thanks to you," Downing replied.

If Stezhnya noticed the unchecked admiration in Downing's voice, he made no sign of it.

"How did you know?" Downing asked.

"I understand men like Neely, sir," Stezhnya said with a shrug. "They're not to be trusted. I didn't trust him from the beginning."

Downing nodded. "You told me. Several times as I recall. I should have listened to you."

"Looks like whoever he sold us out to had their own agenda."

"You think Neely's dead?"

It was hard to judge whether the upturned corner of Stezhnya's mouth was a half grin or a sneer until he said, "Seeing as we're both covered in his blood, and what our own men suffered, it would be hard to convince me he's anything but, sir." After a pause, he said, "What do you want to do now?"

Downing didn't want to admit it, but he hadn't thought of anything else up to that point. He couldn't believe Neely had betrayed them, although he'd lined up a set of alternatives for each phase of the operation. With Neely dead, Downing would have to rely on his secondary sources of information inside the NSA and other U.S. intelligence networks. Sometimes that information was untimely, or even tended to be inaccurate if current.

"To be honest, I had a backup plan for just such an eventuality, but I didn't honestly think we'd have to use it," Downing finally replied.

"I take it that means you want me to recall my men from the United States?"

Downing nodded. "All units go on the alert immediately. You'll leave with your in-country team at dawn."

"Understood. And what about this new threat?"

"You're the tactical expert, here. What do you propose we do about them, or…him, perhaps?"

"You think it's Cooper behind the attack."

"What other explanation do we have for Neely getting killed? Grant you, Neely wasn't that bright, but he would have considered Cooper an ally. Maybe he trusted him to protect his family. We knew they were trading information about the New Corsican Front before we even approached Neely about him."

"Who do you think this Cooper really is?"

Downing sighed and didn't reply for a time. "If I don't miss my guess, I'd say he's some type of covert operations specialist, possibly even military or ex-military. It seems odd, however, that he operates with significant impunity."

Stezhnya appeared to give Downing's statement some thought, but before he could conjure a reply his cell phone rang.

"Yeah?" He paused to listen, then, "What? What did you just say?" Another long pause. "No, I understand. Thank you for the report. Keep all channels open in case there's been a mistake. And by the way, put units three and four on alert."

Stezhnya slowly closed the cover to his phone. When he turned to face Downing, his complexion had paled. "The team in the States is dead. Dead! I swear to you, sir, this Cooper is now the sworn enemy of the Apparatus. I vow to you this night, before this operation is complete I will dangle his head on a pole for the entire world to see!"

"I don't doubt it, Alek," Downing said quietly.

Downing saw the murderous hate in Stezhnya's eyes. Under normal circumstances he would have counseled Stezhnya to not let anger and his taste for revenge become an obsession, but he knew it wouldn't do any good. The man had a right to be angry. Part of it was stupid pride—Downing knew the pride because he'd dealt with many soldiers like Stezhnya before—but another part was justified rage. To have lectured the man now would serve no purpose but to fuel his anger.

Instead he said simply, "Every man must do what he thinks is just. But be aware that I don't want anything to distract you. The mission must come first. Then you may seek whatever retribution you feel is fitting for Cooper. Is that understood?"

"Yes, sir," Stezhnya said, his voice barely audible through clenched teeth. "Perfectly. But I wish to go on record by saying I think the mission could suffer if we don't eliminate this Cooper as soon as possible."

Stezhnya knew Downing wouldn't be able to ignore the statement.

"What makes you think so?"

Stezhnya turned some in the seat to face Downing. "Let's examine this man closely for a moment. Since we executed our initial operation against the French-Arabs, Cooper has been one step behind us. That team of thugs you hired initially to throw him off the trail did anything but. He knew about Hagen, and he had enough savvy to track my men to the warehouse in Atlanta."

"So what?"

"You say that as if it's unimportant," Stezhnya said. "This man took down that gang, and the hit team we sent to Hagen's, to speak nothing of his assault against my men. Those the were the finest trained men in the Apparatus. They were the best, sir.

"Now he's found his way here and most probably he masterminded the attack on us and the assassination of Neely. Obviously, this man operates without discretion or restraint, and it seems he would have the sanction to operate with impunity where the American government is concerned. Do you honestly believe this man will stop now?"

Downing was silent for a time, and then said, "Most probably not. And I am no longer sure what to believe. Very well, Alek, I will leave it to your discretion as to how and when to deal with this man. But I meant what I said about no compromises to our mission."

Stezhnya nodded and sat back, obviously satisfied with Downing's answer. "Do you think the prototype will be ready in time for our operation in Tehran?"

It was Downing's turn to express gravity. "If it isn't, Alek, heads will roll."

NONE OF THE MEN who survived Bolan's assault stood by and risked apprehension.

Neely played his part to perfection. He lay in the pool of "blood" that formed around his body, utterly still until the ambulance came and hauled him away. Bolan remained hidden in a gloomy, dank basement restroom of the building across the street until Grimaldi arrived at the specified time with a rental car. He dropped his large briefcase, which had held the street clothes he'd exchanged with his disassembled rifle and blacksuit, into the back seat.

"Going my way, sailor?" Grimaldi cracked as Bolan got into the car.

"Aren't I usually?"

"Looks like Hal pulled out all the stops on this one," Grimaldi replied, looking back at the morbid scene as he steered the car into traffic.

"You nailed it," Bolan said. "The Man wants this resolved quick."

"Good thing you're in that business."

"Yeah." Bolan checked the sideview mirror for tails.

"I think we're clean," Grimaldi said.

"Probably, but I don't want to take chances."

"Still got some doubts about Neely, eh?"

"I'm not sure what to make of him," Bolan said. "My gut tells me he's trustworthy."

"But?"

Bolan shook his head. "I don't know. There's just something rotten about this whole thing."

"Well, you said before the purpose here was to send Downing a message," Grimaldi replied with a shrug. "Make him jumpy. Based on what I just saw back there I'd say you succeeded."

"Let's hope so. For now, they think Neely's dead and they're probably aware I took down the last of Stezhnya's team in Atlanta. That should be enough to send them over the edge."

"You really think this plan will work?"

"It better," Bolan said. "I don't think either Downing or Stezhnya is the type to let sleeping dogs lie. There's too much at stake for them now. They know I'll keep coming after them until they take me out of the picture."

"And if they don't?"

"They will," Bolan said in a way that left no room for argument. "They won't be able to help themselves. It'll be like bringing the bear to the honey."

"More like lambs to the slaughter," Grimaldi said with a smile.

BOLAN WATCHED from the window of Neely's apartment as two customized SUVs came to a stop in front of the dilapidated building and disgorged a well-armed band of hardmen. They moved like Downing's security force from earlier that day, but this time they wore jungle fatigues and toted full-auto assault rifles.

It left no question as to their intent.

Bolan waited until the welcoming party disappeared inside the front door, then crossed to the rickety bed. He'd donned his blacksuit in anticipation of the enemy's arrival. The Desert Eagle hung at his side in military webbing, and grenades and other ordnance dangled from the shoulder straps of his web belt.

After Grimaldi dropped Bolan at the apartment, he'd headed to pick up Roger Neely from the morgue and escort him safely to the airport. Two NSA agents would then accompany Neely on the flight back to Washington. Brognola had told Bolan because Neely cooperated it was unlikely he'd face formal charges, although he was through with the NSA. Bolan had silently wished him well.

Bolan finished securing equipment for his combat ensemble, checked the action on his FNC, and then moved toward the door to greet the newcomers. There wasn't any turning back this time. The numbers were running down and he knew from this point forward it was going to get hairy.

The Executioner stepped through the doorway, mind and body as one.

CHAPTER SEVEN

Bolan met the first wave of gunners as they approached his position on the third-floor landing. He raised the FNC and stroked the trigger, the reports of autofire reverberating in the confines of the narrow stairwell as a volley of 5.56 mm NATO rounds headed straight for a collision course with human flesh.

Chest shots slammed the first man into a wall, and a second gunman tumbled into a third. The remaining part of the stairway crew ducked out of sight, obviously unprepared for a full-frontal assault by their enemy, but equally not prepared to die just because they bunched up in the fire zone.

Bolan gave them no quarter, triggering his weapon repeatedly in short controlled bursts to maintain his advantage. If all went as planned, he'd keep them on the defensive. The Executioner ceased firing long enough to yank a Diehl DM-51 grenade from his webbing. He primed the grenade, its antipersonnel sleeve in place, and tossed the bomb with practiced ease. It bounced off two steps before reaching the mid-landing. The crew behind cover produced shouts of surprise just a moment before the grenade exploded.

Bolan hadn't waited to view the results; he knew what the bomb could do. He bounded up the steps, heading for the top floor. He wanted to take out most of them now, but a survivor or two was part of his plan. Bolan grinned at the idea he'd pegged Downing and Stezhnya perfectly. Yeah, these were definitely not the types to let it go easily. The festivities earlier that day had embarrassed them, at best, and they couldn't lose face. It would undermine their leadership in the eyes of subordinates. Men wouldn't fight for leaders they didn't trust.

The Executioner reached the fourth-floor landing and stepped into the hallway. He knew from the initial encounter that his enemy had split into two groups. Bolan counted on the fact the second crew would attempt to cover the rear entrance via the back stairs. They appeared as if on schedule.

Bolan knelt, raised the stock of the FNC to his shoulder and squeezed off a short burst. The first gunner's head exploded as a pair of high-velocity slugs blew holes through his face. By sheer luck, the man's comrades managed to evade the soldier's fusillade by taking cover behind the door frame. Bolan didn't step off the assault. He triggered a few more bursts to keep the enemy pinned down. He needed them on the defensive while he whittled at their numbers.

Two of the survivors burst from cover and charged

up the hallway—one hugging each wall—their weapons blazing full-auto. Bolan let them burn away most of their ammo before risking exposure and triggering his own weapon. He heard the bullets buzz past his ears, and his nostrils burned from the spent gunpowder and cordite. Smoke began to the fill the hallway, a lung-searing combination of the gases being emitted from the concert of various weapons.

Bolan steeled his mind against the threat of instant death from the jacketed steel burning the air around him and concentrated on the approaching enemy. He held back the trigger on the FNC and watched as the first of the pair fell under a burst of deadly 5.56 mm stingers. The man continued forward even after his midsection exploded in a reddish geyser, and he struck the hardwood floor chin-first and continued in motion another few feet.

The second man was determined not let the death of his comrade distract him, but he couldn't help himself and he let his eyes turn in that direction of the fall. Bolan used the moment to prop himself on an elbow, the muzzle of the FNC canted upward about thirty degrees. He stroked the trigger once more and confirmed the kill as the rounds drilled through the bottom of the enemy gunman's chin and blew off the top of his skull.

Bolan next turned his attention to the sound of scrambling at the far end of the hallway. He saw shadows fall on the wall, cast by those obviously in a mad rush to leave, and then heard the footfalls descending on steps. Bolan jumped to his feet, quickly frisked the deceased in the hallway for identification. Finding none, he set off in pursuit of the fleeing crew.

The smart thing would have been for them to get to a position on the lower ground and wait to ambush Bolan. Unfortunately, someone had called a tactical retreat, and the Executioner planned to make full use of the blunder. Once he emerged through the door leading from the hall and a second that opened onto the landing of the rear staircase, he paused to listen. He could barely make out the sounds of boots on wood as they stomped down a flight of steps somewhere below.

Bolan began his own descent as he ejected a magazine from the FNC and inserted a fresh one. He pushed through the rickety screen door and rushed into the alleyway behind the apartment building. A look in both directions soon revealed his quarry. Three men were rushing down the alley for the street out front, where they had parked their vehicles. Bolan had his own car waiting.

The crew didn't appear to notice the Executioner sprint in their direction as they piled into one of the waiting SUVs, which they had left manned by a driver. The SUV engine roared to life and then lurched from the curb, the tires emitting a squeal of protest. Radials against hot pavement left a cloud of bluish smoke and the acrid scent of burned rubber in the air as Bolan emerged onto the street.

Several drivers who had already locked their brakes to avoid hitting the SUV that had veered directly in their path now leaned on horns and cursed Bolan for causing a similar ruckus. The soldier ignored them as he leaped behind the wheel of his rented Jeepney and brought the engine to life. He exercised a bit more discretion, waiting precious seconds for a break in traffic before giving chase.

The soldier weaved around vehicles trying to catch a glimpse of the SUV over the roofs of the vehicles separating him from his quarry. For a heartbeat or two he thought he'd lost it, but then he spotted the SUV as it made a sharp right turn at an intersection fifty yards ahead. Bolan took the same turn, and thanked his good fortune to note only one vehicle separated him from the runners.

Bolan recanted the thoughts of "fortune" when he saw one of the men lean from a rear passenger window of the SUV to level a machine pistol in his general direction. The guy squeezed off a number of short volleys. His attempts to hit Bolan were less than effective. In fact, some of the rounds came dangerously close to striking the sedan caught between them. Bolan watched the oncoming lane, hopeful he could catch a break in traffic, but he saw nothing but a seemingly endless line of cars. They approached an intersection and Bolan knew he had one chance.

To pass a smaller, more maneuverable vehicle like the sedan on the right was tantamount to suicide—not to mention the risk of striking a vehicle stopped at the cross street, but the signal had just turned yellow and the driver of the sedan had decided to stop. He was obviously oblivious to the fact the SUV's pursuer was on his tail. The light turned red at the moment the sedan reached a full stop, and Bolan tromped the accelerator and swerved to the right. The Jeepney fishtailed, but the big American kept it under control, knuckles white from the grip but shoulders and body loose. Years of experience had taught Bolan that stiffening the body against centrifugal forces reduced controllability of any vehicle, especially one as large as the Jeepney moving at better than fifty-five miles an hour.

Bolan could see the flash of sunlight on metal in his peripheral vision as he blasted through the intersection. He escaped a collision, assaulted only by an angry horn and screeching brakes. Bolan wiped the sweat from his forehead. The Jeepney didn't have air-conditioning, and he couldn't risk taking one hand from the wheel to crank down the window. What kind of rental didn't come equipped with AC in a climate like the Philippines was nothing short of mind-boggling.

The chase continued along the road, and within five minutes they had left the city limits of Manila. The road remained pavement here, although it was rough and narrow in comparison to its condition within the city. That came as no surprise to Bolan. Considering the economy, there was little incentive for the government to invest in major repairs on the less-traveled routes. A few times, Bolan hit ruts that showed through the shimmering heat too quickly to avoid.

He gritted his teeth with each bone-jarring impact.

"SAY THAT AGAIN," Alek Stezhnya demanded into the field phone. He couldn't believe what the man on the other end said, even though he'd asked him to repeat it. "No, don't tell them to do a goddamn thing. Just tell them to get back here. We'll be ready for them."

Stezhnya hung up the phone and looked at Downing with an incredulous expression.

"What is it?" Downing asked.

"Our strike team failed," Stezhnya replied.

"Which one?"

"Both of them," Stezhnya said, already in motion and headed for the special weapons cached in a storage locker adjacent to Downing's office.

The Russian-American commando emerged a minute later with an M-16 A-3 carbine, a Daewoo K-3 machine gun and a passel of belted ammunition for the K-3. He looked at Downing as he unfolded the bipod of the K-3 and set it on a long, wooden table nearby.

"Why are you staring at me?"

"I thought I was clear with you earlier. We have a mission to accomplish, and I need you leading it. I already told you that I wasn't going to let this Cooper interfere with our plans. You can't abandon this mission to go participate in some ritualistic hunt due to a misguided personal vendetta."

"I won't need to hunt him, sir," Stezhnya said. He did nothing to hide the death's-head grin. "He's on his way here. And this is not a personal vendetta. No disrespect intended, sir, but it seems you haven't considered another possibility."

Downing's eyebrows rose. "And that is?"

"That the mission is in jeopardy as long as this man lives," Stezhnya said as he stuffed the cargo pockets of his jungle fatigues with spare magazines for the carbine. "Not only has he proved himself a formidable enemy, but he has demonstrated a tenacity unlike any man I've ever faced. And so I've concluded that he'll keep coming and keep coming until either he's destroyed us or we've destroyed him. I would much rather meet him on familiar territory, and on my terms."

"So what I hear you proposing is that he won't quit until one of us finishes it."

"It would seem so," Stezhnya said as he loaded the last of his equipment. "Maybe you see it another way, sir. And now would be the time to say something if you do. Otherwise, I need to prepare for his arrival."

Downing appeared to give it careful consideration, although Stezhnya already knew the man didn't have any choice. It was plain and simple fact. Cooper wouldn't relent until they killed him. They wouldn't be able to conduct effective operations if they had to keep looking over their shoulder every five minutes. They didn't need that kind of distraction, and Downing knew it as well as Stezhnya.

"Very well, Alek," Downing said. "Deal with this man as you see fit, but make sure this time we get the job done right. We can't afford any more delays."

"Yes, sir," Stezhnya replied with a nod. "Are you armed, sir?"

Downing shook his head. Sterhnya reached to his side and withdrew the Hungarian-made PA-63. Chambered for the 9 mm Makarov cartridge, the PA-63 was a modern version of the Type 64M pistol commonly seen throughout Russia during the cold war. Downing snatched the pistol out of the air with the reflexes of a man half his age.

"How close is he?" Downing asked.

"Very close," Stezhnya replied. He adjusted the Daewoo K-3 for comfort and headed for the door.

"Good luck," Downing called.

Stezhnya stopped to look at him. "It's Cooper who'll need that, sir."

MACK BOLAN STRUGGLED to see against the dust churned from the wheels of the enemy vehicle.

The chase had long since left behind anything resembling the civilized, modern world and proceeded along the crude, rut-covered road on which they now traveled. Bolan wondered if the term "road" was actually appropriate. He didn't personally consider the thing much more than an earth-packed trail, and while the Jeepney he'd rented was tough, it wasn't nearly as adequate for handling this terrain with quite the same efficiency as the SUV he chased.

Nonetheless, the soldier had known this was a possibility and now he had to deal with whatever might come. As they moved deeper into jungle terrain, the greenery and foliage formed a canopy overhead and darkened the area considerably. Bolan slowed enough to improve reaction time, but still maintained a speed that allowed him to keep his enemy in sight.

They wouldn't get away this time.

The road suddenly straightened after a few twists and turns, and in a heartbeat the Executioner realized that escape was hardly their plan. The packed, red-mud earth ahead suddenly erupted in a geyser of dust and clay chunks, and bullets began to zing off the Jeepney's body. Bolan had figured driving straight into an ambush was a possibility, and he was ready for it, reaching into the center console and closing his fist around a metal handle. He kept one hand on the device, the other wrapped around the steering wheel, his eyes watching the road for just the opportune moment.

Bolan saw that moment looming toward him. Instead of slowing, he increased speed and then twisted the handle and pushed down. Grabbing the satchel in the seat next to him, he kicked open the door and dived out of the vehicle. He hit the road hard but rolled through the impact and came to his feet unharmed. Bolan didn't wait to witness the effects of his moving bomb, but he could certainly hear them. As he dropped into the foliage off the road, he turned in time to see the after-effects of the crunching and crashing noises. The Jeepney nailed a guard shack constructed from weak materials—apparently it had only been designed to provide shelter from the rain—and plowed through before penetrating the wall of a much larger and substantial building.

Bolan ducked his head just a moment before the Jeepney exploded with enough force to rattle his teeth. Shouts of anguish replaced the dying echoes of the explosion, and a few men emerged from the building completely engulfed in flames. Other men rushed to aid of the human torches, while others rushed toward the building with garden hoses to attempt to keep the crackling flames confined.

The Executioner picked his way through the dense jungle until he reached the perimeter. He did a quick count and noted that at least five buildings made up the jungle complex. One of them was low and well camouflaged, in addition to the fact it was nearly three times the size of any of the others, which drew Bolan's interest. If Downing and his people were working on a new weapon to combat terrorism, the Executioner was betting it was in that building. Therefore, it had to be his first target.

Bolan moved along the perimeter, which was lined with an electric fence. This puzzled him, since an electric fence in the middle of the jungle was asking for nothing but trouble. On closer inspection, he noticed some oddities about the fence—particularly the strange boxes secured to each pole—and a secondary study caused him to frown. It wasn't an electric fence he was dealing with here, it was a self-defensive perimeter. Each box came equipped with a significant explosive charge, which in turn propelled chemical agents. These were most likely biotoxins or thermals. It was crude but particularly effective and clever for this terrain. Birds and other jungle creatures generally wouldn't set it off, since the charges were geared to explode with dead-man switches. In other words, a loss in wire tension—such as would occur if the fencing were cut—would cause the charges to ignite. They would also blow if significant weight were placed against them, usually in excess of a hundred pounds. At ten feet high, that meant no way to climb them.

Bolan looked up and shook his head. The garrison here had obviously erected the defense in a hurry, because they hadn't bothered to cut back the foliage. The Executioner had lucked out by finding a tree branch directly above him that would permit entry without ever going near the wire. The sound of boots crunching on the jungle floor merely served to speed him on his way.

The soldier grabbed a vine for leverage and went up the tree as naturally as if climbing a ladder. All of his years in jungle fighting, the hours and oftentimes days of surviving as a sniper while waiting for his target at some location had toughened his mind and body. He learned what vegetation he could eat safely, and which to avoid at any cost; he knew how to move through jungle terrain with very little to no noise; and he knew how to climb trees quickly in a pinch to avoid enemy patrols.

Bolan watched as the group of five armed troops passed directly under him and stomped along the fence line, searching diligently but without care for their enemy. They didn't quite act like the crews he'd faced in the urban jungles of Manila and Atlanta. No, this crew was significantly more lax.

Shimmying across the thickest branch of the tree, Bolan passed harmlessly over the wire and dropped to the ground on the inside of the perimeter. He studied the area around him, but no threat emerged. He could hear occasional shouts, a few he thought sounded like Russian, but he didn't let it concern him.

The target he sought lay ahead.

Bolan reached the large building unchallenged and made his way through an unsecured door at the rear. The interior was comparatively cool. A deep thrum resounded in his ears, sank nearly to his chest, and Bolan could tell the building had a significant power source. He kept his back pressed to the cool metal as he became one with the darkness, letting his eyes adjust to the gloom.

The door he'd come through opened suddenly, and

Bolan whirled as he dropped to one knee and leveled his FNC in the direction of the noise. Through the door stepped a tiny, petite figure and in a wisp of light Bolan could see the feminine features of the new arrival.

"Whoever you are, show yourself," the woman said quietly. "You're walking into a trap."

CHAPTER EIGHT

Bolan lowered the FNC and stepped close enough that the woman would be able to distinguish his shadowy outline in the gloom. "Okay, I've shown myself. Now what?"

Her head whipped around and Bolan realized her back had been to him. "Damn you."

Bolan heard the faint click of a semiautomatic pistol being decocked and realized that she'd had a weapon pointed at his midsection.

"Don't sneak up on people like that," she added in a strained whisper. "I could have killed you."

"Yeah, but you didn't," Bolan replied. "What's your name?"

"Crystal Julian," she said, her pace quickened. "Dr. Julian, actually. But we don't have time for that now."

A roaring noise sounded very close to them, probably a secondary explosion caused by Bolan's Jeepney. The sound of automatic weapons fire had stopped, so the enemy was no longer firing indiscriminately at shadows.

"We need to get out of here," Julian protested.

The Executioner shook his head. "No dice, lady. Here is exactly where I need to be."

"I know you think that," she said. "And I know you're here to destroy the *Hadesfire*. And that's what they're expecting you to do. Now you can go about your mission and get killed, or you can take a chance and come with me right now, Mister…?"

"Matt Cooper."

"Well, then, Cooper, you want to face me or two dozen angry men armed with assault rifles?"

"Angry men with assault rifles is my specialty," Bolan said with his best smile. "Smart, independent women are what worries me."

If she'd been affected one way or another by his quip, she didn't give any indication. Instead she jerked her head toward a darkened hallway in the opposite direction of the alcove where Bolan had been standing when she first walked in. The lighting improved as they walked, much to the credit of the lights recessed into the floor similar to those found in a movie theater. Julian made an abrupt, ninety-degree turn to the left. At first it appeared she would walk right into the wall, but then Bolan realized she had entered a small alcove off the hallway. A moment later he heard the clang of a heavy metal door opening and his eyes were flooded by bright light. Metal-grate steps led downward.

Julian turned and smiled at him, just a trace of smugness at her lips, and Bolan caught his first good glimpse.

She was abou...
wide-set blue eyes stu... CODE
of glasses perched on her butto...
and in the brightness of the stairwell he was; bright,
just the hint of freckles. Her long brown hair large pair
flow naturally from her head like a waterfall all the way
to the small of her back.

She didn't say anything, but instead appeared to take
a moment to size him up before heading down the steps
with a gesture he should follow.

As they descended, Bolan said, "Excuse me, maybe
this isn't a good time to ask, but where exactly are we
going?"

"This is an equipment access tunnel. It leads to a
truck dock near the edge of the compound. They offload
equipment there and bring it down to a freight elevator
that takes it up to the hangar."

"What hangar?"

She pointed at the ceiling just inches above Bolan's
head. "The one above us. The one where we have the
Hadesfire."

"You mentioned that before. What is it?"

Julian came to a grinding halt and whirled on him.
Bolan had to stop short to keep from bowling her over.
She put her hands on her hips and tossed him a furious
expression. She looked more like a cross schoolmarm
and less like a doctor, whatever her specialty. It became
immediately apparent to Bolan he'd said something offensive, but he couldn't imagine what.

"You mean, you're not here to destroy the *Hadesfire?*"

...ow what it is," Bolan replied. ...estroy it?"

...ed on her heel and proceeded to march down ...allway, her pace quickened. "Well, that's just fine, because I would have drawn the line right there in helping you. It's a fantastic machine, and it will help our country combat terrorism. That baby is my project and I won't let you or anybody else ruin everything I've worked for. You—"

She stopped and turned again when she paused from her rambling long enough to realize Bolan wasn't following on her heels anymore. The Executioner stared at her.

"What?" Julian asked.

"Are you through?"

"With what?"

Bolan ignored her sarcasm. "Does this *Hadesfire* have anything to do with MGT theory?"

"How do you know about that?"

"My government invented it," Bolan said. "How about yours?"

She walked toward him, jabbing her finger as she said, "Now listen, Cooper—"

"I'm done listening," Bolan cut in. "Now it's your turn. I know about Downing's so-called plan to combat terrorism in the U.S., and I know he probably has most of you brainwashed to think this whole operation is sanctioned by official channels. The truth, and I don't know if you're interested in it or not, is that Downing is presently viewed as public enemy number one at the highest levels. It's my duty to eliminate that threat and to make sure nobody stops me from doing that."

"So you're nothing more than an assassin. Just a gun-for-hire."

"Look, Doctor, I'm not a gun-for-hire and I don't get my kicks out of wanton violence. What I plan to do is accomplish my mission and stop Downing and his goons. Now if you're going to help me, I call the shots from here out. You got it?"

Julian appeared unaffected by the Executioner's imposing presence at first, but she just as quickly appeared to soften. She didn't seem exactly "all there" to Bolan, but that didn't really surprise him. Most scientists he knew possessed a bit of flakiness—maybe eccentricity better described that particular personality trait within the scientific community—and he'd have to learn to forgive these quirks or simply not accept her help. At the moment, he didn't see the latter as much of an option.

"Okay, fine," she said. "Now can we get out of here before they discover us?"

"Sure," Bolan said. "Where exactly will this take us?"

"I've already told you it leads to a loading dock."

"And from there?"

She smiled as she reached into her pocket, withdrew a set of keys and dangled them in front of her face. "From there, transportation out of the camp."

"So they're just going to let us drive out of here, huh?" Bolan asked.

"I can get us the wheels, pal," she said. She turned and marched for a door at the end of the hallway, adding, "The rest is up to you. I assume you can handle it."

Bolan shook his head, rolled his eyes, then hurried to catch up. He couldn't explain it, but something told him he could trust Crystal Julian. He didn't have much of a choice, anyway, but he didn't plan to let on to that little fact. Once they were free and clear where he could get some running distance, he'd probe deeper into her story. Right now, however, he planned on tending to business.

Julian led him up a steep incline that emerged onto a truck dock, just as promised. She stopped short of the dock area and stepped back to let Bolan take the lead. She pointed at the truck—what appeared to be a commercial version of an old military deuce-and-a-half—and Bolan nodded before risking a glance around the corner. The light had faded considerably at the approach of dusk, and would serve as a great cover. Pandemonium seemed the order of the day. Downing's men seemed to have the fire under control, and on occasion Bolan could see armed patrols scouring the perimeter.

Julian peered over his shoulder, a hand resting lightly on his shoulder. "What are they looking for?"

Bolan tried to ignore the magnetism of her touch combined with the wisp of perfume. "Not 'what,' who."

She nodded. "You."

"Yeah."

"Sorry, I suppose it should have seemed obvious, but I didn't see the way you actually came into the camp. I only happened to spot you as you entered the hangar building."

"As you've already pointed out, we can discuss all this later. You go for the truck first. I'll cover you."

She nodded, tapped him for what reason he couldn't tell, then dashed for the passenger door of the truck. Bolan kept one eye on her while he leveled the muzzle of the FNC in the direction of open ground separating Downing's men from the truck. She made it to the cab without incident, and as she climbed inside Bolan made his own break for it. He rounded the far back corner of the truck and vaulted off the dock. A shout resounded from an unseen location, but Bolan got the gist: someone had spotted them.

The Executioner opened the door and climbed into the cab in one smooth motion. He reached into his shoulder holster and whipped out the Beretta 93-R. He verified the selector was at single-shot mode before passing it over to Julian.

"Here."

She looked at him with express horror. "You're kidding, right?"

"I drive, you make sure nobody gets in here with us. Or even close."

"But—"

"Look," Bolan snapped, "There's no time to argue about this. Now take the gun and give me the keys!"

She obeyed, albeit with reluctance and disdain, and Bolan cranked the ignition. The massive diesel engine rumbled to life. "When you said truck, I was thinking more along the lines of pickup style. These things are rugged, but they aren't known for speed."

"Beggars can't be choosers, Cooper," Julian shot back with a half grin.

"Story of my life," he replied, slamming the stick

into second and popping the clutch while steadily applying the gas pedal.

The giant machine leaped from the dock at the same moment two armed soldiers in camouflage rushed for it. Bolan swung the wheel to the left enough to take out one of the assailants with the front bumper. The unfortunate gunner's colleague managed to leap aside and avoid the five-thousand-pound vehicle as it roared past him in a surge of flying brush and foliage. Bolan poured on the best possible speed by shifting to third gear and whipping the steering wheel back and forth to improve traction over the slippery terrain.

Bolan glanced in Julian's direction when an oddity flashed in his peripheral vision. He shouted and jammed a finger in the direction of the passenger window. Julian turned with surprise to find one of the enemy troops had managed to latch on to the passenger-side running board.

Julian began to scream with surprise as she raised the Beretta and successively squeezed the trigger. The reports were deafening in the confines of the cab, and although she managed to pop off five rounds not a single one hit the target. The man reached through the now open window and grabbed her by the throat. Julian let out a choked squeal of outrage and dropped the pistol. Bolan muttered a curse when he heard the weapon clatter to the floorboard.

The Executioner reacted with battle-hardened skill.

With his left hand securing him to the truck cab and his right around Julian's throat, the attacker had no way to prepare for the eventuality he now faced. It came in the form of a gaping, dark hole at the end of the .44 Magnum barrel held mere inches from his skull. Bolan shouted for Julian to cover her ears, and the moment she complied he squeezed the trigger. Blood and gray matter splattered Julian's shirt and the better part of the cab roof.

The woman opened her eyes when the pressure released on her throat to find no sign of her assailant. She wiped away the small amount of gore that had splashed onto her right cheek and then mouthed a thank-you at Bolan even as her entire body trembled noticeably. He nodded, then pointed to the Beretta at her feet. Julian immediately retrieved it.

Bolan aimed the truck for the same gate he'd approached earlier, but this time he didn't plan to stop. He could see the muzzle-flashes of the weapons as they winked at him, but the roar of the truck engine as he went to fourth gear drowned most of the reports. The occasional tinny sound of bullets striking the truck's metal shell caused the hairs to stand straight on Bolan's neck, but he pushed it from his mind and focused on what lay ahead of them.

I'm no closer to mission completion even if we get through this thing, Bolan thought. Yeah, finding Crystal Julian had definitely thrown a monkey wrench in the works.

Undaunted, Bolan put the truck through its paces and blew through the flimsy wood and steel-rivet gate with explosive fury. The truck had overdrive, fortunately, and Bolan put it in fifth. The engine groaned in protest, but he added enough pressure to the gas pedal that the truck quickly compensated for the lower than average speed. Bolan could hear the power converter torque under the hood and the vehicle really began to pick up speed.

"We made it!" Julian yelled.

A quick look at the gas gauge confirmed Bolan's concern. He'd earlier noticed the needle at the full mark, but now it bounced just below three-quarters. One of the stray rounds had probably punctured the gas tank, but he saw no reason to bring that to Julian's attention. She'd suffered enough trauma for the moment and Bolan didn't feel like adding to her troubles.

The roar of flames, autofire and men's voices faded almost instantly and left only the high-pitched whine of the engine to fill their senses. Bolan became lost in thought as he almost steered his way along the road. The odds had definitely turned against him. So far, he'd done all he could to take the fight to the enemy, but it seemed circumstances to this point had prevented him from crippling the enemy on a permanent basis.

For one thing, Downing's army was much larger than he'd anticipated. The original intelligence he'd gathered from Neely had led him to conclude he was up against a relatively small armed force that happened to be highly trained. From what he'd just seen, that didn't appear to be the case anymore. Downing had obviously been recruiting and training his little private army for the better part of his last few years of silence, heralded by the fact he'd all but seemed to drop off the face of the Earth.

The fact the NSA hadn't chosen to keep tabs on a

man in Downing's position also held some surprise for Bolan. A guy with Downing's contacts wouldn't have been able to cover his tracks quite so neatly without a bit of help from insiders. Bolan recalled Price pointing out during the mission briefing that Downing was far from a fanatic. But that didn't mean he didn't have fanatical people working for him. Alek Stezhnya certainly sounded like he was a bit over the edge, trained soldier or not, and when someone with Downing's brains recruited someone with Stezhnya's devout sense of patriotism and duty, that made for a very dangerous combination indeed.

Now there was another twist—a female scientist who would have appeared up until the moment he contacted to her to have sworn allegiance to Downing. Yet she'd reacted with vehemence at the suggestion. It wasn't impossible to believe she'd been duped; Downing had quite a reputation to be charming and persuasive, a fact he'd proved on repeated occasions during his tenure at the NSA. But the Executioner wasn't entirely ready to subscribe to Julian's purported "innocence." She'd have to do much more than keep him from falling into a trap to prove she wasn't another one of Downing's cleverly hatched plans.

"Okay, we're almost out of time, so start explaining," Bolan finally said. "What's the real story behind your working for Garrett Downing? And what's this *Hadesfire* thing you keep yammering about?"

"Oh, the *Hadesfire* is more than just a thing, Mr. Cooper," she said with surprising composure. Obviously she felt safe enough she could fall back to her old role of haughty and spirited. "It's the ultimate weapon of small-unit warfare."

CHAPTER NINE

"Don't talk in abstract terms," the Executioner replied. "Start from the beginning."

"The *Hadesfire* does possess the capabilities you mentioned earlier," Julian began. "The multi-geo transversal functionality, I mean."

Bolan nodded for her to continue.

"You must sit in the very highest circles of government to know anything about this technology at all," she remarked offhandedly.

"Actually, it's more the people I call friends that sit in those circles," Bolan replied coolly. "It just so happens they ask for my help on occasion and I usually lend it. Now, about the *Hadesfire*…"

"Yes, as I started to tell you, the *Hadesfire* is the most advanced small-unit assault vehicle currently available. It's MGT capabilities allow it to surmount nearly any obstacle. It can fly, travel over large bodies of water and navigate across even the roughest ground terrain. It's even capable of traveling through mountains, although with its low-altitude flight capabilities that's hardly necessary."

"How did you come into Downing's employ?"

"A friend referred him," she said.

"And who is this mysterious friend?"

Julian hesitated, then shrugged. She had obviously decided to trust him all the way or not at all. Bolan hoped it could be a mutual thing. "A man named Peter Hagen."

Something went cold in Bolan's stomach. So, Hagen had been working on something for Downing and he'd apparently decided to involve Crystal Julian in the plot. The big problem had probably come when Hagen had either learned too much or had some sort of more personal falling out—Bolan was betting that something personal was the woman seated next to him—and that's when Downing decided to take him out. It might have been enough to convince the soldier that Julian had thought she was working on the right side, and when she discovered otherwise she elected to risk her own life and flip on Downing.

"I assume we're talking about the same Peter Hagen who served under Downing at the NSA as a chief scientist in the Advanced Projects Division."

"You know him?" Julian appeared excited when she asked the question.

Bolan shrugged, realizing a moment too late he'd committed himself and there was no turning back now. "In a way. I was there when they killed him."

"What!" Julian exclaimed. "When who killed him? Y-you're saying Peter's... That he's dead?"

"I'm sorry." Bolan couldn't think of any other words to comfort her. "There wasn't anything I could do. By the time we realized he might be in danger, it was too late."

"Those fucking bastards!" She slammed her fist suddenly and very uncharacteristically against the dash, and then yanked it back with a yelp of pain. The metal and hard plastic was unyielding to her soft hand. She held it protectively against her body, and the tremors became visible.

Bolan winced in empathy, then decided to keep his eyes focused on the road.

Julian's breathing grew more labored as she continued. "I'll kill them if I get my hands on them."

"Consider it already done," Bolan interjected.

"Good! I hope they rot in hell!"

They rode in silence for a minute, the Executioner letting it sink in and remaining silent out of respect for her feelings. She'd obviously been close to the guy and it wouldn't have helped his cause to tell Julian that Hagen had known all about Downing's OSI group and his plans to take matters into their own hands. It would remain the better plan at this point to let her think Hagen died at the hands of men who she'd just sworn an oath to make pay for his death. Bolan didn't necessarily like the idea of lying to her, but if he could use it to leverage support then it was his first and best option at this point in the game. He'd already let too many things steer him off the course; he couldn't allow one more.

Finally she turned in the seat so her upper body faced him. "What can I do to help you?"

Bolan spared a sideways glance. "Now you're willing to help me?"

"I'll help you do just about anything," she said. "Just as long as you promise me that you won't try to destroy the *Hadesfire*. Not that you necessarily could if you wanted to."

She'd piqued Bolan's interest. "What do you mean by that?"

"Any machine that can do what she can do must be tough, durable and resilient."

"Sure."

Julian shrugged. "So it only stands to reason she'd be well reinforced and heavily armored."

"How big is this flying pillbox?"

"Take caution with your tone. You don't have the first idea what you're talking about."

"That's what I'm trying to find out," Bolan reminded her.

"The *Hadesfire* is approximately nine meters long and four meters wide," she stated, as if their previous banter hadn't even taken place. "It has a crew compliment of one operator and eight troops, with all the standard tactical equipment, and it's outfitted with a twin-jet engine system that propels it through air as well as over water. There's a lot more technical jargon I could throw at you, but that wouldn't interest you nearly as much as what she can do."

"I'm listening," Bolan prompted her.

"In addition to her mobility, the *Hadesfire* is armed with a GAU-12/U Equalizer and four Stinger SAMs. It sports the latest in forward-looking radar, laser-satellite targeting systems, and one of the most sophisticated global communications systems in the world. In short, Cooper, the *Hadesfire* could put a missile onto a spot no larger than the rear end of one of this country's mosquitoes, and within seconds report back the status of that target."

Well, there was certainly no question Julian had passion for her work. It also sounded like she knew her stuff where it concerned the *Hadesfire*. The only question that remained now was her loyalties. Bolan decided no time like the present to play that card; he'd deal the hand and see if she upped the ante.

"If you were so worried about me destroying your little project, why did you choose to help me?"

"Because I chose not to help Downing. And now hearing that Peter is dead, and Downing's men are responsible, I'm glad I did."

"Were you and Hagen lovers?"

Julian chuckled. "Hardly. Peter was like a father to me. My mother lost my father to another woman, and I lost my mother to a pill bottle. Peter Hagen was an instructor at Carnegie Mellon for a couple of semesters."

"I thought Hagen was at MIT."

She nodded. "That's where he was educated, yes, but he consulted and taught all over the country. I just happened to be lucky to have him as an instructor. When he told me about this job, I jumped at the chance to work with him. It wasn't until about two months after I got here that he told me he wouldn't be joining me."

"So why stay?"

"Peter convinced me to hang out by saying our long-distance work relationship wasn't permanent. He said he'd come as soon as he was finished with some research in Atlanta. He claimed he needed to be in the States because it had the best information." She sighed, then added, "Like I said before, I thought I was working for a legit operation."

"What changed your mind?"

"Alek." She said Stezhnya's name with unadulterated disgust.

"The Russian-American," Bolan prompted.

"Yes, that's the one." She let out a nervous laugh. "It's a joke to think that I'd convinced myself I was in love with that unspeakable bastard."

"I understand from my sources that he's heading up Downing's little private army."

Julian nodded. "They call themselves the Apparatus. When I first arrived, Garrett explained they were a specially trained security detachment for the operation. That's when I met Alek and he charmed the pants right off me. Literally. Don't look at me like that. Eight months in the middle of the jungle without some diversion can get to a girl."

"You weren't a prisoner," Bolan said. "It looked to me like you could have left any time you wanted."

"I could have, but all I ever heard from Garrett and Alek was how important it was to maintain secrecy, and all that was at stake if we didn't complete the mission. I did what I did out of duty, Cooper, and I'll be damned if I apologize to anyone for that."

"Never asked you to," Bolan said. "Committing to duty is one thing I understand well."

Julian only nodded.

Bolan looked at the gauge again. "We have maybe two miles to go before we're out of fuel. I think the tank got hit."

"Oh…lovely." Julian threw up her hands. "What do we do now? I have a cell phone, but I doubt it works out here. Garrett made pretty sure we were isolated from the outside world."

Bolan shrugged as he began to slow the truck. "Won't need it. I have friends who'll be coming along soon enough. For now, we need to get out of sight. I'm sure Stezhnya's Apparatus won't be far behind us."

The soldier continued for another mile until he saw a break in the brush and he slowed in time to take the truck off road. When he was convinced they had ventured far enough that their position from the road would be obscured entirely, he brought the massive truck to a stop and killed the engine.

"Let's bail," Bolan told her as he grabbed the satchel and jumped from the truck.

The soldier knelt in the deep foliage. He studied his surroundings and then reached into the satchel and removed two straps tucked away. He folded them out and had them extended and attached to connectors at the satchel's base by the time Julian made her way around the truck. He stood and slung the satchel over his head, pushing his arms through the straps. He yanked them tight and adjusted the weight for comfort. Julian had been watching him with interest, but now when he looked at her she frowned.

"So what exactly do you plan to do now?"

"Prepare for eventualities while waiting for the cavalry. We go on foot from here," Bolan said. He looked in the direction of the setting sun and turned right ninety degrees. He then yanked a compass from a pouch attached to his webbing as he walked away from the truck.

"Um, go where exactly?"

Bolan ignored her question at first, keeping his focus on their position and general distance. He pointed toward the north. "Manila's in that direction, probably about ten klicks."

"Egads! That's over six miles, Cooper," Julian protested.

"I know," Bolan replied with a grin. He looked at her feet and saw she wore tennis shoes. Well, it wasn't the ideal footwear for a jungle trek, but it would be a far cry better than had she had on flats or heels. "We probably won't have to make it all the way back to the city. Just far enough and deep enough into the jungle until my pilot can pick us up by chopper."

"Fine. But what if your friend doesn't get the signal or runs into the same kind of trouble we did?" She tapped her watch. "I'm no expert, but at best we probably have twenty minutes of daylight remaining, if that. It could be a hell of a long walk back to Manila, especially through the nighttime jungle."

"And it'll take even longer if we stand here and debate it."

"I don't know about you, Cooper, but I grew up in a democracy and we generally put this kind of thing to a vote."

Bolan turned on her and got in close and personal. "Listen, Doctor, I'm not sure if all this charm and wit is a personality flaw or just icebreaker humor. Now maybe in the lab your word is law but out here it's mine. This is what I know and I'm good at it. So from here out we do things my way or we go our separate ways. Are we clear?"

Bolan could tell his words combined with his imposing presence had stung a bit because she winced. Julian said, "Very."

"Good," Bolan replied. "Now let's move out."

THEY HAD VENTURED only a mile and a half, maybe two, when the Executioner heard it.

At first it was faint, almost indiscernible, but then it grew louder. Julian didn't appear to hear it right away—no big surprise she had been huffing and puffing with the exertion since nearly the start of their trek—but Bolan did and there was no mistaking its origin. He had heard chopper blades too many times not to be familiar with them, even from a distance.

"Do you hear that?" he asked Julian.

She stopped, only her silhouette visible in the darkness. Her tiny shoulders rose and fell steadily as she breathed, the rhythm less erratic than when their journey first began. Obviously, she was getting her second wind. Bolan could make out Julian's profile as she cocked her head. She really was a knockout, the soldier thought, one he might have taken more time to get to know under other circumstances, but she had a sharp tongue and irritating mannerism.

"Sorry, I don't," Julian finally said.

"It's a chopper," Bolan said as he yanked a compact flexible headset from a pouch on the military webbing. "Only question now is, friend or foe?"

"What are you doing?" she asked.

Bolan shook his head as he donned the wireless set. He adjusted it for a snug fit and then keyed the transceiver clipped to his belt. It would initiate a homing signal specially designed to send a microwave transmission directly to a satellite linkup. That would sync up with the earlier signal he'd triggered without Julian's knowledge, and the two would be confirmed through the on-board instrumentation of Jack Grimaldi's chopper.

"Striker to Eagle One."

There was no reply but Bolan remained calm. It would take time for Grimaldi to confirm the two signals, and there was no way he'd break communication silence before that. If Bolan didn't receive a reply within five minutes, he could be sure it was enemy or a neutral party flying above and he'd send a signal to warn Grimaldi off. The one thing they hadn't done was agree upon an alternate extraction point. In fact, the pilot probably hadn't expected Bolan to be signaling for rendezvous this early. Still, he'd never let Bolan down before and he wouldn't start now. If the Executioner called for help, he could count on the pilot to be there.

After nearly two minutes, the headset crackled in Bolan's ears followed by that familiar voice, strong and clear. "Eagle One to Striker, code Yankee Golf on your transmission. I have your position marked and locked."

"Eagle One, I copy," Bolan replied. "Good to hear your voice."

"Same here, Sarge. There's a clearing about sixty meters magnetic north of your position."

"Understood. We'll head that way for extraction."

"Roger, that. I'll be there."

"Out, here." Bolan cleared the channel and nodded at Julian. "We got lucky."

"How refreshing," Julian said.

Bolan considered her biting reply and chose not to respond. He didn't think it'd make any difference to argue with her; she obviously didn't get it. And she had prevented Stezhnya from sucking him into a trap whether he wanted to admit it or not. He owed her that much, but nothing beyond. Crystal Julian could best make her case at this point by working with him and providing information, or she could return to Wonderland and take her chances with Homeland Security bureaucrats. Given her general disposition, Bolan bet she'd take the first option.

As they walked toward the clearing, Bolan said, "I'll need every scrap of intelligence you have on both the *Hadesfire* and what Downing plans to do with it."

"Fine, but the most I can give you are the technical details," Julian replied. "I don't have any idea what they're planning to do with it."

"You probably know more than you think," Bolan said. "You just don't realize it."

"What makes you think so?"

Bolan didn't detect a defensive tone in the question so he chose a gentler reply. "You had a relationship with Stezhnya, short-lived as it was."

"And?"

"I'm betting he said something important without you even realizing it," Bolan told her. "He wouldn't have had any reason to think you'd divulge it to outside sources since Downing had the operation under lock and key."

For a minute she didn't reply. Then, "Maybe you're right. I can't be sure I *didn't* overhear something you could use. But you'll have my full cooperation. That much I can promise you."

"Good."

Quietly, Julian added, "See? I'm not a complete bitch, Cooper."

"I never thought you were."

"Stick to the truth," she said. "You're better at that."

The Executioner didn't reply. Instead he focused on the task ahead of them. A sixty-meter jaunt through the jungle would have been little more than a hike in the woods under normal circumstances, but navigating the dense terrain in darkness with an inexperienced companion posed a different challenge. Bolan only had to stop twice so Julian could catch up; it wouldn't do her much good if he allowed them to separate. It took almost ten minutes to reach the clearing, but they made it unmolested.

Even in the gloom Bolan could discern the outline of the chopper and immediately identified it as a Huey-style gunship. Bolan grabbed Julian's arm with the warning to keep low before he tugged her in the chopper's direction. The side door slid aside to reveal the crouched shadow of Jack Grimaldi.

"What's up?" the pilot asked with his usual disarming grin. He had to shout over the drone of the powerful engines.

"Change in plans," Bolan replied as he helped Julian into the chopper.

Once they were inside and airborne, Bolan donned a headset connected to the internal communications system. "Thanks for the lift."

"My pleasure," Grimaldi replied from the cockpit.

Bolan took in his surroundings and saw that the chopper was fully equipped. Not only did it appear to have the latest technology but the back end of the hold sported a full rack designed to hold a full complement of small arms and crew assault weaponry. Bolan glanced to the front of the gunship and saw Grimaldi manipulating an advanced set of controls.

"Looks like you spared no expense," Bolan said. "How did you swing this?"

"I'd love to take the credit, but it was mostly Hal's doing. With apparently a bit of help from the Man."

"That's good," Bolan said. "Because I've learned some things that tell me we're going to need it."

CHAPTER TEN

Personal meetings with the President of the United States had grown infrequent over the years. Stony Man operations had reached a level of efficiency that didn't require micromanagement from the Oval Office.

Harold Brognola wouldn't have preferred it any other way, although this mission had apparently generated the exception and not the rule. The call he had received from the Executioner had been anything but good news, and the time drew near when the President would require more drastic measures. Hence, it didn't surprise him when the Man requested a face-to-face to discuss the present situation and options. Under most circumstances they would have met in some discreet location, but the President apparently had another issue on his hands that had him in the situation room for the past six hours.

The President excused himself from the gaggle of military advisers present when Brognola arrived at the

White House. They moved to a soundproof cubicle off the main meeting area.

"Thanks for coming on short notice, Hal," the President said as he took a seat and proffered Brognola a second.

"No trouble, sir," Brognola replied.

"I suppose you were a little surprised I asked for this meeting," the Man remarked.

Brognola nodded. "Slightly."

"I know you're pressed for time so I'll come right to the point. I've spent the past few hours dealing with a situation that I now believe is related to your mission. Several advisers in there are telling me our best bet is to implement a military solution. I don't know about that."

"What kind of military solution are we talking about, sir?" Brognola asked.

"The permanent kind, Hal. And the kind that could very well put your people in harm's way. Particularly him."

The Stony Man chief only nodded in way of reply. He knew the President meant Mack Bolan. "I appreciate the notice, but I'm not sure I understand."

The President shook his head. "I wouldn't have expected you to. You don't have all the information. I called you here now, at this particular time, because my staff is going to expect an answer from me soon. Not only do they deserve that much, but we may also lose a first strike opportunity if we don't handle this in a timely fashion."

Brognola cleared his throat and shifted in his seat.

He tried not to look uncomfortable but he already sensed he didn't like the direction the conversation seemed headed. "Has there been some change in the situation?"

"A big one. You know, of course, since our new policy against terrorism that our relations with the Middle East have been…well, let's just say less than propitious. This morning during my briefing, the deputy director indicated we might see reprisals for Garrett Downing's attack on the terrorists in Atlanta. Significant reprisals that could go as high up as leadership in the al Qaeda network."

"All due respect, Mr. President, but that's hardly headline news," Brognola interjected.

"It is when you consider who's allegedly at the crux of our concerns."

"And that would be?"

The President lowered his a voice a bit, although those outside the room couldn't overhear them. "There were specific mentions within the SCI that pointed straight to the Mujahedeen-e-Khalq in Iran and the Armed Islamic Group in Egypt. We even have reports that some type of terrorist coalition may be forming up at a secret location somewhere in the Oman Desert even as we speak."

Brognola immediately felt a headache coming on while his stomach started to churn. Unfortunately he hadn't remembered to bring a packet of antacids with him, and he'd already consumed entirely too much of Kurtzman's coffee. To now hear this only added to his physical woes. If this information had actually come out of SCI dissemination in the President's daily brief, it undoubtedly meant something.

Sensitive Compartmented Information was a process where especially sensitive and highly classified information was compartmentalized and then required assigned code words. A majority of the time SCI code words were predominantly centralized to NSA signal intelligence operations, but on a number of occasions the CIA had been known to use similar tactics. SCI was never included in the *National Intelligence Daily*—a narrowly circulated document that summarized the main intelligence items from the day before—which told Brognola the President had been keeping his finger on the pulse of such activities for some time.

"I can see why you're concerned, sir," Brognola said. "But I can assure you Striker's getting closer to some answers. I spoke with him less than an hour ago. He's located Downing's central area of operation in the Philippines, and he's ready to take it down for the count."

"I'm not sure that's going to do much for us," the President replied. "That's my whole reason for dragging you out here at this godforsaken time of the morning. I'm afraid we're running out of time."

"Please, Mr President, I'm asking you to give us a chance to deal with this in our own way."

The Man let out a deep sigh. "Hal, you've known me long enough to know I do what I can to keep a hands-off policy where Stony Man is concerned."

"I do, sir, and I appreciate it."

"Then you also know that there's more than just Downing to consider. We can't afford to inflame an already unstable and precarious position on items of this nature. The Joint Chiefs expect me to act quickly when they bring this kind of thing to me. And I'm not just talking about the politics here. We both know Garrett Downing's a shrewd bastard, and I'm pretty sure he's accounted for this as a part of whatever's in his overall plan."

"Then you must also realize he'll expect just the kind of reaction you're proposing, sir," Brognola replied. "If we allow him to stir up any more unrest than he already has, that'll only add fuel to the fire."

"I hadn't thought of that."

"I'd strongly recommend you do before jumping the gun and implementing action. We've tried this before and it doesn't work. Striker isn't perfect but he's experienced. He understands this enemy better than any man I know, and he seems to have a particularly good hand on Downing."

"How so?"

Brognola thought carefully before answering. The President was offering him a chance right now to make his case, and he needed all his wits about him if he stood any chance of convincing the most powerful man in the free world to resist the urge to act with impunity.

"Striker's pegged Downing as something of a misguided patriot more than a fanatic. I believe the term he used was 'idealist.' You see, Downing knows he's operating without sanction by the United States, and yet he still truly believes he's doing what's right. He obviously loves this country or he wouldn't have served it for as long as he did. We trained him and taught him everything he knows where it regards making war and combating terrorism."

"You almost sound sympathetic, Hal," the President observed. His eyebrows rose and he added, "I hope you aren't suggesting we simply turn the other way and hope your man gets a handle on it."

"Not at all," Brognola said, shaking his head. "But I'm convinced we need to give Striker a little more time. I think Downing's trying to build as much public support for his organization as he can above all else. He's trying to portray a specific image. Now according to the intelligence we've just received, a man named Alek Stezhnya is the real muscle behind the organization. He apparently heads up a private army for Downing calling themselves the Apparatus."

"You still haven't told me why you think it's better I not give our elite military units the go-ahead to launch a strike."

"There won't be any need to, Mr. President," Brognola replied evenly, "because Downing's people plan to do it for us. If anything, I think the Oval Office should go on record and completely disavow Downing's actions. I think if you make it public, he'll jump the gun to prove himself and his so-called antiterrorist strategies, and that's when he'll make mistakes. Striker should then be able to blow this thing wide open."

For several moments, the President didn't say anything. Brognola could understand the man's position. It was just one of those situations that could go either way. Even if the President went along with him, he knew it would only buy Bolan maybe twenty-four hours at the outset. If Downing had the time and resources to institute those kinds of widespread operations, they were already losing the battle.

"All right, Hal, I'll give you forty-eight hours to close the situation."

Brognola exhaled loudly, which then made him realize he'd been holding his breath.

"In its entirety," the President added with emphasis. "If it's not resolved by that time, I'm sending in the heavy guns."

"Thank you, sir. But you should know you've already sent in the heaviest gun you can. Striker will come through. I guarantee it."

"Let's hope so," was the reply. "For all our sakes."

EVEN THE TROPICAL, evening breeze couldn't cool Warren Levine.

That's because his blood boiled every time he thought about how Roger Neely had embarrassed him in front of his superiors and how that, in turn, had led him to a reprimand when he could have had a medal. At first Levine had thought about submitting a report that simply said he'd tailed Neely and seen nothing unusual. After losing the man the previous morning, Levine returned to his quarters and caught an encore Red Sox game. Then it was off to bed.

At somewhere around 2:30 a.m., he was roused from a fitfully deep sleep by the ringing of a phone, which was followed by an angry voice of the DDFO at the other end. After suffering through nearly a five-minute tirade—and just *how* had the boss found out

Neely had given him the slip?—Levine was told to back off.

"So I take a reaming and a gig in my permanent file just so I can be told to back off," Levine muttered as he slammed the receiver into the cradle. "That's just great."

Levine then rolled from the sweat-soaked sheets. He'd been waiting for them to come fix the air-conditioning system for weeks, and they still hadn't shown up. He thought all the U.S.-government contractors overseas were incompetent dicks, and because of that he had to suffer through the heat. It only served to foul Levine's temper more. The CIA agent spent three hours in his kitchen with a bottle of whiskey, drinking and cursing and smoking up a storm until he was finally too drunk to stay awake.

At just past noon, the phone woke him from his drunken stupor again and an informant told him that Neely had been shot dead in front of some building downtown by an unknown sniper. Through questioning of witnesses and other individuals—by either bribes or coercion—Levine eventually had the name Garrett Downing dropped in his lap. That's when it all came together and Levine became totally enraged.

He ended up at the morgue and caught sight of a very live Roger Neely being escorted by a swarthy looking character in a flight suit to the airport. Levine had thought about tagging the guy right there, but this new dude interested him even more. Levine had gathered all the intelligence he could over unofficial and official wires regarding the deaths in Atlanta and the claims by Garrett Downing that he was responsible.

Yeah, so suddenly a bunch of very heavy shit goes down and all right here in Manila. First the hush-hush phone call from the DDFO to tail an agent of the National Security Agency—the same guy who looked pretty alive and well to Levine—and then he's told to back off and keep his mouth shut. Now he gets word of Neely buying the farm and somehow Downing's name comes into it? No way, Levine wasn't buying that bullshit. Something heavy was definitely going on in the South Pacific, and Levine planned to find out what it was. After all, he was the section chief for this part of U.S. intelligence operations, and he didn't like being kept in the dark.

Levine managed to get pictures of the man who escorted Neely to the airport, but a database search didn't reveal anything. Once he'd confirmed Neely's departure on a flight to the States, Levine paid someone to keep tabs on the escort while he returned to Neely's apartment and searched the place thoroughly. He didn't find anything connected to Downing, but there was some heavy weaponry and that led him to conclude someone would be coming back.

Levine sat on the apartment and eventually his vigilance paid off. After a major fire storm inside—with plenty of autofire and explosions to sweeten the pot—the battle moved outdoors where another mystery player attired in some sort of commando outfit appeared.

That's when the phone call came from his informant to let him know the man who'd escorted Neely to the airport was on the move again. So Levine stuck with the guy throughout the afternoon, following in a cab and racking up the dollars to do it, as the guy made some rounds to some very strange locales throughout Manila. Eventually the track circled back to the airport where the guy finally took off in a military-grade chopper with military-grade weapons on it.

It was nearly 2200 hours when the chopper returned and off-loaded three passengers. At first, Levine thought his eyes deceived him, but hell no! He would be damned if one of those occupants wasn't a woman, not to mention the pilot and GI Joe in the black ops gear making his second appearance for the day. Well, there was no way he could let this thing go. Levine knew the only way to get the information he sought was to grow a pair of gonads the size of brass baseballs, and risk detection to find out what they were up to. The CIA agent dashed between the cover of fluid drums and other exterior equipment stacked near the hangar until he got close enough to be within earshot of the new arrivals.

By the time he reached them, the woman had gone inside the small private hangar building while the two men remained outside. Levine could see they were talking while ground staff began to refuel the chopper. There was still a bit of noise from the planes taking off, but Levine couldn't get any closer without risking detection. He cocked his head and listened to what he could.

The men were conversing about some camp, and talking something about the jungle. It was apparent that they had just returned from some type of operation south of Milan. Levine kept hearing a strange word—he eventually figured out it started with *Hades*—but he couldn't make out the rest of it. But what was it? That was more important. It seemed the pair he'd been tracking most of the day didn't have much of a clue about that themselves.

Their conversation then turned to the topic of operations being planned by Downing. The commando was telling the pilot how he believed Downing was planning to use as-yet-unknown locations to conduct tests of the Hades-something-or-other. So that was it! Levine figured the men were some kind of government heavyweights, maybe black ops or the NSA's Covert Action Group, here to snuff out Downing and his Office of Strategic Initiative. So it was probably OSI gunners the big guy had gone up against that afternoon. He was some kind of military agent.

It all began to fall together for Levine, and it probably was NSA or Homeland Security pulling strings. He'd most likely been pulled off Neely's trail because they didn't want to risk him colliding with any allied operators; well, so-called allies anyway. They weren't going to work with him, that much was sure. Levine had lost face and brownie points in Washington—points that would have guaranteed his next assignment was a cushy one—and somebody owed him for that.

At least that's the way he saw it. Levine had spent two years in Nassau before this, which had turned out to be a typically boring assignment, and then before that he'd seen tours in South America, Central America and Africa. His requests for transfer to central Europe had been repeatedly denied, and it was only a cousin in records that even got his name in front of the selection committee for consideration as a station chief. That and a very large box of very expensive cigars sent to two of its members. So when Levine got news he'd been selected as a section chief, he was so excited he didn't even bother asking where. He didn't think he'd care.

That's when he heard his duty would be a minimum of three years in the Philippines with a next guaranteed station-of-choice bonus if he did a good job and minded his p's and q's. That was the big difficulty, though—minding anything in the Philippines. The place was always out of control in one way or another, and Levine knew he'd have his work cut out for him. So he'd done more than a year here, and the only thing it got him was divorce papers by special courier and a return to the tequila train. So yeah, someone owed him this chance, the way he saw it.

It didn't take but a minute for him to formulate a plan. He was going to be a part of this operation one way or another. The two men were now talking of how they were planning to go back to wherever the commando dude had just come from. Great! This would be Levine's chance to blow the thing wide open and take all the credit. He wanted out of this place once and for all, and this seemed like an opportunity too good to pass up.

Levine began to wonder just how he could stow away on board that chopper without being seen when the answer virtually presented itself. He turned to see the woman calling to them, waving her arms, and they broke conversation and jogged toward her. A minute later, after a brief discussion, all three disappeared inside the hangar.

And Warren Levine whispered thanks to Lady Luck as he sauntered to the chopper as though he didn't have a care in the world.

CHAPTER ELEVEN

"Forty-eight hours," Harold Brognola announced. "That's the best I could buy you with the Man, Striker. I'm sorry I couldn't do better."

"Don't sweat it," Bolan reassured him. "It's enough."

Brognola gave Bolan a brief rundown on the rest of his conversation with the President, and then asked, "Okay, what's your plan and how can we help at this end?"

"I'd start with getting me any intelligence you can about the groups we'll be up against, and about what's going on in the Middle East."

"Done. But I'd assumed if you were able to shut down the Apparatus and Downing's operation there, that would act as a deterrent to the unrest in Iran and Egypt."

"I doubt it," Bolan said. "It sounds like Downing's already beaten us to the punch. I'm sure he's had moles in place for months stirring things up. That's why it's important for me to get details on what's happening there."

"Fair enough. We'll get the info to you as soon as possible."

"Thanks."

"I trust you have a plan for what's going down there. You need anything?"

"No, Jack's appropriated good air support and my plan is simple. I'll do what Downing least expects."

"Return and hit his camp?"

"Right. It's important to put the *Hadesfire* out of commission before Stezhnya's people can put it to real use."

"From what little we know about it, that doesn't sound like it'll be easy," Brognola pointed out.

"Yeah, but I have one advantage they're not counting on."

"Yes, I know…Dr. Julian. Although by now I'm sure they've figured out she's no longer in the camp. They'll be searching for her, and from what I gathered in your earlier report it sounds like she could be playing both sides of the fence to protect her own interests. Do you think you can trust her?"

Bolan paused to fix the scientist with a wary glance, but she didn't appear to be paying any real attention to him or his conversation. She seemed more focused on the portable computer that Grimaldi had brought along, which contained a link through Stony Man's superprocessors. Since boarding the chopper she'd been using its satellite communication abilities to linkup with the *Hadesfire*'s computer system and upload its specifications.

"For now," Bolan said cautiously. "She's agreed to help me find its weaknesses. Once I have that information I'll be able to exploit it."

"All right, sounds good," Brognola said. "We should have all that intelligence to you within the hour. I'll make it top priority."

"Thanks. Out here."

Bolan disconnected the call and then walked to where Julian sat. She had apparently hacked into the system because over her shoulder Bolan could see electronic blueprints that were obviously of the *Hadesfire*. Structurally speaking, it looked as impressive as she'd described it. It also appeared complex, and Bolan couldn't really make heads or tails of it from this view. Obviously, Julian was much more familiar with it.

"The *Hadesfire?*" he inquired.

She nodded, absently chewing at her lower lip. "I'm inside the system and, so far, it would appear no one's detected me. They must not have its monitoring and security systems enabled."

"Or maybe it's just that your activity in the system wouldn't trigger any warnings," the Executioner pointed out.

Julian looked at him, visibly impressed. "I hadn't thought of that. Very good, Mr. Cooper."

Bolan shrugged. "What exactly are we looking at?"

"Well," she said, turning back to the screen, "these are the completed technical mappings of its electronic and mechanical systems." She pointed to a gray-colored area with superimposed crisscrossed lines of white and blue. "That component is called the central core. It's the heart and soul of the *Hadesfire*. You can think of it as the brains of the operation. All software and data programs are served from its networked repository. It monitors all of the electronic circuitry aboard the system, not to mention most of its mechanical functions."

Bolan's eyebrows rose. "Why would you design it to be that vulnerable?"

"It's not as vulnerable as you think. That core is self-powered with a fail-safe battery system that will service it to the sacrifice of all other nonessential systems. Not only that, it sits at the central part of the *Hadesfire* infrastructure with strictly interior-only access, and is protected by thirty-two-inches of homogenous armor constructed from a titanium-based alloy."

Jack Grimaldi, who had been listening from the distance of a nearby couch with interest, rose and joined the pair at the laptop. "That's pretty significant. Even the black boxes aboard major aircraft aren't protected anywhere near that well."

"And they survive major crashes," Julian said with a nod.

"Sounds to me like the way to stop this thing is to hit key mechanics."

"If you can," Julian challenged. "About the only way to bring the *Hadesfire* down by destroying its mechanical functions is to hit it while it's still on the ground. If the Apparatus manages to get it airborne before you can do that, you don't stand a chance."

Bolan laid a hand on Grimaldi's shoulder. "He does.

You're looking at one of the best pilots in the world. He has many years of air-combat experience."

"Which won't do him a bit of good if he can't catch his target."

"What are you talking about?" Grimaldi asked.

Julian looked him square in the eyes. "The *Hadesfire* sports a CFM-560 jet engine with a short-range backup. Both act as the primary propulsion source. Not only can it travel by air and sea, it's much faster than any helicopter. It can also achieve great speeds, but because it's so much smaller it has a maneuverability not found in conventional jet fighters."

"Okay and fine," Grimaldi replied. "But from what I see of its aeronautical specifications, it doesn't look like it's capable of great ranges. Even if they run, they wouldn't get far."

"They wouldn't have to." Julian returned her attention to the Executioner. "Listen, I'm trying to help you. You seem to keep forgetting that I designed and constructed many of the systems on the *Hadesfire*. It harnesses unspeakable capabilities, and you don't want to underestimate those. You're talking about a weapon that can go just about anywhere, over any kind of terrain, at any time."

The Executioner may not have liked it but he had to admit she made a good argument. He wasn't up against just flesh and blood this time. Not like that was ever the easy part. But a cache of trained mercenaries toting assault rifles didn't seem anywhere near the threat as the *Hadesfire*. Whether Julian was trying to help or not wasn't the point as much as that he had to trust what she was saying to him.

Bolan excused himself and headed for the door to the hangar, motioning Grimaldi to follow. Once they were out of earshot—the door closed behind them—the Executioner got straight to business.

"What do you think?" he asked the pilot.

"You don't really want to know what I think, Sarge."

"I do, Jack," Bolan replied. His expression said it all for Grimaldi.

"Okay, fine. I think you should trust her."

"Why?"

"First, I happen to think she's been straight with us from the beginning, since she seems to have neither the time nor the personality for bullshit. Second, she saved your behind out there in that encampment when the Apparatus had set a trap for you."

"I knew what I was walking into," Bolan said.

"But she knew better than you did, Sarge," Grimaldi reminded him. "You didn't have any inkling what Downing had planned, and where this *Hadesfire* is concerned you didn't have a clue."

Bolan nodded in way of acknowledgment.

"Look, you asked for my opinion and I'm just giving it to you." The Stony Man ace pilot waved in the direction of the hangar. "And it isn't like she's hidden anything from you. She could have let us go back to that camp and kept totally quiet about hitting the *Hadesfire* before it got off the ground."

Bolan nodded. "I'd considered that. That was quite a clever little test you threw at her."

Grimaldi gave him a nod. "I trust you completely *and* I trust that gut-level instinct of yours. If you say she's rotten, then I got to put my money on you because you've never let me down. But if you think about it you'll realize she's being straight with us, and I bet you'll learn to trust her."

Bolan nodded slowly. "She sure has a way of keeping me on my toes. I haven't met anyone quite like her before. She's one of those types you can learn to love and hate all at the same time."

"In my neck of the woods, we'd probably call her a real b—"

"I get the point," Bolan said with a wave, not letting him finish the statement.

Grimaldi smiled. "I figured you would."

"Time to get cracking."

And with that the two friends entered the hangar to prepare for their assault on Downing's camp.

ALEK STEZHNYA WATCHED as his crew put out the last of the flames.

It had taken the resources of more than two-thirds of the garrison to put out the fire caused by Cooper's explosive entrance into the camp. What had him even more disturbed is that Cooper had somehow managed to penetrate the camp—he still wasn't sure for what purpose—and then to escape unmolested. His pursuit squad had lost the trail in the heavy jungle, and on their return the team leader reported a military chopper had extracted Cooper, most probably from a predetermined LZ.

"We're out of time," a voice said next to him.

Stezhnya turned to see Downing at his side. The

work lights set up by the salvage crew provided the only real light. The remainder of the group not assigned to salvage had been put on rotating guard duty of the makeshift hangar for the *Hadesfire*. They had to protect the ship at all costs, as it was the key to the success of their mission.

"We can't wait any longer," Downing continued. "I gave you the opportunity to bring Cooper down and you failed. I gave you the chance. Now it's—"

"My apologies for the interruption, sir, but with all due respect there's no need to say it. You have kept up your end of this bargain and now I will keep mine. I will lead the Apparatus on our mission and I will complete it with success. When it is finished, I expect you'll give me leave to finish my business with Cooper."

Downing nodded. "Agreed. There was no attempt on my part to throw it in your face."

"I never dreamed you had, sir," Stezhnya replied, and he meant it.

"I'm not sure I want to tell the other thing I came to tell you," Downing said. He turned and looked directly into Stezhnya's eyes. "I feared it might distract you from our mission."

"What is it?" Stezhnya asked, but even as he finished asking he knew what Downing meant. He could see it in his eyes. "Crystal?"

"Unfortunately, yes," Downing replied with a frown. "She's missing. I've heard rumors that she was spotted with our intruder. She may have gone to the other side, or she may have been a hostage. Knowing her as you do, I thought you might have an opinion."

"I have none."

"Then how about an educated guess?"

"I would say the first scenario's the most likely one, sir," Stezhnya said. "If she were a hostage, it would be her captors whom I would feel sorry for much more than her."

Downing couldn't seem to resist a light laugh. "Too true."

And they both knew it. One could have accused Dr. Crystal Julian of a good many things, but timidity wouldn't have ever been one of them. She was opinionated and tenacious—traits that many interpreted to be little more than simple precociousness—but Stezhnya had come to admire these things about her. Not to mention her talent between the sheets. In a number of respects she was a real spitfire beneath all the pomp and circumstance of her education and intelligence.

If Stezhnya had come to understand anything about the woman it was that she existed within a state of duality. On the one side she was tender, warm, caring and capable of great passion. On the other she could be gruff, cold and callous with very little regard for the feelings of others. All told, she didn't really turn out to be as complicated as he'd first thought once he understood her almost split personality. The warm and passionate woman he'd grown intimate with was Crystal, and the stiff bitch ass was that *doctor* part of her; the scientist with the cold, calculating mind and the shrewd sense to flaunt her superior intellect over others as a matter of pure scientific subjugation. Stezhnya didn't mind admitting he cared very little for that latter person.

So to him it was Dr. Julian who had succumbed to her misguided sense of patriotism. What puzzled Stezhnya above all else was that he'd made the choice to throw in his lot with Downing because, while they still had little chance of success, he believed more in Downing's motives for liberating America than he did the majority of the politicians. They hadn't done a thing to prevent the invasion of American soil by terrorists from every corner of the globe.

In some eerie way, almost as if he could read Stezhnya's mind, Downing said, "When are people going to understand, Alek? What will it take to open people's eyes? When are they going to start looking around them and seeing, *really* seeing, what's happening to our world? Slowly but surely we're being annihilated by a group that cares only for bloodshed and their own religious views. They call *me* a fanatic and terrorist, but they won't look at what's happening right under their own noses."

"I understand, sir. I wish I had the answers, but unfortunately I'm a mere soldier."

"You not any mere soldier, Alek, you are a patriot!" Downing said, thumping the palm of one hand with the back of the other. "Don't ever underestimate your worth to the security of our nation. If we aren't willing to take on this responsibility, then we could hardly expect others to be willing to do the same thing. We live in a society today that seems more unable than ever to draw the line of what we'll accept and what we absolutely will not. We elect representatives in a free and open system to represent us and speak for us.

"The Aryan Nation, the Jewish Defense League and the ACLU are as guilty of being allowed to spread terror through our country as the Arabs. And the sad thing about all of this is that it's we, the American people, who have allowed these travesties to continue. We have permitted the unjust treatment of our people and we have refused to do a thing to improve the security of our nation."

Stezhnya had heard this same ranting—a ranting that had practically become Downing's trademark speech—a thousand times. Oddly, he'd never grown weary of hearing it. Downing had a way of rejuvenating a man's spirit. His words made absolute sense. He had a gift for gathering men under his leadership, uniting them with a common cause, and instilling in each and every one of them a sense of patriotism and loyalty toward that cause. There were a few among the rank-and-file that were in this only for the pay, but the vast majority of them were there to secure the blessings of the American people. Like Stezhnya, they felt it was their God-given right and duty to protect the nation from those who would defile its security and sanctity.

"It is an injustice, sir," Stezhnya said.

"Injustice nothing, man!" Downing bellowed. "It's a travesty!"

Well, travesty or no travesty, they were going to settle their business with the terrorists once and for all. In all probability, Cooper would soon return in the hopes of taking out the *Hadesfire* before they could launch. It seemed the only viable option at his disposal, and Stezhnya knew he was right because if he were in Cooper's situation it was exactly what he'd do. He also

knew, like Crystal Julian, that the *Hadesfire* would be
at her weakest when she was idle.

Stezhnya remembered Julian's words—"That's
when the central core would be most vulnerable."

He shook his head and blinked with the sudden realization of what Downing had said. Yes, they were definitely running out of time. If they didn't react soon,
Cooper stood a fairly good chance of taking them out
while they were unprepared, and that wouldn't help their
mission. Then again, it wouldn't have put them entirely
out of the game. They, of course, had a backup plan. Like
all good military strategists, Downing had taken certain
steps to ensure their success in the event of any outcome.

Of course, he hadn't shared the details of that plan
with Stezhnya. He'd simply assured him that if they
failed—a possibility Stezhnya considered very remote—they did have a contingency they could fall to.
Stezhnya hoped that wouldn't be necessary. With the
Hadesfire under his command, Stezhnya and his hand-
picked team of elite soldiers would ignite the flame of
war throughout the Middle East. They would pit terrorist against terrorist, taking the focus off America and
putting the war back in its proper perspective.

And when the Islamic militants and the Jewish left-
ists and all these other radical groups had reached a stage
where their numbers dwindled, then the OSI would strike
at the heart of the exposed operations and eradicate the
vermin once and for all. And nothing would ever again
threaten the peace and stability of the American nation.

And then, Stezhnya would settle his score with Matt
Cooper.

CHAPTER TWELVE

Mack Bolan performed action checks on his .44 Magnum Desert Eagle and FNC.

Multiple tools of war hung from his military web belt. The reverberations of the chopper blades pulsed through his body, enhancing the sensations already in place by a surge of adrenaline. Jack Grimaldi had already signaled less than two minutes remained until target. What lay ahead left Bolan with a fresh resolve. Whatever happened tonight, lives hung in the balance. If they didn't stop Downing and the Apparatus from launching the *Hadesfire*, their mission would reach a whole new threat level.

The Executioner couldn't let that happen.

The first option they had considered involved a full-out air assault against the hangar sheltering the *Hadesfire*. The chopper included a forward-mounted Phalanx chain gun and twin 80 mm rocket pods—more than enough firepower to do the job—but Crystal Julian squashed it when she revealed the structural specifications of the hangar.

"From the outside it looks like just a prefab steel building. In reality, its uprights are buried in ten feet of reinforced concrete with a stem wall foundation. There are steel uprights placed every ten feet to reinforce the interior, each of them a foot thick. There are also heavy blast doors that can isolate sections of the hangar, and evacuation systems to extinguish flames up to temperatures of five thousand degrees Fahrenheit."

"Well, so much for huff and puff and blow your house down," Grimaldi had replied.

That left the Executioner with only one logical option. Using infrared scopes, Grimaldi would hover at an insertion point just above the target. Julian had advised since it was the largest building it would give off the greatest heat source, particularly since it required significant power to keep the precious electronics cool and metal dry in the midst of the jungle. Fourteen power generators buried beneath the building provided most of this, and there was no real way to contain all of that heat even given its careful design to thwart observation.

Once inside, the Executioner would go to work and access the *Hadesfire*'s interior by using the command codes Julian provided. They changed regularly—a failsafe built into its vast security systems—but she had managed to retrieve them from the central core. The master code would override any of the security defaults in place unless it had been reprogrammed. Julian seemed skeptical at such an outcome. If anything, Stezhnya and Downing probably realized any attack would be immediately forthcoming and rush to get the *Hadesfire* as far from there as possible.

Before their departure, Grimaldi had elected to ask the unthinkable. "And just what the hell do we do if they manage to get this thing airborne before the Sarge can knock it out of commission?"

Julian's reply had been as cold and unyielding as frozen steel. "Pray."

Bolan would leave most of that to clergy and others better suited to it. He planned more swift and direct action if that occurred. While the chopper might not have been able to catch it, the President had promised Hal Brognola complete support. That included military resources. Bolan didn't want to call in cavalry, but he would if left with no other options.

The soldier felt the sudden slowing of the chopper. He rechecked the Swiss-style descent harness, then slipped his lead line through the D-style carabiner. Bolan then stepped to the side door of the chopper and yanked on the handle. He pushed outward and slid the door aside. The beating of blades intensified as a gust of humid night air slapped him in the face. Undaunted, Bolan fed the line through the eyelet of the personnel winch dangling just outside the door, cinched it, locked it in place, then turned and stepped into nothingness.

Bolan felt the heat of the friction through his neoprene gloves as he descended quickly and steadily on the line. Grimaldi kept the chopper rock-steady during the drop, the chopper not wavering even slightly as it hovered mere feet above the treetops. The Executioner continued downward through a break in the trees and in less than thirty seconds his boots touched the rooftop of the building. He quickly disengaged the rope from the carabiner and headed for the venting stack protruding from the rooftop.

In all their grand scheming, neither Downing nor Stezhnya had believed someone would attempt such an assault. They hadn't bothered to secure the vent in any way, and it was child's play for Bolan to detach one of the mesh panels. He stuck his head through the relatively large opening and saw that the stack terminated at a cross duct about three yards below the roofline. Removing a multipurpose tool from his web belt, the soldier found the metal cutters and carved a man-size hole in the duct.

The Executioner had his entrance. He squeezed through the opening feet-first and controlled his descent by bracing hands and feet against the sides of the vent stack. When he was close enough to the opening in the duct, he released his hold and dropped the roughly five remaining yards to the floor of the hangar.

Bolan immediately knelt and drew the Desert Eagle. He tracked the muzzle 360 degrees. As his eyes adjusted to pseudo-haze of the dim lights above, he realized he'd landed in some kind of large storage room. The shelves lining the walls were sparse, and what sat on them appeared to be mostly spare parts. A lot of it looked like additional control modules, memory sticks, digital boxes and other bits of sensitive electronic equipment.

Gadgets Schwarz would have a field day in here, Bolan thought in passing, envisioning how Able Team's electronics wizard would light up at a chance to tinker with this equipment.

The Executioner returned his attention to the matter at hand. He'd committed the hangar layout to memory. Julian said there were no real sentries other than those at the front entrance. Bolan knew the rear entrance wasn't guarded, and that was where he planned to make his escape for pickup. There also wouldn't be any bystanders—the scientists and technicians working on the *Hadesfire*—to worry about since it was very early in the morning. Although none of it would matter in a few minutes unless he got to work, since they hadn't exactly arrived with stealth.

Bolan moved over to the door and pressed his ear to it. He could hear the sounds of frantic movement, and shouts or voices speaking frantically as associated with a flurry of activity. That didn't fall in line at all with what Julian had told them, and Bolan could immediately sense the reason for the enemy's urgency. It became more apparent when he heard the mechanical cough followed by a sputter that indicated the attempted start of cold aircraft engines.

The soldier pulled back hard on the door as if to rip it from its hinges. He burst from the room and into a long, narrow corridor that opened onto a partial view of the *Hadesfire*. Bolan sprinted for the opening, his FNC held low and at the ready. He came into the open to find a few uniformed guards standing vigil near the *Hadesfire* while others in lab coats scrambled to accomplish whatever duties had been assigned them.

Bolan adjusted the selector on his rifle to 3-shot

mode, and double checked that all innocents were clear before taking his targets. He dropped to one knee, raised the FNC to his shoulder and squeezed the trigger. The first two fell under the assault with gaping wounds to their chests before their comrades could even react to the situation. If they had been expecting some sort of attack, they certainly hadn't planned for such an open and brash one by the enemy.

Another pair of sentries scrambled to swing their machine pistols into acquisition. Bolan grabbed cover near some pallets stacked with equipment and took the first with a fifty-yard head shot. The 5.56 mm NATO slug slammed through the man's skull like a ballpoint pen through rice paper and deposited him against the wall. The second Apparatus gunner managed to bring his weapon to bear and sight on Bolan's shoulder. The soldier whirled in time to see the enemy gunner sighting on him and dropped flat on his back just as the guy leaned back on the trigger. A flurry of slugs buzzed the air where he'd stood.

Still on his back, Bolan reached to his shoulder holster and whipped the Beretta 93-R into play. He snap-aimed in the enemy gunner's direction and squeezed the trigger twice. One of the 125-grain rounds cracked the man's sternum and continued onward to his spine while the second blew a hole through his heart. Blood visibly sprayed his shirt and a nearby wall as his corpse doubled over and collapsed to the unyielding metal floor.

No further sentries showed up to resist him, and the lab-coated bystanders had apparently decided it better to remain hidden or simply to get out of there, since the hangar suddenly appeared abandoned. Bolan got to his feet and experienced only a momentary silence before it was interrupted by another cough and sputter of the *Hadesfire* engines. This time, however, the sputter turned into a roar as the engines came to life.

Bolan shook his head in disbelief before sprinting toward the craft. He would have to make his entrance through the underbelly and could only hope it hadn't already been sealed from the outside. He stopped short when he reached it, as the path through a belly hatch was still open, but it was blocked by the hulking form of an Apparatus soldier. Muscles rippled beneath the olive drab T-shirt worn by the human roadblock.

The guy turned, yanking the camouflage cap from his bald head and cracking his knuckles. He then reached to his side and drew a knife with a blade that had to be a good sixteen inches long. The murderous intent etched in his features made it abundantly clear to the Executioner what he had planned next. The big man started marching purposefully toward the soldier's position.

Bolan saw no reason to waste time and aimed the Beretta. The attacker stopped only a moment to consider this new turn of events, then let out a bloodcurdling scream to accompany the charge. Bolan didn't hesitate. He squeezed the trigger, the report from the pistol hardly audible above the warming engines of the *Hadesfire*. The slug drilled into the man's skull. The body continued forward and Bolan simply sidestepped to avoid the grisly missile of flesh.

The big American holstered the pistol and rushed to

the hold. He jumped onto the metal ladder and scrambled upward through the well toward the main compartment. He'd nearly reached the top when he felt the walls and rungs beneath his feet begin to vibrate. This was it! Downing and his people had managed to make the *Hadesfire* operational before he could destroy it. The only way he could stop it now was to neutralize the crew and try to contact Julian or Grimaldi for help to pilot the blasted thing.

Bolan experienced sudden pain as something grabbed his ankles and yanked him. He struck his chin on the ladder, and the back of his head slammed into the unyielding steel of the ladder well. The soldier dropped to the ground, his ears threatening to burst as the engines powered up and the *Hadesfire* lifted away in a wash of hot air.

And then a world of darkness threatened to close on Bolan as something encircled his neck even before he could formulate his next move....

JACK GRIMALDI COULDN'T be sure what surprised him more, the fact he'd managed to get away from the drop point without ground troops putting a hole in the undercarriage of the chopper, or the fact somebody now held a gun to his head.

Things had seemed to start off okay. After confirming Bolan had descended safely, Grimaldi flipped a switch for the winch retractor and then lifted away from the tree line. Once clear, he turned the chopper and headed back for the camp outskirts, determined to buy his friend as much time as he could. Grimaldi was just about ready to release the first set of rockets when he felt something hard and cold pressed into his ribs.

The Stony Man pilot turned and found himself staring into the tired, haggard face of a dark-eyed stranger, much younger than him, who wore clothes that reeked of cigarette smoke. When he spoke, his breath was easily as atrocious and saturated with the odor of cheap booze. Surprisingly, the guy had still possessed enough sense to don a headset before attempting to communicate with Grimaldi. Fortunately, he'd put one on that was internal only.

"Who the hell are you?" Grimaldi asked.

"I'm the guy who'll blow a big hole right through your heart if you don't shut the fuck up," the man replied in a menacing rumble.

The man's attitude didn't scare the Stony Man pilot; it only incensed him. "You kill me, we go down and burn in this thing together. So unless you're ready to take the stick, pal, I'd keep the threats to yourself."

"You are in no position to threaten me."

"Neither are you," Grimaldi said. "So you want to go back and forth or you want to talk?"

"First, you land this bird."

"Uh-uh," Grimaldi said, shaking his head emphatically.

Now *that* would have been a death sentence. His ability to fly this bird was the only thing keeping him alive at the moment, and he planned to use that to its maximum potential. If he set the chopper down—particularly in any civilized area—that would be the end of him and their mission. And he wasn't about to abandon Mack Bolan. He didn't give a damn who this stow-away was or what he threatened to do. There were just some things that wouldn't happen no matter what, and that was one of them.

"You work for Downing?" Grimaldi said, circling high enough above the trees to prevent being taken out by any stray rounds that might venture their way.

The man snorted. "Are you kidding me? That guy's a piece of shit. And don't be all pretending like you don't work for him."

"I don't," Grimaldi replied. "I'm here to stop him."

"Yeah, you and your commando friend. Right?"

Grimaldi kept his mouth shut.

"Don't bother acting stupid or trying to deny it," the man replied. "I've been following you all goddamn day, and I know exactly what's going on here."

"You think so, huh?"

"I *know* so, pal." He spit. "I might have been born in the dark, but it wasn't last night. I get a phone call from the DDFO last night, telling me—"

"Who?" Grimaldi cut in.

"DDFO," the man repeated with irritation. "Deputy Director of Foreign Operations. The name's Levine. I'm the Philippines section chief for the CIA desk here."

"Well, then, why the hell are you sticking a gun in my ribs?" Grimaldi asked with just a slight dramatic emphasis of indignation. "We're on the same side, stupid. You know how much trouble you just bought yourself?"

"Not as much trouble as you if you don't shut up and let me think," Levine threatened.

"Yeah, well, while you're doing that you might also want to think about what's happening below," Grimaldi shot back. "Look, I won't bullshit you. This Downing character has apparently built some kind of super-weapon and he intends to use it to further the cause."

"You mean this Organization of Strategic Initiative he kept squawking about in that earlier broadcast."

Grimaldi nodded. "That wasn't seen by everyone, only targeted members high in government. The same people you and I work for."

"You talking about the director?"

"Tip of the iceberg, friend," Grimaldi replied. "I'm talking about right up to and including the President of the United States. Weren't you ordered to lay off this mission by your people?"

"Yeah," Levine answered, not concealing the suspicion on his face. "How did you know?"

"Never mind that." Grimaldi was becoming frustrated with his boneheaded captor. "Where do you think that order came from? It came straight from the top, man, the same place where *our* orders came from. Now right at this moment a very good friend of mine's on the ground and trying to knock this weapon out of action. And he damn well better make it because if he doesn't, ally or no ally, you won't survive this trip. I'll kill you with my bare hands."

Levine seemed to chew on that for a bit, and Grimaldi left him to it. The CIA man knew Grimaldi was telling the truth. He'd apparently elected to disobey orders for whatever reason, but they could deal with that later. Right now he had to do what he could to help out

Bolan and be ready for the extraction. That time drew shorter by the minute, and the last thing he had time to do was to sit around arguing loyalties and sides with Levine. He couldn't afford the distraction.

Neither could the Executioner.

"All right, so let's suppose I believe you," Levine said. "Who's the girl you brought back to Manila?"

"She was one of the scientists who helped build this doomsday weapon," Grimaldi replied truthfully. He didn't know what Levine's clearances were but he didn't really give a damn right at the moment. "Whatever Downing plans to do with that thing, we're here to make sure it doesn't get off the ground."

"And what if it does?" Levine asked.

Before Grimaldi could reply, the air in the chopper was filled with a sonic shriek and something streaked out of the trees and accelerated away at an unbelievable speed. Grimaldi could only stare at the blue-white trail left in the path of the object as it rocketed away from their position. He didn't have to guess at what it was. They had successfully launched the *Hadesfire*. To make things worse, he hadn't received the signal from Bolan to indicate his readiness for extraction.

Grimaldi checked his watch and noticed it was two minutes past the agreed-upon time for contact.

"What the fuck was that?" Levine said, pointing at the *Hadesfire*'s trail.

For the first time in some while, Jack Grimaldi found himself unable to speak.

CHAPTER THIRTEEN

Agymah Malik slammed the telephone receiver into its cradle.

He tried to contain his anger, but he simply couldn't suppress the quiver of hatred and loathing that ran through his lithe, athletic figure. Beads of sweat glistened against his dark complexion and soaked the collar of his tan silk shirt. He took several deep breaths, shoved his hands into the pockets of his tailored wool slacks and left his office. He crossed a great room and walked through the open double doors onto the balcony of his home.

The sandstone mansion overlooked the verdant oasis on the outskirts of Cairo. This was *his* city. With a population of more than six million people, Cairo bordered the city of Giza on the banks of the Nile, and drew great wealth from a variety of areas. And as a businessman, Malik had diverse interests. Some of those interests weren't wholly legal, but Malik didn't let that bother him. He had founded nothing short of a principality on his investments, and he paid good money to ensure its security.

Now something ominous threatened that security. He'd begun his career as a freedom fighter with the Armed Islamic Group—GIA—first protesting the policies of his government and its leaders and later actually participating in more "practical" matters of persuasion.

Eventually, Malik realized he took little pleasure in bombing buses with children aboard, even the children of the Westerners. He'd never considered that to be courageous, and he saw little benefit to the GIA. His aims were more about bringing stability to his own country and its people. Far too long the Egyptian people had been oppressed under the financial wherewithal of their neighbors, and Malik had a dream to change that. One day he believed he would bring prosperity to his countrymen, and he'd never have to dirty his hands again with the slaughter of innocent women and children.

What the hell was honorable about killing the weak and unarmed?

Malik eventually served as a protector for the head of the GIA, but again he took no real satisfaction from such mundane work. After the rapid decline in their numbers, he elected to leave the organization. He first learned to read and write English from his brother, a doctor and naturalized U.S. citizen, and then began to explore uncharted territory in the Egyptian business world. With investor backing and the will to succeed, Malik ruthlessly eliminated the competition by any means at his disposal. Now he stood on the brink of an unprecedented alliance with the Iranian revolutionaries, Mujahedeen-e-Khalq.

Malik took another deep breath of the hot desert air and it made him feel only a little better. He'd expended almost five million dollars of his own money for the operation in Oman, the reason for the phone call, and still they couldn't seem to acquire a single piece of solid intelligence on American military efforts to subvert their organization. It seemed his contacts in the United States were as much at a loss as he was.

And then there were the almost laughable private disclaimers by U.S. politicians regarding the activities of an American named Garrett Downing. In public they neither supported nor denounced the man. How they could feign complete ignorance of this man in front of the entire world bordered on insanity. It was a clever ruse, Malik would admit that, but a ruse all the same and one to be dealt with swiftly and decisively.

To some degree he was equally puzzled by recent events in the Philippines that seemed somehow related to what had happened in Atlanta. Of course the New Corsican Front, who had for the past several years claimed they were a peaceful political group and nothing more, denounced American actions after the massacre in Atlanta, both before and after the incident. Malik's informants had spoken of well trained commandos with military explosives and weaponry at almost every turn in the whole sordid situation.

Yes, that had him very disturbed. But he couldn't let on to his guest—whose arrival was pending—that this had taken place. He had to keep quiet long enough to finish his work in Oman. He would eventually learn the truth behind the entire charade, and then he would deal with it appropriately. It would not do for Kiyanfar to find out.

As if on cue, Malik observed a white Mercedes-Benz stop at the front gate and await permission to enter. He smiled with satisfaction. It was good to let the new arrivals wait. He didn't want to seem anxious, although it was hard to keep such appearances. The truth was that he was very excited. This newly formed alliance with the MEK had already turned out to be one of the best ideas he'd ever had, not to mention what it would do for him in the eyes of members within the al Qaeda leadership. They had already proved a great financial resource, and supported him with the idea unity was the key to victory. Of course, the money they had provided didn't come anywhere close to the financial backing of the pilot utility project he'd brokered in Oman. That had served as the perfect front through which to funnel his latest operations.

Malik turned on his heel and walked purposefully but unhurried through the mansion as the new arrivals made their way up the drive adorned by cactus and fruit gardens. Soft music echoed through ceiling speakers spread throughout the spacious abode. Malik descended a wide, spiral staircase and three of his bodyguards greeted him at the bottom. Two toted machine pistols on shoulder slings while his security chief wore a .357 Magnum revolver with a four-inch barrel in shoulder leather.

Malik still carried a pistol himself, in a holster at the

small of his back. He'd learned at a very young age that one couldn't be too careful. He was considered a dangerous man but also respected. Most looked the other way at his questionable business activities, mainly because the bribes he disbursed to underpaid officials charged with running an underfunded police regime kept him out of a dank, dungeon prison. He had no false sense of security or invulnerability. Agymah Malik had survived this long by being careful and seizing the advantage when it seemed easy for the taking. He wasn't about to let his guard down by thinking that twenty or thirty soldiers armed with machine pistols and spread throughout the grounds were foolproof protection.

Anybody could be hit if the assassins wanted it badly enough.

The security chief opened the door and stood aside to let his men accompany Malik onto the front porch. Malik threw up his hands in welcome as his visitor emerged from the back of the Mercedes. It was only the second time he had ever met the man who now stood in front of him. Their first meeting had been rushed and business-like in the back of a very dark and dingy bar in one of the worst parts of Istanbul. Turkey provided a decently neutral ground for such meetings, where neither party had the advantage and both were equally hated by the local citizenry.

The visitor's name was Behrouz Kiyanfar, and he was the leader of one of the most powerful revolutionary units in Iran. The MEK was perhaps one of the best equipped and trained fighting forces ever established.

They had begun small and ill-equipped, but as time went on their membership grew exponentially and soon they had amassed a fighting force of more than ten thousand members. In addition to their attacks against the Iranian government, primarily dignitaries and politicians, they were extensively tied with smuggling of arms to similar groups in neighboring countries. They provided protection to members of other groups in the Islamic jihad, but due to limited financial resources they were in constant need of almost support from outside influences.

Seeing an opportunity, Malik had moved on that need.

"Behrouz Kiyanfar," Malik greeted him in a warm, congenial tone, "welcome to my home."

Kiyanfar stepped forward and studied his host a moment with a casual expression. He was about Malik's height, with tough, leathery skin and dark, piercing eyes. A full beard protruded from his strong chin and jawline, and wrinkles lined his eyes and forehead. In short, Kiyanfar had the weathered look of a man who had fought many battles and endured all the greatest hardships of a brutal, untamed desert country. Malik could see that harsh, inhospitable and unforgiving conditions had hardened Kiyanfar's body and mind.

After a long and stern appraisal, Kiyanfar's granite-like features appeared to relax some. "It is indeed a pleasure to see you again."

Kiyanfar reached out and grabbed Malik by his beard, pulled him forward and kissed both sides of his check before anyone knew what was happening. The guards stepped forward in the next moment, reaching for their machine pistols. Kiyanfar's driver burst from the Mercedes and rushed to protect his master.

Malik raised his arms and shouted a few, terse orders at his men. "Stop! This man is my guest and you will treat him with the respect deserving of that honor!"

All parties calmed and lowered their weapons.

"I apologize," Kiyanfar replied, turning to assure his own bodyguard. "I should have warned you that I was ordered to greet you traditionally under the terms of the new fatwah regarding alliances."

"There is no reason to apologize, my brother," Malik replied smoothly, staring daggers at his men. "Please, come into the shade. I am sure you're hot and tired after your journey, and I would consider it a privilege if you would permit me to show the finest comforts of my home."

"That is most kind," Kiyanfar replied. "And after this, I would like to rest before we conduct our business."

Kiyanfar whispered something to his assistant, then followed Malik into the mansion. The tour didn't take long, and once they had completed it Malik's servants led Kiyanfar to the guest quarters where he could rest. An hour later and a servant led Kiyanfar to a rooftop dining tent that overlooked the city. The sun had begun to dip toward the western horizon and soon it would be time for prayers. Neither of the men followed the pure faith of their ancestors.

"I do come from a very strict sect of the faith," Kiyanfar noted. "Yet, I have found that the path upon which God has set my feet is that of a soldier. There seems something very impractical about matters of faith in such circumstances."

Malik smiled. "The same might be said of business-men like me."

Kiyanfar observed the city as they drank tea and smoked from a very large hookah. "Indeed it is a beautiful city, just as you told me at our last meeting."

Although the rooftop was fully shaded from the sun, Malik squinted and replied, "I was born to live here. I will die here."

Kiyanfar frowned over his glass. "Let us hope that won't be necessary, Agymah."

Malik nodded, then said, "It truly is a pleasure to have you here, Behrouz. I believe I mentioned before that the actions of your followers have reached the ears of even my own people here in Cairo."

"Really?" Kiyanfar appeared impressed with this bit of revelation. "I believed our cause against the government had died with their announcement of the cease-fire."

"Your cause may have been reduced to a smolder for the time. But I *never* believed it had died."

"It might have," Kiyanfar replied. "Had it not been for their breaking of the agreement between our peoples. We were a dying force. But their most recent activities have rekindled the spirit of our fighting men. Every day we recruit more young, strong warriors and every day we draw closer to ultimate victory. This time we will not fall for their treachery as we did before."

It was Malik's turn to smile. "Yes. The bureaucracy

within the Iranian government *has* sown dissension and mistrust among their ruled masses. This is not a new story. But I sometimes wonder if you've asked yourself why this sudden turn of events. Why in these times of greatest turmoil, especially following the war in Iraq with the Americans and the growth of influence by Western powers, do you suppose they chose now to stir up trouble?"

"I am not sure I understand."

"Nor do I. I am simply asking if it doesn't seem to you that the timing of your enemies is a bit off."

"How so?"

"With so much civil unrest, it would not seem beneficial for them to violate a cease-fire with your people. They can ill afford such problems. Additionally, they seem to have no motive for it."

Kiyanfar waved away the very suggestion. "They have never needed a motive. They oppress my people because of our beliefs. They have fallen to the ways of the Westerners. The blind lead the blind within our government. And now because they have not the resources to combat the real threat to our society, they choose to create trouble between us so as to remove the focus from their own shortcomings."

"So you're saying they have removed the glory of your people through their ignorance of tradition."

"Exactly," Kiyanfar replied with a curt nod.

"I believe in a very similar cause," Malik said, changing the subject a bit. "It's my wish to restore the glory of the Egyptian people to the times of the pharaohs. We have long suffered the plagues of starvation and poverty. I believe I can return us to the height of our riches and stature. And I want freedom from repressive government just as you. What I am not certain of is who my enemy really is."

"You don't honestly believe some other group is behind this war between my people and our government," Kiyanfar said with a barking laugh. "Or suggesting that you believe the American's whispered claims of how they have nothing to do with this Garrett Downing? He's purported to be a some self-proclaimed liberator, and yet he apparently held a significant office within the American intelligence circles."

"I'm no longer sure what to believe," Malik replied smoothly and quickly. He sat forward, tapping the hand-carved clay table with his finger and added, "Of course I do not succumb to the preposterous claims by the Americans, but I also cannot believe that after years of peace your government would blatantly violate its cease-fire agreement with you."

"I would be more than happy to show you the pictures of our dead if you need convincing."

"That is not necessary," Malik said. "I have no doubt of your losses. In fact, that's the reason I asked you to come. I know you need more support, particularly in the area of weapons. I, on other hand, need protection for my business operations in Oman. That is why I think we could help one another, Behrouz."

Kiyanfar pulled the pipe from his mouth. "Agymah…my friend. I have already provided all of the men I can spare for your operations. Now you ask me for more?"

"I know it seems a great burden, but when you've heard my proposal you will most likely find it very hard to deny me such a simple request."

"I'm intrigued by your enthusiasm alone. Please continue."

Malik took a deep breath. Now was the moment for which he had waited almost six months. He had obviously made a good impression, otherwise a man like Kiyanfar wouldn't still be seated here. He couldn't blow it now by seeming as an opportunist. It was of paramount importance he convince Kiyanfar of the promise in his words and the totality of his vision.

"When I left the jihad to form my companies, I came to realize that the key to survival lie in the acquisition of powerful allies. I believe you know this, as well."

Kiyanfar nodded.

"It occurred to me," Malik continued, "that if my operations are to remain profitable and you are to achieve victory against your enemies, we would be stronger if we were to combine our forces and take this war back to where it originated. I want to get operations under way in the very heart of Tehran. This will not only assist your people, but it would most likely rally cause for your support. It would also deter the focus of our enemies on the operations in Oman."

Kiyanfar took a long sip of his tea and then gently returned the pipe to his mouth. He looked onto the rich, colorful gardens spread across the grounds. Malik could tell the wheels were turning inside the head of his Iranian ally.

Finally, Kiyanfar said, "What you propose might be

possible. However, my people bear a vast majority of the risks where it involves loss of life."

"This is true. But I can promise you that for a temporary measure I will provide you with the very best equipment. You will have all the small arms and munitions you need, and it will bring you closer to your goals."

"What do you mean?"

"When word of such an operation reaches our brothers, it will undoubtedly bring with it the support of al Qaeda, and this in turn would provide the funds necessary to the continued health of both my business operations and your war. It will also draw out those who are working for the Americans. They will no longer be able to deny the actions of this mercenary, Downing. We can then exploit their involvement by spreading propaganda that American subversives are actually behind the entire situation, and are attempting to overthrow your government."

"Perhaps your plan could work," Kiyanfar admitted. "But you are making many assumptions."

"Such as?"

Kiyanfar laughed. "First, you are convinced the Americans are lying with their story of this rogue intelligence agent who has decided to finance total war against our brothers in the New Corsican Front. Second, you also proclaim the majority of the public will believe the American intelligence community would actually attempt to create a coup of bloodshed within the Iranian government."

"And both of those are exactly reasons why this plan

would work," Malik replied. "It's certainly no secret the United States has manipulated rather unstable situations in other countries in the hope of overthrowing what they perceive to be a dictator. Think of the number of examples we could name right this moment! If this story about Downing isn't a fraud, the Americans will soon decide a first-strike initiative is the safer and more logical option. If they do that, they will strike at every known operation and that will include our efforts in Oman. They already know we're there. It's only a matter of time before they launch an air strike or some covert operation against us. Think about how much we stand to lose if we do not put the focus elsewhere."

"I cannot deny the wisdom of your argument," Kiyanfar finally replied after nearly a minute of silence had elapsed between them. "I will ready my men for this operation and submit our requirements as soon as possible."

"Excellent, excellent," Malik replied. "You will not regret it."

"Let us hope not for your sake," Kiyanfar replied.

The threat in Kiyanfar's voice wasn't lost on the Egyptian.

CHAPTER FOURTEEN

Mack Bolan hadn't initially sensed the presence that pulled him from the ladder well of the *Hadesfire*. There was a lot of noise distracting him.

However, there was no ignoring the feeling of a shadow crossing over him, followed by something being slung over his head. Bolan turned just slightly in time to avoid having his throat crushed by a thick rope and managed to raise his forearm near his head, a reactionary movement that came from years of training. Rope made a crude garrote, but it could still prove lethal in the hands of an experienced user. Bolan's particular attacker seemed anything but that. The soldier was sideways to his assailant now, had made it to his knees, and his well-calculated and well-timed movements gave him the advantage.

Bolan reached down, grabbed the back of his adversary's boot and yanked forward while simultaneously rising from his position. The maneuver threw the assailant onto his back. Bolan was on the guy in seconds, but his enemy was just as fast. The man launched a kick to Bolan's face that nearly knocked him unconscious. The soldier's head reeled from the vicious assault, but he shook it off.

The attacker slipped free and regained his feet nearly as fast as the Executioner. The glint of the hangar lights on steel revealed that the Apparatus hardman held a large combat knife. When the mercenary charged, Bolan sidestepped the attack and delivered a knife-hand strike to his would-be assailant's wrist. The terrorist shouted with a mix of pain and surprise, and the knife fell from numbed fingers.

The man whirled and reached for his side arm, but the Executioner cleared the Beretta from shoulder leather first. He snap-aimed on the enemy gunner and squeezed the trigger twice. The first 9 mm slug hit the terrorist in the right chest, punching through a lung. Blood erupted from the man's mouth in a foaming spray even as the second round struck him in the chin and then traveled on to rip away the lower part of the jaw. The man began to twitch and shudder as blood spurted from the open, gaping wounds. Bolan stepped forward and put a mercy round through his head.

Bolan didn't wait for a new pair of Apparatus soldiers to announce themselves.

As soon as they came through a door near the launch pad, Bolan dropped and rolled for cover. The air around where he'd been a moment before was suddenly filled with a hail of bullets. Bolan completed his roll and settled into a kneeling position, Beretta held at the ready, now in 3-round-burst mode. He triggered the first trio of bullets, shooting the weapon from the closest terrorist's grip with the first two rounds and catching him in the ribs with the third.

Bolan immediately followed up with a second volley, but he couldn't see its effect because the sudden whoosh of heat and flame washed over his head and forced him flat to the floor. Stray rounds had obviously found their way into the fuel containers.

Sparks had done the rest.

Bolan lifted his head at the sound of screaming and immediately noticed the remaining opponent was awash in flames. The human torch wailed and cried for mercy. Bolan gave it to him with a triple-burst head shot.

The Executioner swept the hangar with the muzzle of the Beretta but no further threats remained. Bolan holstered the pistol in favor of the FNC, double-checked the assault weapon's action, then palmed an AN-M8 HC smoke grenade. He crossed the hangar, bound for the door he knew would lead him to a corridor that terminated at the back entrance.

An immediate response met Bolan as soon as he opened the door. The rounds slammed into the door frame and ricocheted off the door but missed the Executioner as he'd made his entry in a crouch. Bolan tossed the smoker and immediately followed with an M-67 fragmentation grenade. Thick, white clouds of smoke immediately enveloped the hallway, drifting slowly and lazily upward toward the vast open ceiling above.

The fragmentation bomb exploded a moment later, and Bolan could hear the screams of more Apparatus soldiers who had laid in wait for him. He tossed another M-67 into the corridor. The smoke thickened but did nothing to hide the flashes or contain the blasts and smell of cordite. Bolan felt rounds buzz over his head but he continued forward on his belly, undaunted by the odds stacked against him. Bolan had grown rather accustomed to battling superior numbers. He'd never quite grown comfortable with it, but he was used to it.

Bolan estimated he was about one-third of the way down the hallway when he sensed his proximity to the enemy. Smoke still obscured everything ahead, and the last thing he wanted was to crawl right up nose to nose with the enemy. After a moment of consideration, the Executioner realized just how surprised the Apparatus gunners would be at that.

Bolan crawled another five yards, then got to his feet and charged through the smoke. He emerged to see a cluster of terrorists on the retreat, and nearly ran into one. The soldier launched a buttstroke to the groin area of one of the gunners, and watched with satisfaction as his surprised opponent collapsed. Bolan was now in a position beyond the smoke where he could see clearly the enemy numbers: there weren't many. Most had probably succumbed to the grenades.

The Executioner immediately lowered the FNC to hip level and held steady on the trigger to spray the area with autofire. The terrorists dropped where they had stood, unable to respond to the surprising emergence of the black-clad specter from the smoke and destructive fire. Their training had not clearly provided most of them with live-combat conditions. Most had probably assumed they would be on the offensive against unprepared and untrained fanatics.

Two of the soldiers managed to escape the initial onslaught by ducking into the alcove adjoining the corridor, the same alcove where Bolan had first met Crystal Julian. Bolan rushed their position and reached the alcove unscathed. He no longer had the advantage of surprise, but he had something the Apparatus didn't: unquestionable experience in the heat of battle. The Apparatus gunners opened up on Bolan simultaneously but their aim was ineffective. In their haste, they made the deadly mistake of expending most of their ammunition.

Bolan got the first hardman with a sustained burst that stitched from crotch to head like a needle through satin. The gunner dropped his weapon and danced backward under the assault. His back finally reached the wall and he jerked a few more times as Bolan added another short burst for good measure. The man was little more than a hunk of bullet-riddled flesh by the time he hit the floor.

Bolan whirled and caught the second gunner with a short burst. The man had apparently tried to reload while Bolan dispatched his partner, but he wasn't fast enough to eliminate the threat. The soldier's shots cut a swathe of destruction across the enemy's midsection and he began to drop. A follow-up burst struck him in the chest and left gaping exit wounds. One of the rounds struck an artery in the neck, and blood spurted everywhere as the man's body hit the deck with a dull thud.

The Executioner kicked open the back door and keyed the evacuation signal by flipping a switch on the transceiver clipped to his equipment belt. He then shoulder rolled in time to avoid being chopped to shreds by a pair of gunners charging his position, their AK-74s ablaze. He went to one knee and fired the FNC on the rise. The weapon echoed in the jungle air with a thunderous report. A burst of 5.56 mm NATO rounds took the first gunner in the chest, tearing holes through his back and ripping apart heart and lungs. He left his feet and crashed against a nearby piece of equipment. The second attacker tried to avoid Bolan's fire, the initial volley missing vital organs and catching him in the legs as he dived for cover. He hit the jungle floor hard and died under a fresh salvo before he could recover from the assault.

The Executioner met two more attackers before he could get to his feet and head for the open point where Grimaldi would pick him up. He took the first one high in the chest as the man brought his assault rifle to target. The high-velocity slugs slammed into his body, seemingly pinning his arm to his side and spinning him away.

The second man simply began to swing the muzzle of his weapon in Bolan's direction, furiously unloading a barrage of rounds. He'd obviously chosen to forego aiming in favor of speed for purposes of self-preservation. Bolan rushed to cover behind a heavy ground vent in time to avoid being perforated by a hail of 9 mm slugs from the shooter's foreign-made machine pistol. Bolan waited until he'd stopped firing and heard the pop of a magazine, then emerged from cover just enough to snap-aim the FNC and blow him away. The man's head exploded under the impact of several 5.56 mm rounds.

Bolan crouched and turned to his rear flank at the sound of boots slapping moist jungle ground. Four more Apparatus hardmen appeared from the side of the hangar. Bolan could hear the movement of men and equipment now, which meant the whole damned camp had gone to full alert. The Apparatus gunmen were obviously unaware their enemy was close enough to engage, and they emerged directly into the spotlight shining from a sentry tower perched atop another prefab building.

As the gunners armed with AK-74s charged his position, scientists and technicians who had vacated the hangar burst from their hiding positions and tried to escape. Bolan ensured they were clear, concentrating solely on the armed opposition. He couldn't simply cut them down in cold blood. First of all, they were unarmed. Second, he couldn't assume they were guilty of any real crime, as it was entirely possible they had all been duped the same way Crystal Julian had.

Bolan made a beeline for another ground vent as he triggered the FNC again. Two of the four fell under the soldier's superior marksmanship. He kept moving, confident that tactic would prevent the remaining pair from flanking his position as they were trying to do right at that moment.

The Executioner was right.

He suddenly changed direction at the last moment, heading directly toward the enemy instead of away from them. At less than ten yards, Bolan knelt and opened fire. The FNC chattered as Bolan swept the muzzle in a biting figure eight and cut his opponent down. The remaining Apparatus troops turned to escape, obviously realizing the odds had been evened. Bolan raised the FNC to his shoulder but the sudden sound of rotor blades distracted him.

The engines of the chopper roared in his ears. Then there was the sound of the Phalanx chain gun and the whoosh of 30 mm rockets as they burst from their pods. The spotlight blinked out a moment later in a grandstand display of showering sparks and bodies falling from the roof. The tower toppled mere seconds after the two men manning the spotlight sailed from its peak.

Bolan broke cover and raced toward the winch-controlled cable that lowered to the ground. He keyed up the system and shouted into the microphone for Grimaldi to raise the winch. He clipped the carabiner to the safety line just a moment before his feet abruptly left the ground. The chopper went straight vertical at significant speed. Bolan almost lost his grip but kept his cool. Something had obviously spooked Grimaldi enough that he felt the need to get away as quickly as possible. Well, that was just fine with Bolan. He'd learned over the years to trust the pilot's keen intuitions nearly as much as he trusted his own.

As Bolan reached the top of the chopper and stepped through the open door, he found himself looking down the barrel of a pistol. It was held by an unkempt-looking man, his face grimy with the dirt and heat of a very long day, and a jaw that had long passed the five o'clock shadow stage. In fact, he almost looked like some kind of street bum.

"You got some explaining to do, mister!" the man said.

Bolan didn't wait for any more chitchat. The Executioner dropped to his left hip and swung his right leg out in a trip sweep that easily toppled the guy. The maneuver took the man by complete surprise and he lost control of his pistol, which hit the decking of the chopper and bounced out of reach. Bolan jumped onto his opponent and pinned the man's shoulders with his knees. He fired a rock-hard punch to the man's forehead, slamming the back of his skull against the deck. The single punch was enough to knock him cold.

Bolan reached into a pocket of his blacksuit and retrieved a pair of plastic riot cuffs. He turned the man over and slapped them on his wrists, then got wearily to his feet and staggered to the cockpit. He tapped Grimaldi on the shoulder and the pilot turned, grinning sheepishly.

The Executioner reached for a headset and donned it. He jerked a thumb in the unconscious passenger's direction and said, "What gives, Jack?"

"Sorry, Sarge, but he was listening. Said if I warned you he'd cut the line before you got aboard."

"Who is he?"

"Stowaway. Guy works for the Company, or so he says. Smelled pretty liquored up to me."

Bolan shook his head. This mission had grown more interesting by the minute, *and* more complicated. "Once he comes to and we get the full story, I'll let the Farm deal with him. You saw?"

"The *Hadesfire* got away. Yeah I saw. I'm sorry about that, Sarge."

"So am I," Bolan replied.

"Especially since we don't have a clue where it's going."

"I think I know exactly where it's going," Bolan replied.

"Where?"

"The Middle East."

AFTER SEVERAL HOURS of questioning, Mack Bolan managed to get the entire story from Warren Levine and how he'd become involved in the situation. Once he had the information, Bolan contacted Stony Man Farm to discuss their options with Brognola and Price.

"We should let Levine's superiors deal with him. Obviously the guy's been in this business a bit too long," Price said. "We'll contact the head of foreign operations first thing in the morning and get him off your hands."

"Fine," Bolan replied. "For now, I have him restrained and he's sleeping it off."

"Poor bastard," Brognola chimed in. "I've seen too many like Levine waste away in hellholes like that one."

"Yeah, I can understand," Bolan replied. "It doesn't mean I can agree, though. We all have to make choices, and Levine made his. Now he'll have to live with the consequences."

Bolan didn't mean to be harsh, but he didn't think there was any other way to look at it. He knew a lot of good men had an alcohol or drug addiction, and it was disappointing. Bolan had learned through the years not to get too preachy about such things. It happened to even the best men, the most well-intentioned.

"So you have an idea about the *Hadesfire*," Brognola said.

"Yeah," Bolan replied, sitting on a bunk in the rented hangar and willing his mind and body to stay alert. "I'm betting based on the activities you reported in the Middle East that Downing and his team are about to make their play. We have to stop them before that happens."

"Are you going to need support from the military?"

"I know the Man has his finger poised over that button, but I'd prefer to use the time he offered first. Intervention by armed U.S. troops would only mean a publicity nightmare for America and these other countries. The situation over there's hot enough already. That would just add punch to Downing's alleged crusade. Better we keep it under wraps as long as possible."

"That was our assessment, as well," Brognola replied, which was another way of saying he knew Bolan would say that. "Well, the offer is a standing one. Any time you want help you just say the word."

"Our best bet is to get there as soon as possible. I'll need regular feedback on where the hotbed of activity is."

"You're thinking wherever that it is, the Apparatus will be there, as well."

"Right."

"Okay, Striker, you're still calling the shots on this one. Just don't hesitate to call us for help if you need it."

"Understood. Out, here."

Bolan disconnected the call and then stopped to stare absently at the drab wall of the hangar. Grimaldi had already left to prep the jet, and Julian was out like a light in a nearby bunk. She had finally decided to catch up on some much needed rest. Bolan wished he could do the same, but at times like these a fitful slumber escaped him. He'd catch a few winks on the trip over.

They were now bound for one of the most hostile regions on the face of the Earth, a place where they would be unable to trust anyone, and where they had very few contacts. And being Americans they would definitely stand out among the populace. Every turn in the road would be a risk. But the Executioner would adapt and overcome any circumstance that crossed his path, for he'd walked this road before.

He could simply add it as another bloody mile.

CHAPTER FIFTEEN

Mack Bolan managed to grab a few hours' rest aboard the flight.

He stretched in his seat, then stood and started a pot of coffee. He shook Julian awake. Bolan had elected to bring the scientist with them since she possessed critical technical knowledge about the *Hadesfire*.

"Feel better?" Bolan asked as he waved a cup of coffee under her nose.

"Yes," she said, taking the cup gingerly from him.

Bolan took a moment to study her features more closely. She was truly an attractive woman. It was too bad she had a personality so diametrically opposed to her good looks. In other circumstances she was attractive, but that brusque personality was difficult to take. He dropped back into his seat and looked at his watch.

"It'll be time to go spell Jack soon," Bolan said.

"How long have you been doing this kind of thing?"

The question surprised him. "What kind of thing?"

"You know…all this fighting for truth, justice and the American way," she shot back.

Bolan returned her stare with a humorless one of his own. "Let me guess, you think I have some sort of Superman complex?"

She actually smiled now and curled her legs up on the oversize seat, resting her chin on her knees. "I suppose that's one way of looking at it. Although I was thinking more along the lines of Dudley Do-Right."

Bolan shook his head, then reached to the bag beneath his legs. He pulled the FNC from it and began to strip down the weapon. He got down only to the working parts and then proceeded to spray them with a cleaner and light lubricant. He then repeated the efforts for the Desert Eagle, choosing to keep the Beretta locked and loaded in shoulder leather. For some reason he couldn't explain, he still didn't trust entirely the woman seated next to him. She had shared a relationship with the enemy and that didn't sit well with him.

The soldier decided the weapons could soak in the solvents while he watched the cockpit instrumentation. He left them on the small table in front them, refilled his coffee cup and then headed for the cockpit. As he reached the cockpit door, Julian called to him.

"I didn't get the chance before to thank you for pulling my ass out of Downing's camp. If you hadn't come along when you did, I'd probably be strapped to some table right now and tortured for information." She let out a visible shudder. "Or something worse I don't even want to imagine."

Bolan thought a moment about his reply. It seemed

Julian was being sincere enough. He settled for, "Sure thing."

He entered the cockpit and squeezed himself into the copilot's seat. Grimaldi nodded an acknowledgment at his friend before giving his full attention to the instrumentation and navigational systems. The pilot was a rock, no question about it. He'd been on enough missions like this one that to go without sleep for many hours came almost naturally. Staying awake for longer periods of time became a matter of conditioning the mind and the body. And lots of coffee didn't hurt, either. The Executioner offered his cup to Grimaldi, but the pilot declined with a wan smile.

"No, thanks, Sarge. I'd prefer to just grab a little shuteye if it's all the same to you. Coffee's for later down the road."

"Go ahead. You sure as hell deserve it."

Grimaldi nodded. He would simply plot the remainder of their course and then lay back in his seat and sleep while Bolan kept an eye on the instrumentation. It wasn't the first time the pair had done something like this, and it sure as hell wouldn't be the last.

"What's the word back there?" Grimaldi asked, gesturing with his head in the direction of the cabin. "Is our little angel awake?"

Bolan nodded with a knowing grin. "Yeah, she's a handful."

The flier shook his head. "She's a pain in the ass is what she is. But I guess I can understand your bringing her along. I just hope I'm not stuck having to baby-sit when we get to wherever we're going."

Bolan decided to be noncommittal in his reply. "We'll see what's what when we get there."

"So what's the verdict back at the Farm on this whole deal?"

"Hal called me about an hour ago and advised things are getting stirred up in Tehran."

"Tehran?" Grimaldi echoed. "I take it that means we should plot a course change for Iran?"

"Probably," Bolan said. "Things have been unstable between the Iranian police authorities and citizens with established ties to the MEK over the past couple of weeks. There's a similar story brewing in Egypt. I'm betting it's Downing behind all of it. This has probably been his plan for months."

"It would make sense," Grimaldi said.

"Sure," Bolan replied. "It wouldn't take much to work groups like that into a frenzy anyway. Washington's plan to privately deny any involvement with Downing while playing deaf, dumb and blind in the public sector probably did more harm than good."

"Well, I'm sure they made the best decision given the circumstances," Grimaldi pointed out. "And at least Hal was able to buy us a little more time."

"Yeah. Let's just hope twenty-four hours is enough, because that's all we'll have by the time we get to Iran."

"Do you have a plan?"

Bolan nodded. "I'm betting Downing and Stezhnya won't risk using the *Hadesfire* within the city. It's not the kind of weapon that would prove effective. That means they'll have to apply more conventional means of combat while they're in Tehran, and that's something I can counteract."

"So where does the *Hadesfire* fit into all of this," Grimaldi said. "Because I can tell you that the speeds I saw that thing traveling at only a jet fighter would be even remotely effective against it."

"I'm not so sure on that yet," Bolan admitted. "Hal said the President mentioned activity in the Oman Desert. Intelligence circles have already touted it's some kind of terrorist operation, maybe small unit training or even a terrorist coalition of sorts."

"Well, whatever it is or whoever's behind it, it sounds like a large operation."

"Yeah. Just the kind of operation a killing machine like the *Hadesfire* would be perfect for."

"So I don't get something," Grimaldi said.

"What's that?"

"The connection between the unrest in Iran and Egypt and this business in Oman. Those places are pretty remote to one another. Not to mention Tehran and Cairo are major cities, capitals in fact. Yet you could basically view the Oman Desert as a no-man's land of sorts."

"It doesn't make much sense," Bolan agreed. "But I'm sure there's a connection. Let's hope Tehran holds the answers."

GARRETT DOWNING HAD never known such ecstasy. He'd never experienced any fantasy as intense as the one in which he presently found himself. In short, nothing could compare to the sensation. The *Hadesfire* was more perfect than he could have ever imagined it. No other craft on Earth could measure up to it. He could literally feel her energy, manifested by the ceaseless thrumming from stem to stern, course through his veins to the very center of his being.

A few times Downing bothered to withdraw from his trancelike meditation and glance at Alek Stezhnya. In large part he could tell that it didn't make much of an impression on the military man. Stezhnya was a professional soldier and leader of soldiers, and he seemed almost unimpressed by the advancements in technology. That was okay, however. Downing could be impressed enough for both of them.

The results in the craft's performance had already far exceeded anything Downing could have imagined. He chose not to share his elation with the others who had accompanied them. They would arrive at their arranged rendezvous point within the hour. The plan called for them to fly into Iranian airspace below radar and airdrop the Apparatus into a remote area a few miles outside Tehran. Trucks awaiting them at the drop point would then transport Stezhnya and his team into the city.

At first, Stezhnya had tried to convince Downing to remain in the Philippines until they could send the all-clear on their mission objectives, but Downing dismissed the idea out of hand. It was important that a leader go where his men went, and although he left military tactics to Stezhnya, he also knew the value of maintaining a presence with subordinates.

What Downing didn't want to admit, and would

never have disclosed to anyone else, was his distrust of those he oversaw. Yes, they were well-trained and he had every confidence in Stezhnya's abilities. But these men were soldiers of fortune, guns for hire, mercenaries; they weren't men of vision or intellect and they did little real thinking beyond the barrel of an assault rifle. They enforced their views through bullets and bombs, and most couldn't see that imagination and resolve were the best ways to advance an ideal.

Downing had always considered himself a man of vision. He received high marks during his formative school years, and by the time he entered the Naval Intelligence Service many had marked him as a young man who would go far. The predictions were all accurate. After completing his military service he joined the ranks of the NSA and moved up quickly. Eventually his talents and hard work allowed him to take on the roll of second in command at the NSA.

That's when he quickly learned to command the respect of underlings. He made interagency contacts to facilitate support in advancements in counterintelligence tactics and technology. Most importantly, it was Downing's vision that permitted him to move forward unhampered by the normal bureaucratic red tape that seemed to bog down most government leaders, tying their hands and feet with political bonds too cumbersome to overcome.

These were the kinds of traits he could only hope to instill in men like Alek Stezhnya, where brute force overwhelmed matters of logic and higher problem-solving. Downing supposed he looked down on these men in a way. Of course he was operating somewhat out of his own element. He'd worked regularly with those of near equal intellect—in some cases even superior intelligence—in near country-club surroundings. But for the past six years of his life he'd spent a majority of his time hiding in rundown apartment buildings among the uneducated and disadvantaged citizenry of third world countries, and endured morose and near intolerable conditions in the name of a greater cause.

Now, the very government he'd served for so long, had privately disclaimed him to former colleagues—not to mention implemented a smear program throughout intelligence circles—and cursed his good name to select allies in other nations. Publicly, they denied any affiliation to him. This burned deep in parts of Downing's heart and mind no words could describe, and only strengthened his already steely resolve.

The *Hadesfire* and the operations of Stezhnya's men would only signal the beginning of his new war. He would use every tool, every resource, to eradicate the terrorists that threatened his nation. And when they were beaten, he would totally and utterly wipe them from existence. They would become a memory as the Roman Empire had become. There would be no place they could go he wouldn't find them. Then the entire world would remember his name.

Yet Downing was a realist. He didn't aspire to godhood and he wasn't insane. He merely did what he did out of a sense of duty and loyalty. He had family and friends in America, loved ones whom he missed dearly. He had committed the ultimate sacrifice by choosing to sever those ties to protect them from repercussions. They had known his self-appointed mission wouldn't be popular with the alleged authorities in America. Downing could only hope that most believed in him and his cause, and the would go on believing his actions were based on the best interests of the American people.

Now, as he neared the culmination of his work, Downing reflected on the fact he would have done it all over again given the chance. All the stress and agony and rejection was about to pay off, and Downing knew it was only because of his perseverance and his belief in one single purpose: that the American people had the right to live in peace, as did their generations to come.

In many respects, he found it rather difficult to understand why men like Matt Cooper couldn't understand that. They hadn't been able to find a scrap of information regarding this man, and yet Downing felt he knew Cooper perfectly. Or at least he knew the type. Cooper obviously carried with him many of the same ideals as Downing. That the two of them could be bitter enemies seemed almost impossible to him.

Downing would have disagreed with anyone who thought Cooper as little more than a loose cannon. Downing had seen the man in action right up to the point they launched the *Hadesfire*. Cooper wasn't some bloodthirsty gun-for-hire, such as Stezhnya would have liked all those around him to believe. No, this was a man of clearly high moral purpose; a man on a mission; a man who considered what he was doing as duty. Downing could understand such noble concepts. In fact, he could relate to them much more than he could Stezhnya's motivations.

"You are quiet, sir." Stezhnya's deep voice cut through Downing's musings.

"Am I?" Downing replied with no hint of pretentiousness.

Stezhnya merely nodded.

"I suppose I am. I have a lot on my mind."

"You were thinking about our mission, sir?"

"I was thinking about a great many things," Downing said. He expressed mild indignation. "I have many more stressors than I would prefer right now. The next eighteen hours will reveal the criticality of our situation. Our mission *must* succeed if we are to gain support among those back in America."

"I agree failure isn't an option," Stezhnya said. "But I'm not confident this will gain support for either of our causes."

"What do mean by that?" Downing interjected. "I thought our cause was united."

Stezhnya's smile couldn't have been classified as friendly. "I beg your pardon, sir. I suppose I misspoke. I was merely referring to the OSI and the Apparatus."

"The Apparatus is part of the OSI, Alek," Downing said in a frosty tone of voice to match his change in expression. "Need I remind you the Apparatus wouldn't even exist without my support?"

"I need no such reminder, sir," Stezhnya said more quietly this time. "You bring it up quite often. In fact, I sometimes wonder if it's not something you choose to hold over my head."

"I'd be careful. There are some things even you may not say to me with impunity."

"I do not intend to be disrespectful, sir."

"You could have fooled me," Downing snapped. "The bottom line is that while the Apparatus operates with autonomy, it doesn't operate at all without my approval. You are more to the OSI than mercenaries. You are the elite guard assigned to protect the OSI's ultimate objectives. Understand, Alek, that I am a part of this collective, as are you, and as is every other member of the Apparatus. In other words, we are the OSI and as one unit we should be united in our objectives."

"I want freedom for our country just as you do, sir," Stezhnya said with some zeal. "I have never made that a secret, neither have I strayed from the goals as you've outlined them. But I must also think of my men and to some degree show I'm as responsible for their welfare as I am of my own. If I didn't lead by example, you couldn't hardly expect these men to follow me into combat."

"I would agree with you entirely on that point."

"So it's well and good you've conceded that point," Stezhnya said. "Because in truth my only goal is to accomplish all of our objectives and keep my men alive. So far, our track record hasn't been good on that count. One more disaster and I can assure you that we won't have any men to lead into battle. They will abandon me as a spineless and incompetent leader."

"I'll leave such intricacies to your own devices where it concerns your men," Downing said. "I'm only trying to impress upon you the need for unity of objective and singularity of purpose. If we can accomplish these things, then in many respects we have already won."

"I can appreciate your position, sir, but we have hardly won. We are about to go against some of the toughest fighting men in the world. They are hardened combatants with experience, trained to survive in some of the harshest climates known to man. They are religious fanatics, yes, which makes them dangerous and believers of dying for their cause. They won't surrender and they won't quit until every last man has fallen. They will also have the advantage of being in their own element. We will be in unfamiliar urban surroundings for this first strike, and fighting against far superior numbers. So I don't think it wise to believe we have already won. Let us see how this first mission progresses, and then when we are through you will truly have a measure for knowing whether we have truly succeeded."

Downing had to admit Stezhnya's speech, albeit somewhat impassioned, had impressed him. "I'll concede the point in favor of maintaining good spirits. But understand this much, Alek. The survival of our cause depends on the skill of the men *and* their leader."

If Stezhnya had thought to respond, he gave no sign.

And Downing took satisfaction in the mere fact he had the final word.

CHAPTER SIXTEEN

"Mr. Cooper," said Kalik Subaharam, a captain in the Tehran police unit. "Let me be the first to welcome you to Iran."

"Thanks," the Executioner replied with a nod.

As Subaharam took a seat behind his desk and studied the large index card in front of him, he added, "And to warn you not to interfere in the affairs of this city or its people. Such activities could subject you to detainment, interrogation and perhaps even confinement."

Bolan shook his head. "I'm not here to cause trouble."

"Ha! I'm sure." Subaharam turned the large card face-front to Bolan. It was about six by nine and stamped with the seal of the Iranian government. "And yet here is an official mandate from the first vice-president's office that one Matthew Cooper receive all diplomatic courtesies and be treated in accordance with the stipulations recently enacted between our respective countries."

Bolan kept his expression impassive as he said, "How nice."

"Quite," Subaharam said. He dropped the card on the desk and folded his hands over it as he leaned forward and studied Bolan. "In truth, we both know I am not bound to extend you any diplomatic courtesies whatsoever."

Yeah. Bolan knew it was the truth. There was no official U.S. representation, political, ambassadorial or otherwise in the country; the conservative politics of the nation didn't permit it. In fact, the protecting power in Iran was Switzerland, and Bolan knew if he bought any sort of real trouble in the country he wouldn't be able to get much support from Swiss officials. They would be, after all, neutral in such affairs. That meant the Executioner was on his own and bound to rely on only himself for support.

"However, since the order comes from my superiors I will comply. Although naturally I'm curious as to the real purpose of your visit."

"Would you believe improving public relations?" Bolan attempted a smile.

Subaharam shook his head. "No. But I have a theory, I think you are here due to the recent unrest between this department and the Mujahedeen-e-Khalq."

"You could say it's a main point of interest," Bolan said. "So in a way, that *is* public relations."

"I am a serious man, Mr. Cooper," Subaharam said. "It doesn't sound as if you take this seriously."

Bolan frowned and an edge crept into his voice. "I think you misunderstood me. I take this very seriously.

Seriously enough that I came a long way to see if I could help rectify your situation."

"The 'situation' to which you refer will soon be in control."

"Don't bet on it," Bolan shot back. "Look, we might as well stop fencing each other. Let's be clear. I'm definitely here to look into your problem. Mainly because we think your problem really starts with our problem."

"And what problem would that be?"

"Are you aware of the recent activities in my country? Particularly the massacre of innocent people in Atlanta?"

"I am," Subaharam replied. "Your press fascinates me. They keep us so well informed we almost cannot justify the expense of maintaining the ministry."

He was, of course, referring to the Ministry of Intelligence and Security—known as VEVAK by the initials of its Persian translation—the primary tool of the government leaders to oversee security and intelligence operations internally and abroad. Very little was known about the activities or areas of operation where it concerned VEVAK, since there was little distribution of literature on it. The Executioner knew that if Stony Man had very little on them, they would be no less enigmatic to America's other intelligence agencies.

"This would be due to that little thing we call the U.S. Constitution," Bolan said. "And you can't believe everything you see."

"It doesn't matter," Subaharam cut in with an irritated tone. "You still have not explained what your rogue agent has to do with the recent unrest of the MEK."

"Propaganda makes it sound as if the Iranian police were the aggressor," Bolan replied. "Fortunately, I like to stick to facts. That's another way of saying I don't believe it. There's no advantage in breaking a cease-fire with a group that's been relatively out of the picture for the past decade."

"That's an astute observation, Mr. Cooper. Perhaps I misjudged you."

"Seems more obvious than anything. Let's face it, your agency stands nothing to gain from domestic clashes with radicals. You have your hands full with the drug-running and prostitution, not to mention enforcement of Islamic views."

Subaharam's expression remained stony.

"I see from that look we agree," Bolan continued. "I believe Garrett Downing has started this unrest in your country."

"To what end?"

"To further the cause of his own organization," the Executioner replied. "For what it's worth, my government has nothing to do with Downing. I know most don't believe it, but I don't really care. I think it makes sense that association with a man like Downing wouldn't benefit Iranian-U.S. relations one iota. Downing has his own agenda. He wants to eradicate every last Muslim he *thinks* might be a terrorist."

"You believe he's here in Tehran."

"Maybe he's not here personally but I know his goons are, and that's not going to wash."

"Well, it would appear this *is* a matter for us to handle internally," Subaharam said. "I will say again that I don't want outside interference."

Bolan shook his head. "Sorry, but no dice."

"You have an alternative suggestion?"

"We work together. This is your city. You know it much better than I do. You know all the most logical hiding places for the MEK. You give me that information and I'll make sure this comes out good for both sides."

"I cannot permit you to roam Tehran without an escort," Subaharam said, shaking his head. "I'm sorry."

"You want to tag along, fine by me," Bolan replied. "But you pull your own weight. One thing I can tell you about Downing's people is that they're well-trained and well-armed. I'm sure their first priority will be to stage some kind of major spectacle."

"Where?"

"Where would you find large groups of people this time of morning? Think about the proximity of those locations to concentrations in MEK members."

"That's easy," Subaharam stated. "The town market on the lower side will have many shoppers after morning prayer. Most of those who were officially part of the MEK lived under a self-imposed poverty. This is a poor part of the city and most would still reside there."

"That's a start."

"Fine," Subaharam said, rising and grabbing his uniform cap from a nearby hook. "I also know a man I think can help us. If there is any talk of unusual activity in the area, he will have heard of it by now."

Subaharam led Bolan down a flight of back steps in the police station and into a lot where they kept their vehicles. As they walked toward Subaharam's car, he said, "If this alleged group you've told me about actually exists, it could mean significant bloodshed."

THE LOWER SIDE OF TEHRAN actually turned out to be on the southern outskirts, and poverty definitely ran rampant judging by its looks.

Apartment buildings that lined narrow, trash-packed streets of half dirt and half-broken asphalt were pockmarked and run down. Children who played along the broken, sagging sidewalks wore little more than rags. Men were the best-dressed in semiclean robes and traditional garments, and the women were somewhere in the middle of the quality gap but wore the most clothing to hide their faces and all other revealing features. On occasion, Subaharam would pass a female who hadn't covered herself appropriately and slow his car.

Bolan looked hard at him a couple of times, in which case Subaharam would either appear to make a mental note or scribble something on a pad before continuing. The ride from the police station to the central part of the marketplace took nearly a half hour. Subaharam pulled his car to the curb, and Bolan stepped from the air conditioned interior into the already building heat of early morning.

Subaharam nodded toward a small, single-story building that appeared healthier than the others around it. "The business of the man I spoke about."

Bolan studied the furniture in the window. "An antiques dealer?"

"I would say more like a dealer in junk, but you are correct."

That struck Bolan as odd. What would a seller of trinkets in the poverty-stricken downtown of Tehran know about the Mujahedeen-e-Khalq or the threat of outsiders to peace between MEK and Iranian authorities? Of course, Bolan had been in such situations before and wondered much the same thing. This was Subaharam's domain, and he knew things Bolan couldn't possibly have known. He'd have to trust the Iranian policeman's judgment whether he liked it or not.

Subaharam joined Bolan on the sidewalk, such as it were, and added, "It would be wise that you not speak unless I indicate otherwise. As far the people here, you're an outsider and not to be trusted."

"Does that include you?" Bolan asked forthrightly.

Subaharam smiled. "Let us not quibble, Mr. Cooper. I have already given my word to cooperate with you and I will. But it is difficult enough to get these people to speak to me. It will take much more to get them to talk to me in front of a Westerner."

Bolan considered that and then nodded. "Reasonable enough. After you, Captain."

Subaharam led Bolan up three rickety steps onto an equally unstable porch. He yanked on a small cord and the tinkling of a bell resounded from somewhere within. Bolan did a quick inspection of his surroundings, watchful of any potential ambush locations. An attack from a rooftop seemed unlikely given most of the buildings along this area were one or two stories. A frontal assault was also unlikely since morning prayer hadn't quite ended. Satisfied he'd made it ahead of the enemy's plans, Bolan looked at his watch.

"What time before the crowds start picking up?"

"A half hour, at best."

"Then we better get our information quick."

"Agreed," Subaharam replied with a short nod.

He yanked on the cord once more. Another minute elapsed before the door opened slowly and a middle-aged man stared up at them. The wheelchair he sat in took Bolan by surprise but he quashed any reaction. The man had gray hair and a long beard to match, with eyebrows that grew uncontrollably above eyes of milk chocolate brown. An unfiltered cigarette dangled from his lips, and he closed one eye in response to a wisp of smoke that curled into it while he studied his visitors.

"Neshbi," Subaharam greeted him in English. "It is agreeable to see you again."

The man's quiet reply dripped with a tone of suspicion. "Oh, really? I wonder about that. But I must assume your intentions are good." He looked at Bolan, then back at Subaharam. "You bring an American with you? Here?"

"This man is from the United States, yes," Subaharam said. "He seeks information, and that information is of great interest to me and my superiors."

"What kind of information?"

"Do you really think it's a good idea to stand out here and discuss such matters?" Subaharam countered.

The man called Neshbi studied Bolan a little longer then wheeled his chair aside so they could enter. Once inside with the door bolted behind them—a fact that made Bolan edgy—their host led them to a small room in the back. In other circumstances it could have been described as "cozy," but the junk that lined the walls and floors removed any qualification for the title. Bolan and Subaharam had to wind their way through the path to a nearby couch.

"Now what is it that's so important you couldn't just phone me?" Neshbi asked after offering them coffee, which both declined.

"This man is Mathew Cooper, an agent of Homeland Security in the United States. He has information that might explain the recent outbreak of fighting between the Mujahedeen-e-Khalq and my department. One that he claims is not the fault of either side, but has apparently been incited by a third party."

Neshbi looked at Bolan and said, "He is correct."

For a long moment dead silence followed. When Subaharam finally managed to get his voice back, it was menacing. "You're telling me that his claims are true?"

"Yes," Neshbi replied.

"And why did you not bring this information to us before now? Why make me come to find you?"

"If I remember right, my debt to you is paid in full," Neshbi replied. "I don't owe you anything."

"You owe it to your people as a citizen of Iran!" Subaharam's face grew visibly red even through his dark complexion. "Don't you forget that! And don't also forget that the terms of your release can be rescinded at any time if it is found you have participated in criminal activity."

"Not reporting rumors to the Tehran police is hardly criminal, my friend," Neshbi replied with a derisive laugh.

"No," Subaharam replied. "*That* would actually be treason."

At that moment Bolan almost found himself in agreement with Subaharam. He didn't know the situation here at all, but it appeared these two men had a relationship that went beyond what was established or even permissible. The laws governing the conduct of citizens and their dealings with the police in Iran were significantly more strict than in the United States. The Iranian police—and this was especially true of those in the capital city—had discretion that went even above those of the Moscow police at the height of the USSR's political influence in the world. Any citizen caught violating laws or withholding information that resulted in civil disobedience and unrest could quite possibly result in immediate arrest, and execution if convicted by government court officials. Such convictions probably weren't too hard to obtain given the right type of evidence, even if that evidence was circumstantial.

Neshbi cleared his throat, crushed out his cigarette and immediately lit another. As he waved out the match he looked at Bolan. "I would like to hear what this man says. If I like what I hear, I will tell you all that I know."

"And if you don't like what you hear?" Subaharam asked.

"Then you may have to cut out my tongue or even separate my head from my body, because I will not speak a word of what I know."

"You want to know why I've really come here, don't you?" Bolan interjected. "You're worried about whether or not I'm going to use this information against your people."

Neshbi looked surprised. "You are a wise man, that much I can see. How did you know this?"

Bolan nodded at Neshbi's left forearm, which was only partially concealed by the robe he wore. "I saw the markings on the back of your forearm when you lit that cigarette. You were in prison for crimes against the Ayatollah. Only political insurgents are given that mark. I know, because I've seen it before. You were once a member of the MEK."

Bolan turned to look at Subaharam. "And I'd bet you were a guard in the prison at the time Neshbi came through. That about cover it?"

"How could you have known that?" Subaharam asked.

"Simple," Bolan replied. "You knew as well as I did that someone from the outside had to be involved in stirring up war between the MEK and Tehran police. I figured that much even before I walked into your office. And the reason is, you know the MEK well enough to know they couldn't be behind this, just as I do. But it was also seemed like you knew more than that. Call it an instinct, but it was clear you had other ideas about this."

"That proves nothing, Mr. Cooper," Subaharam replied in a not so convincing tone. "It is pure conjecture."

"Is it? First, you're the right age and rank to have served in the prison detail during the peak of the MEK resistance. New cops always start with correctional details at the political prisons. Second, you seem to know a lot about their methods. Not common knowledge among most. Finally, why of all places would you pick *here* to get information? Especially from a man who clearly used to be a member of the MEK. It's obvious you two know each other."

For nearly a minute neither man spoke. They simply stared at each other as if engaged in some type of telepathic bond. Bolan knew by the silence alone that he'd hit the nail on the head. Why they had chosen to hide this information wasn't clear, but he knew they'd never tell him anyway, so it didn't make much difference. Bolan wondered if the two men weren't somehow related, but being on opposite side of the tracks, as it were, they were hiding this fact from scrutiny.

"Whatever's going on between you two is none of my concern," Bolan finally said. "Will you help me or not?"

Subaharam nodded and Neshbi began to speak. "I cannot tell you I have information about who might want to rekindle the hatred between my people and the government. But we are certain it was started by an outside influence."

"Any idea who that influence might be?"

"At first I thought maybe your CIA," Neshbi said through a cloud of smoke. "But that view has since changed. Now I am unsure who is behind it, but I think they are trying to threaten the Mujahedeen-e-Khalq's alliance with the Egyptians."

"What alliance?" Bolan asked.

"You did not know?" Neshbi asked, and he began to laugh. "They have formed an accord with the Armed Islamic Group."

"For what purpose?" Subaharam asked.

"What else? The utter destruction of the West."

CHAPTER SEVENTEEN

Behrouz Kiyanfar despised the Egyptian jihad.

He'd despised it since a young, half-naked wisp of a boy. He'd spent most of that time running through the poverty-stricken streets of Tehran in search of anything he could steal so he might feed his mother. His father had been off fighting against Iraq or other enemies and never returned. To this day, Kiyanfar had no idea what actually happened to his father, despite the small fortune he'd paid to get to the truth.

So Kiyanfar's mother died of a broken heart, his two younger siblings of starvation, and it literally burned in his gut.

Kiyanfar had only formed this alliance with Agymah Malik to solicit the cooperation and funding of al Qaeda. The fatwahs of al Qaeda insisted, even demanded, the cooperation among all groups. Kiyanfar believed there was strength in such unions, but only if the allies served the common cause. Kiyanfar served the goals and ideals of al Qaeda, but it seemed Malik was in this only for his own personal gain. That made him a traitor in Kiyanfar's eyes.

One day, very soon, he would kill Agymah Malik.

But for now the arrival of the Americans had to command all of his attention. The weapons cache Malik had promised arrived without incident, and already his men were preparing for the assault against the Tehran police headquarters in the central part of the city. His spies had told him of a recent arrival in Tehran, an American who had gone straight to the police. Kiyanfar had attempted to acquire more information about the man, but got nothing more than a name: Matthew Cooper. The American was some type of agent, perhaps an adviser for the U.S. intelligence services, and Kiyanfar suspected the local law enforcement might be consulting him on what to do about their problem.

All of it was mere conjecture, however.

Kiyanfar gave careful thought once more to Malik's suggestion about the truth in the American denial of affiliation with the man named Garrett Downing. What puzzled him most was the fact he'd heard nothing further about Downing. The Americans continued to deny any involvement with these operations, but they had not publicly disclaimed him. It could have been because Downing was an embarrassment to them, or that they sought plausible deniability if their plan backfired.

When Kiyanfar coupled that idea with the sudden arrival of an American consultant to his country—a man who the Iranian government would consider an intruder into affairs that didn't concern him—he couldn't help but wonder if there wasn't some merit to Malik's suggestions. The entire thing seemed wholly absurd to Kiyanfar, and yet he couldn't overcome the gnawing in his gut. Something just wasn't right.

Kiyanfar turned from where he'd been supervising the offload of weapons at the warehouse on the outskirts of the central market and returned to his makeshift office. He had a number of calls to make to his satellite units spread throughout the city. He needed a count on how many men they could spare to send to Malik's operations in Oman. He couldn't really spare them, but they had an agreement and Kiyanfar was, if anything, a man of his word.

The terrorist had just stepped inside when he heard a shout from one his team leaders. He turned and watched as the man approached him on a dead run. The man skidded to a halt and began talking so rapidly it came out as gibberish.

"Be calm," Kiyanfar said as he held up a hand. "That's it. Now start from the beginning."

"We received word that one of our units in the market is under attack!"

"Under attack by whom?"

"We do not know, sir," the man said.

"Gather your men and your weapons," Kiyanfar ordered. "We will move to support our brothers now."

THE STORY NESHBI RELATED to Mack Bolan went far beyond anything he might have imagined. The sheer dynamics of what was at work here were nearly unfathomable. Bolan had seen many such alliances before, even participated in a number of concurrent operations with Stony Man to put them down, but the magnitude of this particular one gave him every reason to see why the President had his finger on the trigger, as it were.

"It's impossible," Subaharam told Bolan as they left Neshbi's hovel. "I cannot believe that the Mujahedeen-e-Khalq would form any such agreement with the Egyptians. This is a personal war to them."

"Only because they think you started it," the Executioner replied. After they climbed into the car and Subaharam pulled away, Bolan continued. "Let's assume for a second what Neshbi told us is true."

"You must be a lunatic, Mr. Cooper," Subaharam said. "But I will play this game with you for now because it amuses me. Until I grow tired of it."

"Look, you already said you don't want a war with the MEK any more than they want one with you."

"Aha!" Subaharam held up a finger. "But they *do* want a war with us. They have always wanted one. They do not like the rules of Islamic society as have been ordered by our ilams, our religious leaders. They would prefer a more conventional rule. Such thinking would be nothing less than genocidal. Iran would fall to every vile form of social disarray."

"Come off it," Bolan said. He'd about had enough of Subaharam's righteous indignation. "That argument might work for most, but I've been around too long to buy it."

"You have a better explanation?" Subaharam asked, casting a sideways glance at Bolan.

"A simpler one," Bolan said. "Less impassioned."

"And that is?"

"Your trouble isn't with the MEK. This alliance they've formed with the GIA smells rotten to me."

"I do have trouble believing about this, as well," Subaharam said with a curt nod.

"No, it's real. I'm talking about—" Bolan cut it short when he noticed a small girl on the sidewalk frantically waving her arms at them.

Subaharam stood on the brakes and whipped the car over to the curb, stopping just short of the small cracked strip of concrete that passed for a sidewalk. Bolan rolled down the window and the girl raced to them. She immediately began to speak to Subaharam. Bolan exchanged glances with them, seeing the girl point down the street and Subaharam nod with a concerned expression.

Suddenly the girl was gone from the car and Subaharam sped from the curb in a squeal of tires.

"What's going on?" Bolan asked.

"There is some kind of trouble at the end of the street," Subaharam said. "She said something about men and shooting. A battle of some kind."

It felt like chilled fingers walked up the Executioner's spine. It was too late. It had begun and there was nothing anyone could do to stop it now. The Apparatus had obviously beat him to the punch on this one.

Subaharam took a corner so fast it almost felt as if they were on two wheels for a moment. The policeman shouted into a radio as he negotiated his way through the traffic, and Bolan figured he was probably calling for backup.

"They won't get here in time," Bolan said.

"Maybe," was Subaharam's reply.

Both men spotted the trouble almost immediately. A clear delineation existed between the two groups of aggressors. A number of men in traditional Arab garb were visible on the street or set up in the windows of buildings, and facing off against a mixed group dressed in camouflage fatigues and armed with heavy firepower. Bolan recognized their tactics immediately, and the odd assortment of small-arms and crew weapons at their disposal.

The Apparatus had brought their war boldly into the streets of Tehran, which Bolan hadn't anticipated at all. He figured Downing would be more discreet in his operations against the terror groups who had publicly affiliated themselves with the New Corsican Front. He hadn't believed Downing or Stezhnya would operate so openly against a group like the MEK. The whole purpose had been to undermine civil authority within Iran—most importantly where there resided high concentrations of MEK members—and thereby gain public sympathy of the OSI's cause.

In the center of the road, three military-grade, five-ton dump trucks provided some cover for the strike team now advancing along the road. The men in fatigues used the trucks to shield them from the autofire being poured onto them from ahead and above. A couple of innocents trying to escape the maelstrom were unlucky in their flight. They fell to the merciless and indiscriminate cross fire of friend and foe alike.

"Those are not our men!" Subaharam said.

"No, they're not," Bolan replied, and then he was out of the car and moving.

The Executioner reached beneath the loose-hanging cotton shirt he'd wore and drew the Beretta 93-R. The pistol was small defense against a group like that, but if he could attract the Apparatus's attention long enough he stood a chance of knocking down the odds and acquiring one or two of their assault rifles. The Arab gunmen in the windowsills and behind cover didn't even appear to take notice of the Executioner as he sprinted along the sidewalk to flank the new arrivals.

Bolan took the first pair of Apparatus soldiers with 3-round bursts from the Beretta before they could draw a bead on him. He didn't break pace as he reached the fallen gunmen and bent to grab both rifles on the fly. Bolan reached cover at the tailgate of the rearmost truck, holstered the 93-R, slung one of the rifles and then checked the action on the other before rejoining the battle. He jumped onto the tailgate of the truck and peered into the hot, dusty darkness of the dump bed. Empty.

The soldier grabbed hold of the taut canvas covering the truck and hauled himself onto the top. He gauged the scene in a heartbeat, then trained the rifle on another trio of Apparatus gunners weaving their way through abandoned junk cars and vendor carts. Bolan acquired a sight picture with just a small lead on the targets, took a deep breath, let half out and then squeezed the trigger. The AK-74 rifle emitted its distinctive, barking reports as Bolan laid down a furious barrage of 5.45 mm slugs. The impact propelled the first man forward in his

sprint to find cover. His arms pinwheeled in an attempt
to keep his balance but it soon turned futile, since his
brain hadn't yet told the rest of the nervous system he
was dead. By the time his corpse hit the broken sidewalk he'd taken at least seven rounds to the upper body.
Bolan got the second, who stopped to see why fire came
from their own side, with a head shot that slammed the
Apparatus man against the wall. Bolan stitched the remaining trio from crotch to sternum with a corkscrew
burst.

Five down, and a couple more taken out by MEK
gunners above, brought the head count to about ten.
Bolan realized his luck wouldn't hold much longer. Despite the fact he hadn't made any aggressive moves toward the MEK, Bolan knew he'd be mistaken for an
enemy by one of the terrorists sooner or later. He realized in that moment of irony he'd been taking out
Americans in defense of a known terrorist organization.
In Bolan's mind, however, the Apparatus had proved itself the aggressor against a group that had otherwise
been coexisting peacefully with the Iranian authorities.
Bolan didn't necessarily agree with everything about
the government in Iran, nor its policies against its citizens, but he could much less abide the murder of innocent people for a cause that cared only for itself.

Americans or not, the Executioner couldn't have
Stezhnya's men killing unjustifiably in the name of his
country.

"Cooper!" Subaharam shouted.

Bolan turned to his left and saw a pair of Apparatus
gunners rushing toward his position, the muzzles of

their Uzi SMGs winking. He rolled out of their sights, did a backflip off the opposite end of the truck and landed on his feet. He turned to his right and saw Subaharam rushing toward him, pistol drawn and firing on the run. Bolan shouted a warning, but it wasn't in time. One moment Subaharam rushed toward the aggressors and the next he fell under a full blast of 9 mm stingers that ripped open his chest. Hot blood spurted from the gaping holes left in the wake of the autofire and Subaharam skidded face-first along the coarse surface of the street.

Bolan dropped to his belly and watched as two pairs of boots raced toward the back of the dump truck. He rolled beneath the stationary truck, crawled toward the rear and waited until the Apparatus gunners had skirted the back before leveling his AK-74 and triggering a burst. The rounds ripped cleanly through the boots and exposed flesh and bone. Both men dropped to ground in agony. Bolan finished the pair with short bursts to the head. The AK-74's bolt locked back on an empty chamber. The Executioner took just a moment to mentally salute Subaharam's sacrifice, consoled that the man hadn't died in vain.

Bolan abandoned the AK-74 as he rolled clear of the truck, then got to his feet and rushed to the driver's door. He jumped onto the running board, Beretta prepped, and looked inside. The cab had been vacated, the engine left running. Bolan was thankful for his good fortune, as he opened the door and jumped onto the bench seat. He slammed down the parking brake handle, stood on the clutch, dropped the shift straight to second and gunned it. The dump truck lurched forward and the Executioner pointed its nose at the rear of the truck about ten yards ahead.

A few of the Apparatus soldiers who'd been using the other truck for cover whirled in shock to see the massive five-ton bearing down on them. Only one managed to avoid being crushed between thick pieces of iron, steel and glass. Bolan continued to feed gas while he double-clutched into third and let the vehicle do its grisly work. The truck ahead seemed to resist, whether caused by a driver standing on the brakes or the emergency brake.

Bolan eased off the gas and put the truck in neutral. He engaged the parking brake and went EVA. The warrior jumped onto the hood, careful to avoid slipping on the gory spots, and leaped onto the canvas roof of the truck ahead. He hop-stepped along the roof, careful to keep his feet on the crossbars until he'd reached the front peak of the taut covering. Bullets buzzed past his ears, several coming too close for comfort. Bolan peered over the driver's side and spotted another pair of Apparatus gunmen hunched for cover behind the engine compartment frame.

Bolan sighted down the Beretta's slide and triggered a single shot through the head of the first hardman, his skull exploding and dousing his comrade with blood and gray matter. The lone survivor looked up with mixed horror and surprise as Bolan triggered another round. The 9 mm Parabellum bullet punched through the man's top lip, ripping away the upper bones in his face. The impact flipped him from his crouched position, and he landed flat on its back with a sickening crack of skull against pavement.

The Executioner dropped onto the hood of the truck and whirled to see a surprised driver peer at him through the jagged shards of broken glass left from a shattered windshield. Bolan triggered a double-tap, the bullets drilling through the man's throat and chest. Blood and tissue sprayed the driver's compartment. The man's head bobbed queerly on what remained of his neck, and then his body slumped sideways and all but disappeared from view.

The roar of vehicle engines replaced the sudden lull in the firefight. Bolan whirled in time to see two large SUVs round the corner followed by a jalopy panel truck. The vehicles screeched to a halt, and the soldier watched as a band of gunmen clad in robes and turbans went EVA. The group announced its arrival formally with a fresh clatter of autofire. Bolan got out of their sights quickly, although it didn't really appear they were shooting directly at him. Still, the Executioner knew he'd about used up all the good fortune he dared at the moment. In such uncontrolled firefights, he stood a good chance of getting caught in a cross fire.

Bolan heard the sound of approaching sirens, probably in response to Subaharam's radio call. He studied the buildings and spotted a small break between two of them. The soldier couldn't be sure where the makeshift alley led, but it would most likely provide cover and get him out of sight—even if only on a temporary basis— from the new Arab arrivals and the police.

He burst from the cover of the dump truck and raced

for the opening, reaching it just as a hail of hot lead bit at his heels. Bolan had to turn sideways to fit between the slum-style buildings, but thankfully he spotted an opening on the far side that most probably led to the next block. He would have to make sure he cleared out of the area before the Tehran police had time to cordon the area.

Bolan again considered the irony of what had just happened. For the first time he could remember, he had defended a sworn enemy against American citizens; although he couldn't exactly view Downing's Apparatus deserved the title. Still, he had taken the lives of Americans, and probably among them a few foreigners, in an attempt to save the lives of known Iranian terrorists. Moreover, they were terrorists who had allied themselves with the Armed Islamic Group in the hopes of taking their operations into the heart of his country.

Bolan also felt responsible in that he hadn't arrived in time to avoid a major conflict between the MEK and the Iranian authorities. While he didn't necessarily agree with the methods of its police organization, or their enforcement of traditional religious and social views, he had hoped to deter any serious conflicts between those two warring factions that had managed to live in uneasy peace for the past decade. Now all had changed and it meant more bloodshed. The very best he could hope for now was to quell any further outbreaks in the fighting by striking at the heart of the matter.

It seemed to Bolan as if he'd been just one step behind Downing's operations at every turn. The Executioner tried not to let it bother him. He couldn't have done anything to prevent the assassination of Peter Hagen or the launch of the *Hadesfire* out of the Philippines. Nonetheless, he couldn't keep on his present course. He needed to find a way to get in front of the situation. The first and best place to do that would be to go on the offense.

Yeah, it was time for a blitz. And the most reasonable place to start that blitz wasn't in Tehran. It had moved beyond that. Based on what Neshbi had told him, it seemed the MEK had been stirred into action by higher-ups inside the GIA. They were obviously providing the means, both tangible and intangible, to support this "holy war" between Iranian authorities and the MEK. If he could sever those ties, the situation would most likely resolve itself. It would also lead him to the mysterious operations Brognola had spoken of in the Oman Desert.

So now the entire situation had become not just a matter of mission and duty for the Executioner. It had become personal, a question of necessity. Mack Bolan was no longer sure who the enemy was, so he could no longer discriminate between GIA or MEK, Apparatus or other potential factions. In a blitz, every player was a potential target. Bolan would do what he could to keep the purely innocent out of the fray. And God help anyone else.

CHAPTER EIGHTEEN

Thoughts of a dark-haired man, a stranger really, distracted Crystal Julian.

It puzzled her that she would allow herself to become so flustered over Cooper, and yet nothing at all about it seemed strange when she considered he'd saved her life. Then again, she'd saved his hide, as well. If she hadn't diverted him from the hangar when she had, he might have walked right into Stezhnya's trap. That didn't seem to be what occupied nearly every conscious thought process. It had more to do with just the kind of man Cooper was. She found him sexy, attractive; he was a man of passion and duty and honor. Those were traits very difficult to find in many of today's men, particularly those in the same scientific circles as herself. Julian had once promised herself never to become romantically involved with anyone she worked with, more out of fear of complication and distraction than any other reasons, but she'd broken that rule with Alek Stezhnya.

Now Cooper had come into her life, complicated matters, and she didn't know exactly how to tell him how she felt. Strange for a woman, since she belonged to a gender that purported nurturing and sensitivity as basic traits to every member in their ranks. Well, she'd have to reserve that activity for another place and time, because right now the best way she could help Cooper was to keep track of the *Hadesfire*.

No question remained in her mind that the goals of Downing's organization were less than admirable. Downing had proved himself nothing but a manipulator and liar, and Stezhnya was his bootlicking thug. That was another trait Julian had to admire about Cooper; he didn't back off from anything or anyone. He stood his ground and he did what he did based on moral principles. She hadn't mentioned it, but she didn't blame him for Peter's death. There wasn't anything he could have done about that. She believed Cooper partly blamed himself even though it didn't make any sense to do so. Cooper almost seemed like a consummate professional who took a personal interest in certain aspects of his profession.

And there she was thinking about Cooper again. Well, damn it, she couldn't help it. That's just the way it was and it wasn't as if she was really hurting anybody. She had tabs on the *Hadesfire* signal and—

"What?" she whispered as she suddenly noticed the stationary signal had now become two separate signals.

The pilot she knew only as Jack looked up from the magazine he'd been reading, perched on a stool next to a breakfast bar in their hotel suite. "Huh? What'd you say?"

"Nothing," she said, shaking her head. "Just a little fuzz on my computer here. Looks like we have two signals for the *Hadesfire,* but one of them has to be a phantom. Just some kind of weird interference."

"That hookup was arranged by our people," Grimaldi replied. "Some of the best people in the business. If it says there are any problems, we need to get them cleared up. We lose that connection and the Sarge might never be able to find that signal."

She nodded, and then asked, "Why do you call him that? Why do you call Cooper 'Sarge'?"

The pilot shrugged. "Just always have, I guess. As long as I've known him. Has to do with his military background."

"He was a sergeant?"

She turned just in time to see Grimaldi nod before he went back to his magazine. His expression said he didn't really want to talk about it beyond that.

Julian turned in her chair, frustrated that Cooper's friend wouldn't say more about him. The whole thing almost made her feel like a schoolgirl with a crush, trying to pry information about some boy from a younger brother. Not that there was much obvious age difference between them. They weren't as far off from each other as most would have suspected, and in fact it almost looked like Jack was a little older than Cooper. It also looked like they had been friends for many, many years—something she'd noticed just based on the way they interacted.

"The signals are still there," she stated.

The man started to climb off the stool and walk toward her to look when the door opened to admit Cooper. The first thing she noticed was that he looked like hell.

"You look like hell," Grimaldi said, almost as if he'd been reading Julian's mind.

"Nice to see you, too," Bolan said.

"What happened?" Julian asked.

"I'll fill you in shortly," he said. He looked at Jack. "Right now, I need to call Hal and I want both of you to get ready to leave."

"But we just got here!" Julian protested.

Bolan fired a not-so-friendly look in her direction and she quickly shut her mouth.

"Where are we going?" Grimaldi asked.

"Cairo."

"LOOKS LIKE THE MAN was right on the money, Hal," Mack Bolan said. "What he didn't know was just how deep this thing goes."

Hal Brognola directed his voice toward the ceiling speakers. "We've been seeing reports come in all morning about the firefight in Tehran. What happened?"

"The Apparatus started a firefight with the MEK right in the heart of downtown. I managed to take down a good number of them before the police arrived. At that point, I was outgunned and outmanned at least fifty to one, with the low ground to boot. All I could do was split."

"Fair enough, Striker," Brognola said. "I never meant to get you in that kind of a situation. I shouldn't have talked the President out of a military option."

"Yes, you should have," Bolan countered. "The police captain you set me up with is dead. But he managed to get me to one of his contacts. He confirmed the GIA-MEK link, and he also said the GIA had financed a good number of the MEK operations with weapons and other supplies since breaking the cease-fire."

"So they weren't pushed to this on their own."

"No," Bolan replied. "In fact, I think it's really the GIA behind most of this unrest. And we already know who's behind *all* of this."

"Downing?"

"Sure," Bolan said. "Consider this. Downing arranges some sort of major coup and gets the GIA to kick-start a major operation in Oman. But in reality, it's not really the GIA behind it. Instead, it's a former member of the GIA that still has some friendly connections in Cairo, mostly because he's got serious cash to back him. I have a name for you—Agymah Malik. I need the best possible location on him. He supposedly operates as a legitimate businessman, so he won't be hard to find."

"Okay." Brognola leaned forward to a pad on the table and jotted the name. "Anything else?"

"I'm going to Cairo to end this once and for all."

"And what about the situation in Oman?"

"I think it's important to stop Malik first. Downing will keep, since he stands no chance of making his plan work unless he can continue sowing unrest between the various factions. The Egyptian's obviously represented himself as a major player in the GIA. Once the higher-ups find out what's going on, they'll think the MEK's to blame and you'll have total war on your hands. That's when Downing would step in to save the day. I think the Oman operation is to support a mass jihad inside America."

"What if that operation gets under way before you can stop Malik?"

"No chance. I'll be in Cairo well before that happens. Downing will have to stir up a lot more publicity before it would be worth his time."

"Good point," Brognola interjected. "I hadn't thought of that."

"Besides, we're keeping our eye on the *Hadesfire* and its current position. If there's any serious change, then we'll deal with it."

"Okay, Striker, sounds like you have a handle on this and good. We'll contact you as soon as I have best location on Malik."

"Thanks," Bolan replied. "There's something else. Jack just told me Julian may be having trouble with the connection you provided for her. She's getting duplicate signals. She thinks one's a phantom, but she isn't sure. Could you ask Bear to look into it?"

At some point during the conversation, Aaron "The Bear" Kurtzman had rolled into the room. He spoke up immediately. "I hear and obey, master."

Bolan chuckled and then asked, "Any ideas?"

"Not one," Kurtzman said. "I'll spare you all the technical jargon but it comes to the fact we're seeing the exact same thing she is."

"And no explanation for it," Bolan finished.

"Right. We've tested it on this end and everything, connections, transmission rates, blah-blah-blah, are in perfect working order. Frankly, I'm stumped. If there's a glitch in the system, we haven't found it yet."

"I have a bad feeling about this," Bolan said. "Should we consider the possibility there's a second one?"

"A second what? *Hadesfire?*" Brognola asked.

"It's a possibility we haven't considered before. If everything about what Julian has told me about this thing is correct, it would mean double the fun. Just one of these things can do some amazing stuff."

"If there is a second one," Kurtzman said, "it would make Downing twice as dangerous."

"And make Striker's job twice as difficult," Brognola added. "It's something we should consider strongly as fact until we can positively rule it out."

"Hal's right," Bolan said. "Best to get in front of it now."

"Understood," Kurtzman said.

"Anything else?" Brognola asked.

"That should cover it," Bolan replied. "We're out of here shortly. Jack and Julian are packing it up. Jack says we'll be airborne within the hour."

"Okay, then. Good luck, Striker."

THE EXECUTIONER LEFT the hotel bedroom after his call to Brognola. The two small overnight bags they had brought were packed, as was Julian's essential equipment.

Bolan nodded with satisfaction as he walked to the table where she'd been working and stacked the scrap sheets of paper there. He then removed the Beretta 93-R from the holster beneath his shirt and expertly field-stripped the pistol in less than ten seconds. Bolan reached into one of the bags and withdrew his .44 Desert Eagle. He checked the action and then laid it next to him while completing his work on the Beretta.

The second item he'd withdrawn was a gun-scrubbing compound spray developed by John Kissinger. He sprayed the metallic parts in front of him, and the compound coated them like liquid Freon. Then Bolan used a small brush to scrape away the almost dried, tarry particles left behind. Within a minute, the weapon was totally free of spent powder and metal mixed with gun oil, one of the primary causes of slide jam. Bolan wiped it lightly with a silicone cloth, added a drop of oil to either side of the ejection port and exterior slide wells of the receiver, then reassembled the weapon almost as quickly as he'd disassembled it. He reholstered the weapon, locked and loaded.

Bolan moved over to the window and opened the shade. He looked onto the street and saw exactly what he'd expected to. Two men dressed in traditional robes, robes that looked very familiar now, stood on the corner of the street and watched the hotel. Bolan had made sure no one followed him from the marketplace, but he was also confidont in the vigilance of the Iranian government's internal security network. It stood to reason a good number of Americans that came into Iran were under constant surveillance, just as would be Iranians inside American borders.

"Ready to go, Sarge?" Grimaldi asked.

Bolan shook his head and let go of the thick, black shade of mesh that blocked the scorching afternoon sun. "There's some trouble below I should take care of first. You two head out the back way and I'll meet you at the airport."

Julian expressed worry. "What kind of trouble?"

Bolan looked her in the eyes. "Nothing I can't handle."

The warrior nodded at Grimaldi, who gently grabbed Julian's elbow and steered her toward the door in a fashion that left no room to argue. The Stony Man pilot had known Bolan long enough to pick up on the subtleties in his voice and mannerisms.

Julian gruffly removed her elbow from Grimaldi's grip and stopped dead in her tracks. "What, you're just going to obey him without question? You don't have a mind of your own?"

"Actually, I do. And right now it's telling me he needs us to do what he asks and when he asks it. If you're smart, you'll figure that out." He reaffirmed his grip and added, "Now *let's go*."

Julian didn't offer any further argument as they headed out the door, bags in tow. Grimaldi had parked their rental car out back in the hotel's small lot.

"I'll meet you at the alternate rendezvous point," Bolan called as Grimaldi went to close the door. "Fifteen minutes."

The Stony Man pilot nodded, then closed the door after him.

To the Executioner's knowledge, the tails had only been for him. If they hadn't managed a good look at Grimaldi and Julian, the pair could probably get away with pulling out of the hotel lot and drive away without attracting a lot of attention. The vehicle would raise eyebrows, but for the most part they could pass as tourists or otherwise, which made the likeliness of pursuers relatively nonexistent.

That would leave the observers for Mack Bolan.

The Executioner waited until he saw the SUV pull onto the street and drive away, then he left the room and took the stairs to the lobby. Bolan crossed to the desk, checked out, left the lobby and stepped onto the street. The pair of observers turned away and tried to look as if they were occupied with other interests on the busy street. Bolan shook his head as he crossed the street and approached the men without inhibition. The men tried to pretend they didn't see him, but one finally realized the Executioner's intent to approach them and bolted.

The second man, obviously more seasoned than his partner, kept in character and didn't let his mark intimidate him. The problem was he didn't know what had happened until Bolan was on top of him. Grabbing the man's arm, Bolan shoved him off the sidewalk and through the open door of a small pottery shop, out of sight of the crowds. The guy recovered and reached behind him to withdraw a knife, but Bolan had the Beretta 93-R out, barrel pressed under the man's chin, before he could make any further aggressive moves.

"Drop it," Bolan ordered him. He heard it clatter to the floor. "You speak English? Never mind, of course you do."

"What do you want?" the man asked. His tone lacked fear.

"That should be my question," Bolan replied. "Who sent you to follow me? Iranian secret police?"

The man let out a sardonic laugh. "Hardly. The government cares nothing for you…*Americans*." His emphasis on the word told of his distaste. "My people are interested in your activities. You are American, and yet you are combating your own kind. This interests my people."

"And who are your people?" Bolan asked.

The man stood straighter and his chest puffed out some. "I am of the Mujahedeen-e-Khalq. Victory to Kiyanfar!"

"Who?" Bolan pressed.

"Our *alim*."

The Executioner searched his memory for the term. The *alim* was considered a religious leader, a spiritual guide and shepherd for Islam. It seemed odd to hear this reference, since the MEK didn't ostensibly operate as religious fundamentalists. In fact, a good number of them had publicly denounced the traditional ways of Islam in the past. They didn't even support an Islamic platform, as attested by their past struggles against the Iranian government—a government that had been trying to restore the society to more traditional Islamic views. No, this couldn't be about religious fanaticism. It was purely political, which told Bolan something else was motivating the MEK in this fight.

That, and the fact they hadn't shot him on sight.

"Why would your people have any interest in that?" Bolan said. "Don't you despise us all equally?"

"Word of you came to us before your arrival. We know you have fought against the American trying to bring war to our country. We know this man slaughtered our brothers. We plan to take our revenge."

"So you know this attack wasn't promoted by the Iranian government then," Bolan said.

"The *alim* knows the Egyptians are not interested in promoting our cause. We are using them for a time to accomplish our aims so we may deliver our Arab brothers from the murderers in your country."

Suddenly the Executioner understood it all. The MEK wasn't trying to fuel their war with the Iranian government. This simply served as a convenient cover for their own plans. They were deceiving the deceivers. They planned to hand out vengeance for the slaughter of the New Corsican Front operatives in Atlanta, and they knew *exactly* who was behind the scheme. That's why they hadn't gone out of their way to retaliate against the Iranian police authorities.

"I'm on your side," Bolan said.

"You are not a part of the Mujahedeen-e-Khalq. You could never be a part of us. You are our enemy...but you are insignificant."

"I'm an enemy to anyone who threatens my people," Bolan said. He pressed the muzzle tighter against the man's chin. "Take a message back to your leader. Tell him not to get in my way. Simple. You got it?"

The man nodded.

Bolan whirled and walked out of the shop, then broke into a quick jog and headed for his rendezvous point with Grimaldi. The situation grew stranger by the hour.

CHAPTER NINETEEN

Bolan met up with Grimaldi on schedule.

"What next?" the Stony Man pilot asked.

"Head for the airport," the Executioner said. "We need—"

The soldier cut it short to look around the front passenger-side A-post. He'd hoped to not see what he thought he would, but fate wasn't dealing from that deck this night. There they were, three or four of them. It was hard to tell as they approached single file in that blind spot. Bolan could barely see the silhouette of weapons in their hands. "It figures. You packing?" he asked Grimaldi without taking his eyes from the approaching forms.

"What is it?" Julian asked from the back seat, the first time she'd said a word since he'd arrived.

"Yeah," Grimaldi said. He pulled up his shirt and drew a SIG-Sauer P-226.

"What is it?" Julian asked again.

"Company," Bolan said. "Get down in the seat and don't show yourself until we get back."

"And what if you don't *come* back?" she asked, grabbing his shoulder before he could get out of the car.

"Then you drive away," Bolan said, and he and Grimaldi went EVA.

Bolan brought the Beretta into play, thumbed the selector to 3-shot mode and squeezed the trigger. The subsonic cartridges chugged from the weapon and sent a trio of hollow-points in the direction of the new arrivals. The sudden resistance took the approaching gunners by surprise. The first man in line felt the brunt of Bolan's direct assault. All three rounds ripped through the tender flesh of his chest and dumped him on the pavement.

The Executioner tracked on the second in line even as two more gunners split off in either direction. He triggered his second volley even as Grimaldi tracked on one of the pair racing for cover.

It was nice to have a trusted friend and companion right at that moment.

Grimaldi got his bead and took the shot. The pilot loaded Olin subsonic cartridges, the same as used by the FBI, which were 147-grain, soft-nose rounds. This particular round reduced the chance of overpenetrating a human body and taking down an innocent bystander in the process. The 9 mm Parabellum round ripped a neat hole in the target's neck, but the outgoing path wasn't nearly as neat. It blew out the man's throat and neck muscles; his head bobbed oddly on his shoulders as the impact drove him to the pavement.

The Executioner squeezed off another burst at about the same moment Grimaldi took his first shot. The 3-round volley cut a deep swathe across the enemy's belly, tearing out tender flesh and perforating vital organs. The man's howl of agony was audible as the echo of gunfire died in the stifling, early evening air. He toppled to the ground as he stumbled over the corpse of his comrade, and his weapon skittered across the broken, uneven street.

Grimaldi had a fix on his second target before his first hit the ground. The Stony Man pilot squeezed out two rounds, but the first went clear of the guy's head as he ducked at the last moment and the second ripped out a chunk of stone at his heel. Grimaldi held off with his third shot to conserve ammo since the guy made cover before he could get a clean shot. He turned to advise Bolan he'd missed the second target but the Executioner had already bolted from his position, apparently hell-bent on finishing what their enemy had started.

Grimaldi glanced inside the car to verify Julian was okay, then turned his attention to the more critical matters at hand. Movement caught his peripheral vision and he turned in time to see a trio of gunners approaching from his left, an obvious attempt to flank their position. With Bolan tied up, the pilot didn't intend to let the enemy take him down.

Grimaldi ripped open his door and crouched behind it for cover even as the approaching gunmen raised their weapons. He braced his arms between the A-post and window frame, sighted on the leader and squeezed the trigger twice. A pair of 9 mm slugs traveled that distance in seconds. The man stiffened, surprised at the fact Grimaldi had actually hit him, and then looked down slowly to see the blood begin to ooze from his belly. He then stared Grimaldi directly in the eyes with a horrific expression before he collapsed face-first to the sidewalk.

The pair accompanying him realized they had lost the element of surprise and tried to find cover, but obviously they hadn't planned the attack well since there wasn't much in the way to shield them from gunfire. One of the men reached a light pole just as Grimaldi brought him into target acquisition and took the shot. The round caught the gunner in the shoulder and spun him clear of the cover he'd found. Grimaldi followed immediately with another shot that struck the man in the chest and knocked him to the ground. His body twitched for a moment then lay still.

Grimaldi caught the other who had stopped a mere moment to check the leader's condition. The guy apparently saw he had no way out and obviously decided his best option was to go down fighting. He climbed to his feet and charged Grimaldi's position, triggering his machine pistol on full-auto. The Stony Man pilot held his position, undaunted, took careful aim and squeezed off a well-placed shot. The soft-nose round penetrated the man's skull and blew his face open. The guy staggered backward under the force of the shot. His weapon pointed skyward, his finger continuing to jerk reflexively on the trigger as he sent a plethora of rounds skyward. Finally he staggered backward, tripping over the body of his comrade, and collapsed to the pavement.

Grimaldi turned in time to see Bolan approach their vehicle. "You okay?"

The soldier nodded. "Never better."

"Well, if we're done having all this fun, I'd say it's time we get the hell out of here," Grimaldi cracked as he holstered his pistol and got into the car. The comment was merely the pilot's way of blowing off the stress of the moment. Despite his training, it wasn't every day that he faced people hell-bent on killing him.

As he drove them away from the scene, Julian asked Bolan, "Who do think they were? More of Downing's goons dressed like locals?"

The Executioner shook his head. "Not likely."

"More of our MEK friends, Sarge?" Grimaldi interjected.

"I'm betting that's what someone would like to think, but that doesn't seem their style. Not after my run-in with that tail."

"Why would anyone want you to think they were these MEK terrorists?" Julian asked.

"Because someone's trying to fuel the unrest here in Iraq."

"I don't mean to sound like a smart-ass," Julian replied, "but that's not exactly hard to do."

"She does have a point there, Sarge," Grimaldi added with a lopsided smile.

"You're not helping," Bolan told him, but he returned the banter with a chuckle. He kept his eyes on the road and continued. "That police captain's contact told me something very interesting. He said the MEK isn't the least bit interested in fighting a war with the Iraqi police. They don't want dissension inside their borders at all. That makes sense to me."

"A lot more sense than what everyone's tried to lead us to believe so far," Grimaldi said.

"Right," Bolan replied with a nod. "Now they would like to kick off operations in America, but only to rally support for those who they perceive as oppressed brothers of Islam."

"So what else is new?" Julian cut in as she rolled her eyes.

"The bottom line," Bolan said, ignoring Julian's sarcastic wit, "is that this Malik in Egypt is putting out a considerable amount of funds to keep the MEK busy fighting anybody and everybody in sight. They practically had a small army waiting for Stezhnya's crew."

"That's why we're headed to Cairo?"

Bolan nodded. "We've been on the defensive too long. That little fiasco back there proves it beyond a shadow of a doubt. I need to start hitting them at home."

"What about Downing and the *Hadesfire?*" Julian asked.

"They'll keep," the Executioner replied. "First, let's stop the guy fueling this fire. Then we'll deal with those who pretend they want to put it out."

"THERE'S NO DOUBT about it now," Aaron Kurtzman said as he rolled himself into the main conference room in the Stony Man Farm Annex. "The duplicate signals aren't phantom."

"They're both real?" Hal Brognola asked with surprise. He'd just finished pouring himself a cup of coffee. He wished Price had been here to make it, but he'd ordered her to stand down for twenty-four hours for a much needed rest. He'd just have to hope that Kurtzman's evil brew wouldn't eat away the lining of his stomach.

Kurtzman nodded. "As real as you and me, boss."

"So Striker's hunch was right on the money," Brognola said in a huff as he gestured to the pot in offering. Kurtzman shook his head and Brognola added, "There are two of these infernal machines out there."

"That's our official position," Kurtzman said, the "our" a reference to his crack cybernetics team. "If they're using a phantom signal to attempt to throw us off track, then they're doing a whiz-bang job of it. Had us fooled for a while. You can duplicate signals all you want to and you can even make them appear to come from the same source. What you can't do is dummy up satellite analysis via microwave. As soon as we ran an algorithm in our detection program, we discovered two entirely different sources for the signals."

"Could the second one just be a dummy transmitter?"

Kurtzman shook his head and spun in his wheelchair to access a nearby computer terminal. Strong fingers danced rapidly over the keyboard and a moment later the overhead projector spit an image of two red-green outlines on the screen. They were identical in shape and size.

"Here's an infrared sweep we did in a section of the Oman interior about fifteen kilometers outside the town of Manah."

Brognola leaned forward and squinted at the images for a long moment before turning to Kurtzman with a shrug. "Are those our twins?"

Kurtzman nodded. "We believe so, without any other strong evidence to the contrary. I tried to funnel this information back to Julian to confirm, but she's incommunicado along with Striker and Jack."

Brognola sat back in his chair and expended a deep sigh. "I figured as much. He said there might be some time where he wouldn't be in touch." He waved in the direction of screen. "So assuming you're correct about this, what I don't get is how Downing pulled it off."

"Hagen," Kurtzman said matter-of-factly.

"Come again?"

Kurtzman looked at Brognola and the rich, booming tone rose a bit as he became more excited at deciphering the puzzle. "I've given this some thought. Didn't Striker tell us before that Crystal Julian had been building the *Hadesfire* on-site in the Philippines?"

"Sure," Brognola agreed.

"Okay, and she also said Downing was working on something at his end and that's why he couldn't join her right away," he continued. "I'd bet dollars to silicone chips it was a second prototype."

"In case something happened to the first one," Brognola finished. "That makes good sense, Bear."

Brognola found himself in total agreement with Kurtzman's logic. It explained a lot of things that had seemed to elude them up to this point: such as why Downing had Hagen assassinated. After he'd finished the *Hadesfire*, Downing couldn't risk him being caught by the authorities. Hagen was a scientist who had served under Downing, and probably took a large pay-off for the work. But that's where his loyalties would end. If cornered by federal interrogators, Brognola knew that Hagen would have wagged his tongue faster than a puppy's tail. It only made sense. Hagen still had fingers that ran deep through the hairs of certain elements inside the U.S. intelligence community.

"So Downing figures Hagen's a liability and he sends this Apparatus of his to cancel Hagen's ticket," Brognola surmised.

"Yeah," Kurtzman replied. "Only problem is they hadn't counted on coming up against the likes of Striker."

"Neither will the players in Egypt."

"Egypt?" Kurtzman raised his eyebrows.

"Striker's headed to Cairo."

"Damn, he's sure taking a grand tour on this mission," Kurtzman quipped. "So dare I ask what *that's* about?"

"I'm not sure yet," Brognola said. He leaned forward and typed some information into his own terminal relay. "You came in on our last call after the fact."

A passport photo of a dark, handsome man in a well-tailored suit replaced Kurtzman's infrared image.

"Meet Agymah Malik. He's an Egyptian businessman with ties to at least a dozen influential companies all over the world. He's also a former member of the Armed Islamic Group."

Kurtzman whistled. "Striker's had plenty of go-arounds with that crew. Nasty bunch."

"Malik was no exception," Brognola replied. "He started at the bottom of the rung and worked his way up to protection detail for the leader. And then one day he just abandons it for a legitimate operation. Or at least it would seem on the surface."

"What's he into now?"

"Mostly he moves money around, makes a few legitimate contacts and investments to keep up appearances. But deep down the guy's rotten to the core. He makes plenty of cash below-board so he can pay off Egyptian authorities to turn a blind eye to his activities."

"A lot of money changing hands, eh?"

"Enough to interest me," Brognola said. He suddenly snapped his fingers. "Wait a minute! Didn't you just say those images you took were outside of Manah?"

"Yep."

"That's how Malik's doing this then. A couple of years ago he managed to get a series of investors to back a brand-new private sector power project in Oman. In fact, it's the first of its kind and it's under the purview of the IFC."

"Who?"

"The International Financial Company. It's a member of the World Bank Group with nearly two hundred member countries in their ranks. They primarily work in private sector investments for developing countries. They loaned a Gulf-region company called Union Power Corporation over seventy million to build an electric power plant in Manah, plus install lines that connect the grid in Muscat as well as about a half dozen other towns."

"I'm sure the payback will be lucrative," Kurtzman concluded.

"And long-term," Brognola added in way of agreement. "It's just the kind of thing a guy like Malik would sink his teeth into."

"I don't see what any of this has to do with Downing or these *Hadesfire* prototypes."

"Think about it," Brognola said. He sipped from his coffee cup before continuing. "Malik's name hadn't come into this at all until Striker ran down that Iranian police connection in Tehran. That was just a few hours ago. Then I run Malik's profile and come back with a load of intelligence that's just too damned close to the action to be mere coincidence."

"Yeah, there isn't much happenstance in our line of work," Kurtzman agreed. "I'd say you're right and there's a legitimate connection here."

"Believe me when I say I wish there wasn't. But I'm afraid this new information leaves little doubt. Striker was convinced Malik had something to do with all of this, and it looks like he was right."

"Again," Kurtzman replied with a nod. "So, what's the plan?"

"First thing's first," Brognola said. "We need to get all of this intelligence downloaded to Striker's PDA as soon as possible. Once that's accomplished, he'll know how to proceed. You also need to get him clued in to the likelihood of his theory where it regards the existence of a second *Hadesfire*. Tell him about their proximity, but that we don't know how long they'll stay that close."

"I get it. He'll try to hit them both at the same time while they're most vulnerable."

"Exactly. Although he did tell me that taking out Malik would be the priority."

"Don't you think Downing's plans pose a bigger threat, Chief?"

"Maybe," Brognola said, "but it doesn't really matter what I think anymore. Striker has to call the play. I think part of his logic here makes sense."

"In what way?"

"Well, for one thing it seems that Downing's entire plan hinges on the fueling of this fire between the MEK and Iranian authorities. As long as Malik has an outside group to protect his interests in Oman while keeping the focus in Iran, Downing has running room *and* a justification for the righteousness of his cause. Since the Oval Office wasn't that successful with its damage control efforts in Atlanta, I do think Downing still poses a significant threat."

"You mean in the fact that most of the public thinks it was the terrorists that killed those people and not Downing. But you're also thinking that Striker's right about taking the fuel out of the fire. If he brings down Malik, Downing can no longer hide behind the problems of global terrorism. It will neutralize the trouble and exposes his activities."

"Right on both counts," Brognola replied. "So let's get that information to Striker so he can make the best use of it in the shortest time."

"Consider it done," Kurtzman said.

CHAPTER TWENTY

Mack Bolan had a best possible location on Agymah Malik from Stony Man by the time they touched down in Cairo, as well as a confirmation of his suspicion regarding a second *Hadesfire*. He leaned over Dr. Crystal Julian's shoulder as they reviewed the information together—after the Executioner had cleared it to make sure it contained nothing sensitive for his eyes only— and Julian reviewed it with only an occasional hum.

"I don't get it," she finally told him. "I don't understand how Downing could have been building another *Hadesfire* without my knowledge."

"My people think it's the 'other project' Peter Hagen was working on while you were in the Philippines," Bolan said. "And that's also why Downing killed him."

She turned and fixed him with a look that combined realization with horror. "That means he would have—"

"Yeah," Bolan said, not letting her finish the statement.

The Executioner didn't doubt for a second that Downing would have murdered Julian the moment she'd finished the *Hadesfire* and the opportunity presented itself. Fortunately, her selfless act of putting it all on the line to save the life of a total stranger had turned out to be the same one that saved her own life. Bolan didn't bother to mention it out loud—her expression said it all.

She cleared her throat and removed her glasses, quietly folding them and setting them on the table tray in front of her. "Now what?"

"Now I find this Malik," Bolan said. "It's high time someone punched his ticket."

AGYMAH MALIK had his hands into everything. Bolan had considered simply reaching out to the GIA and informing its leaders of what Malik had been doing in their name, but he didn't wish to ignite a full-scale war between them and the MEK. It was better to handle this quickly and quietly.

Getting into Egypt with arms would have proved impossible, even with Stony Man's connections, so they had abandoned the cache of weapons in Iran and hidden them until one of their contacts could retrieve them. That meant Bolan's first mission would be to get his hands on some firepower, and lots of it since he had no idea where he would go from here, or even if he'd have another chance to gear up.

As in most Middle Eastern countries, weapons weren't difficult to come by. The Executioner had been to Egypt enough times that he knew all the most trustworthy arms dealers. He would have preferred to go through official channels, but there hadn't been any time. He had to bring down Malik and do it fast if he stood any chance of curtailing Downing's plans.

It turned out to be good fortune that the man Bolan dealt with when he was usually in Egypt just happened to work his operation right out of the same uptown area where Malik's offices were located, which only made it more convenient for the Executioner to implement the plan he had in mind. Bolan knew the dealer only as Donkor, a name he wasn't even sure was real. It didn't bother him since Donkor didn't know Bolan's name at all, and preferred to keep it that way. It had been— what?—three years since he'd last seen Donkor. He wondered if the guy were still even in business. He was taking a chance exposing himself to scrutiny in broad daylight, but he didn't have much choice. Any other contacts were more remote, and Bolan needed the tools of his trade quickly.

The Executioner instructed the driver of the cab he'd caught from the airport to drop him at an intersection three blocks from where Donkor did business. Bolan covered the three blocks in under two minutes, eventually turning into an alleyway and following it to the end where a long flight of concrete steps descended steeply to a rusted, metal door.

Bolan rapped his knuckles twice in succession and waited less than a minute before the door cracked open. A pair of dull brown eyes peered through the crack from a height about half that of Bolan's. The Executioner stared back at those eyes, and a moment later the door opened just enough to reveal the face they belonged to.

"Well, I'll be a sultan's slave," he said, his voice a rich baritone with a British accent. "I wondered if I'd ever see you again."

"Some people can only hope," Bolan replied with a half grin. "You should be so lucky."

"And you should be dead, shouldn't you?" he asked. He made no move to open the door wider and admit the Executioner. "What do you want?"

Bolan sensed Donkor's suspicious behavior and wondered if he'd made a mistake. He couldn't tell if the man's furtiveness was the result of mistrust at seeing Bolan suddenly, unannounced, or if someone had gotten to him first.

"Why so jumpy, Donkor?"

"Just wasn't expecting you," the man replied quickly...too quickly.

"Don't tell me you suddenly found a conscience," Bolan replied. He shifted position ever so slightly to realign his center of gravity.

"Would that be so tough to believe?"

"Yeah," Bolan replied with a nod. "There's not enough profit in it."

"Maybe keeping out of prison was enough," Donkor said matter-of-factly.

"Sure, when Hell freezes over," Bolan said. "Listen, Donkor, I don't have time for games. I'm here strictly on business so let me in and let's talk about that."

"Yeah, I heard exactly what kind of business you're here to take care of already, American," Donkor said. "And I don't want any part of it. So beat—"

Bolan's foot lashed out, his booted heel striking the heavy door. Even its metal frame and sheeting wasn't about to hold back the pistonlike strength of the Executioner. The door flew backward, the impact knocking Donkor off his feet and sending him sprawling across the cracked linoleum floor of a dimly lit hallway. Bolan advanced through the doorway and slammed it shut behind him, and then walked menacingly toward Donkor who crab-walked to escape the approaching specter.

Two muscular men, native bruisers of the largest kind, emerged from a side doorway as Bolan advanced on Donkor. They rushed his position but the Executioner stood his ground. The narrow confines of the hallway prevented both of them from advancing side by side—not to mention they would have to get around Donkor without stampeding him to death—which gave Bolan the advantage of having to manage only one threat a time. Not that either looked as if they posed any terrible risk. About the only thing they had going for them was their size because their movements told Bolan neither of them was that experienced in unarmed combat.

Bolan waited until the last moment before stepping aside and throwing out his right arm and advancing. The clothesline caught the first attacker in the throat and took him completely off his feet. His body landed hard on the floor and his skull impacted with a sickly crack against the linoleum.

The maneuver came unexpected to his cohort, who barely managed to keep his balance as he tried not to trip over the unconscious form. The man regained his balance and fired a haymaker punch at Bolan's head. The Executioner stepped inside and crouched. The punch glanced harmlessly off his shoulder as he brought his right fist from the knees and caught his enemy with an uppercut to the point of the chin. The man's head snapped backward, the punch was hard enough to have almost knocked him cold. Bolan didn't let up, quite aware that while his enemy wasn't fast he stood a good chance of losing this fight if the man got hold of him with those ham-size hands. Bolan snapped an elbow into the man's solar plexus and knocked the wind from him. He wheezed for air, and Bolan took the remaining fight out of him by ramming a knee into the man's groin. The guy howled in pain and dropped to his knees. The Executioner clapped the man's ears, then drove a ridge-hand stroke into his throat. The guy's hands went to his fractured windpipe and now he struggled to breathe, although it wouldn't do him any good since the damage was done. The man quickly succumbed to the lack of oxygen and collapsed.

Bolan whirled on Donkor as he caught his breath, bent over and hauled the little man to his feet by his shirt collar. He jerked a thumb over his shoulder. "You want to explain the gorillas?"

Donkor threw up his hands and stepped back from Bolan. "Hey, a man must protect his investment, American. It is nothing personal."

"I take anyone trying to kill me personal," Bolan replied. "We've done plenty of business before and never had a problem. Why now?"

"Because I know what business you are here for," Donkor said. "I cannot afford word to get out that I had anything to do with that."

"What do you think I'm here to do?"

"Kill Agymah Malik."

"And how would you know that?"

"You are jesting with me, yes?" Donkor asked, emitting a nervous chuckle. "You must think we are imbeciles over here, that we have no brains whatever. I heard about the firefight in Tehran and that an American was involved. As soon as I heard the description, I knew it was you. And I also figured you'd be coming here next."

"Why's that?"

"Because of Malik's involvement with your American chum, Downing."

"Start your explanation from the beginning."

"Maybe I do not have to explain anything."

"You want to come out of this alive?" Bolan asked. "You have a lot more to fear from me right now than Malik, Donkor. That much I can guarantee. So tell me whatever you know about it, or I'm going to kill you, take what I need from your cache, and make sure it looks like a deal gone bad."

Donkor laughed and put his arms out to his side. "After all we have been through together?"

Bolan said nothing, just stared.

After a moment Donkor's good-humor mask fell. "Malik's been fueling the Iranians for some time now. He's been supplying them arms and equipment to battle the Iranian police."

"That's old news," Bolan said. "You'll have to do better than that."

"Malik's not interested in Iranians," Donkor said more quickly. "He's got his eye on this base of operations in the Oman interior."

"What kind of base of operations?"

"The kind from which to launch strikes against the West. The kind where his so-called team of jihad freedom fighters can rest between missions and plan their next strike. It will make your CIA training camps in the Afghani deserts look like communes for the poor. I hear tell of state-of-the-art equipment, and it's all being financed by monies funneled through his company."

"What's the talk about him still being involved with the Armed Islamic Group?" Bolan asked.

Donkor snorted. "He doesn't care about them, and they care even less for him. But apparently their people have orders he is strictly to be left untouched. That's the only reason they haven't eliminated him by now. Something about Jabari having a weakness for him because Malik once served as one of his personal protectors."

Bolan nodded his understanding. Ishaq Jabari had been leading the GIA movement for more years than anyone cared to count. In his younger days he'd exercised stronger control on them, but these days there were a lot of factions and sects that had broken from the main body. The largest bodies had operated in Libya and Algeria, but their numbers had waned over the years, and the most radical broke off to join remnants of the Egyptian jihad.

"So Malik isn't operating under GIA sanction," Bolan said. "Only the mercy of his former boss."

"Agymah Malik is a respected businessman in Egypt, and most often he is seen in the company of other respectable businessmen. On occasion, however, he has been known to associate with men of, shall we say 'lesser caliber,' and that has cost him some of his untarnished reputation."

Bolan sighed. "Get to the point."

"Malik wants to run a legitimate business because he can funnel money, vast sums of money, through that pipeline."

"What are we actually talking about here? Laundering?"

"Nothing so simple as that," Donkor replied. "Malik is not a fool. He is more interested in controlling something of which there is significantly short supply."

Bolan knew immediately what Donkor meant. "Power."

"Your insight is impressive, American," Donkor replied. "Anyone who can maintain a hold on utility supplies like water and electricity in the Middle East has a significant bargaining position. Malik's an idealist. He is attempting to get back into the graces of not only his GIA counterparts but also those in charge of the larger network of Islamic freedom fighters. Yet, he is not even of the Islamic faith and would therefore have no legitimate interest in the religious fervor of the more devout members. He leaves the jihad to those like the Mujahedeen-e-Khalq and his former GIA allies."

"Now you're making sense," Bolan said. "That's

why he helped broker the deal with the financial company in Washington, D.C., and has operations under way in Oman. He plans to help facilitate the completion of this deal, and then he'll seize control of it by force."

"What you say is right," Donkor said. "I am glad you did not force me to tell you this."

What Bolan decided not to reveal was how Downing played into all of this. Somehow, Downing had discovered Malik's plot. So Downing and the Apparatus had worked behind the scenes to keep the fire going. They wanted to see Malik make this move. And then when the Egyptian did act, Downing's people would be there to pounce on him. But they had to distract the U.S. government from their real intentions, so they implemented the operation in Atlanta to set everyone on edge with the promise of more to come, when in truth they had no intention of any further operations in America. At least, not right now.

Bolan felt stupefied and simultaneously angered that he hadn't seen through the plan until now. He had to hand it to Downing—it was certainly an ingenious plot, to say the least. The Executioner had made one minor mistake on this mission, and that was underestimating the enemy. He planned to rectify that mistake right now.

"You just saved your life, Donkor," Bolan said. "What you haven't told me yet is how you know all this?"

"Whom do you think Malik came to for the weapons he supplied to the Iranians?"

Bolan nodded. "I see. Well now, you and I have

some business to transact. And I know you'll be glad to offer a deep discount in order to keep me a happy customer."

Donkor swallowed hard. "How deep?"

"Seventy-five."

"Percent?" Donkor hollered. "That is robbery, not to mention unacceptable!"

The Executioner grabbed Donkor by the shirt collar and lifted the man off the ground so they were nose to nose. Bolan could see the fear in the little man's eyes, exactly as he'd planned. "Like I said, you just saved your life. Don't screw up a good thing. What I pay you will be enough for you to get out of the country alive."

Bolan set him back on the ground none too gently.

"But I'll never be able to come back," Donkor protested.

Bolan shrugged. "Time to retire then, isn't it?"

Donkor appeared to think hard about it for a minute, then turned and muttered something as he gestured for Bolan to follow. He led him through a heavy steel door and the Executioner made sure to keep Donkor in proximity. He didn't want to end up locked in some gun vault, his flesh rotting off the bone for the next hundred years.

The room beyond that door seemed unremarkable at first glance, but somewhere Donkor activated a switch because the walls suddenly inverted and replaced the sterile emptiness with an arsenal sufficient to equip an entire platoon of U.S. Marines. Pistols to rocket launchers lined the walls, each categorized into its particular area of small-arms class. Bolan nodded, impressed with the state-of-the-art display. Donkor hadn't presented anything close to this on Bolan's last visit to Cairo.

"So...tell me what you need," Donkor said.

CHAPTER TWENTY-ONE

Julian and Grimaldi watched in silence as Mack Bolan girded for war.

The Executioner had managed to acquire all the necessary tools from Donkor he needed to take the fight straight to Malik. When he took out the Egyptian, he'd also remove a big piece of the threat to America. Still, he faced the threat of not one but two *Hadesfire* prototypes, and he didn't relish that encounter. For now, he had enough to keep him busy.

"What's your plan?" Grimaldi asked him.

"I'll go in hard and fast," Bolan said as he donned the remainder of his equipment.

Donkor had equipped him with a customized Beretta Model 96 Centurion, which chambered the .40 S&W cartridge rather than the 9 mm of his Beretta 93-R. It didn't have 3-shot mode, but Bolan had become accustomed to the Beretta's reliability and so it made for an obvious choice. Additionally, he'd picked up a Walther

MP-L submachine gun along with its stubbier counterpart the MP-K. They weren't his first choice, but they were more than adequate for the job ahead.

To top the list, Bolan had selected an M-16 A3/ M-203 combination, and about a dozen 40 mm high-explosive grenades. The HE rounds would definitely work toward clearing away any heavy firepower Bolan might encounter. He was certain a decent guard detail would accompany Malik anywhere he went. Bolan didn't really know what he was up against, a fact he didn't like much, but he didn't have a choice. He'd have to be prepared for anything since his connections and resources were limited in this part of the world.

"What about Downing?" Julian asked. "Are you sure he's still not a threat?"

"He's still a threat," Bolan replied with a nod. "But if I take Malik out of the picture first, that removes the main thrust behind Downing's plan. It's difficult to wipe out an enemy that's already been defeated."

"Yeah, sure," Grimaldi rebutted. "That will just leave Downing and the Apparatus with one enemy to fight. You. And you'll be up against two of those machines of his."

"I've already thought of that, Jack. That's why you're along." Bolan couldn't resist a grin as he passed over a Belgium-made Browning BDA 9 and a box of 9 mm Parabellum rounds, another piece he'd acquired from Donkor. "Just in case."

Grimaldi accepted the pistol and immediately tucked it away.

"Listen," Julian cut in. "No offense to Jack, who's

obviously a fine pilot, but you'll be no match against a single *Hadesfire,* let alone two of them. It has no equal."

"There's no such thing as indestructible," Bolan reminded her.

"Perhaps, but the *Hadesfire* is as close as it gets."

"We'll see," Bolan said as he loaded the Walther SMGs and Model 96 into a new sports bag and headed for the door of the hotel. He had donned his blacksuit and then covered it with a lightweight set of coveralls worn by the maintenance personnel of the building that housed Malik's offices. Grimaldi and Julian had managed to locate a hotel within spitting distance of that building, which would make it much more convenient for Bolan to get away.

"I'm going to leave the over-and-under with you," he said as he headed for the door to the hotel room.

"Check. Good luck, Sarge," Grimaldi said. The pilot tossed him a thumbs-up.

Bolan returned it and quietly left the room.

The Executioner descended to ground level from their sixth-floor room via the stairs. He didn't wish to attract attention, and the single elevator serving all ten stories of their middle-class hotel got enough business to make him feel best to avoid it. Especially since the majority of the hotel appeared to cater to everyone from local urchins to tourists from neighboring countries. That made them stick out like a sore thumb, so they had agreed not to leave the room unless absolutely necessary.

Bolan crossed the street, hands in his pockets, hunched and sauntering as much as possible in hope he'd appear like just another common laborer, returning from a lunch that was too short to a job that didn't pay enough. Nobody gave him a second glance, and Bolan figured he had his dark hair and complexion to thank for that.

The warrior reached the five-story building two blocks away. Malik's offices were on the top floor. He walked toward the front entrance and then thought better of it, opting instead to turn right at the corner and follow the sidewalk to a back alley. A lowly servant wouldn't boldly enter through the front door; there had to be an employees' entrance. Bolan found it within a minute and happened upon two men coming down a small flight of steps just beyond the vestibule, attired in coveralls like his. Bolan tossed them a gesture and the customary greeting in Arabic. The men barely acknowledged him beyond an obligatory reply in turn.

The Executioner allowed himself a smile as he ascended the steps. His role camouflage had passed muster with those he emulated, which meant he'd have even better luck with a crowd that took scant notice of him. The elite tended to look down their noses at those less fortunate. That was good, as the last thing Bolan needed right now was attention.

Bolan decided to find a service elevator, a search that eventually led him to a small corridor on one side of the building. He took the elevator to the fifth floor and stepped off it. The corridor was deserted, but Bolan decided to proceed with caution all the same. He walked to the end, gave his coveralls the once-over, and then rounded the corner and walked nonchalantly toward

Malik's offices. He passed only a couple of men in formal business attire, but they paid him even less attention than the custodians had downstairs.

The Executioner pushed through double glass doors with frosted imprint. He couldn't read any of it, but he figured he had the right place. A good-looking young man sat behind a rather large desk and busily typed at a computer terminal. Bolan scanned the rest of the office, decided it was pretty much deserted—most of its occupants were probably at lunch—and made his move.

The man at the desk looked briefly in Bolan's direction, then returned to his work. Bolan quickly moved over to an eighteen-inch plastic wastebasket, picked it up and walked back toward the man's desk. He stood there awhile before the man noticed him.

He looked up with surprise as Bolan set the basket on the long counter adjacent to his work area, and pointed the Model 96 at the man's head, using the wastebasket to conceal it from any potential observers. The man's eyes widened and he made a sound from deep his throat that sounded like a cry of surprise mingled with a squeal of outrage. Bolan didn't really want to frighten this young man but didn't see he had much choice. The possibility existed this guy was totally innocent of any wrongdoing—perhaps just another pawn in Malik's game—but the Executioner didn't have the luxury of being picky right now.

"You speak English?" he asked.

The man nodded.

"I'm looking for Agymah Malik. Is he here?"

The young man shook his head and Bolan could see the obvious relief in his face.

"Where is he?"

"He is home today," the man said in a hoarse voice. He self-consciously cleared his throat.

"And where's that?" Bolan pressed.

"I cannot tell you!" the man cried. "I will not allow you to harm Mr. Malik. He has been kind to me."

"Maybe so," Bolan replied coldly. "But he's a criminal and a murderer, and he's responsible for the death of a lot of people. That will change before anyone else dies. So you can tell me where he is or die martyred. Your choice, make it now."

The man swallowed hard, his eyes roving to the wide muzzle of the Model 96. Bolan knew he was thinking hard about it. This young man probably did owe Malik a lot, but he was clearly no fanatic. He wasn't on some crusade and he certainly didn't strike Bolan as the type who would be stupid enough to attempt to outwit or overpower a professional soldier. He didn't have that kind of fight in him, and they both knew it.

"I will tell you," the young man said quietly. He gestured toward a pen and Bolan nodded his permission. The man quickly scribbled something on the pad in front of him, then tore off the top sheet and handed it to Bolan.

The Executioner took the paper, scanned it, then shoved it deep into a pocket beneath his coveralls. "Get up. Slowly."

The man did as ordered and Bolan directed him into a nearby office that couldn't be seen from the outer hallways. He found a light switch and shoved the young man inside the room before closing the door and turning the lights on. It was spacious and decorated to suit the finest, most eclectic tastes. How lucky. Bolan had somehow managed to stumble into Malik's office on the first try.

"Is that your boss's computer?" Bolan asked, nodding in the direction of a terminal.

"Yes," the man said with a nod.

"You know how to access it?"

"Yes."

"Good, go ahead and do it," Bolan said. "And if you try anything heroic I'll kill you here and now. Just remember that."

The man nodded and strolled over to Malik's computer. He sat behind a large, glass desk and although it was very thick glass Bolan could see every move the young man's hands made. There was no way he'd be able to pull a weapon on him. He kept just out of arm's length, pistol held at the ready, and watched the man sign into his employer's computer. Bolan couldn't read any of the information coming across the screen, but he wouldn't need to. All he had to do was link up with a very special address through a Web browser and Kurtzman would do the rest.

Bolan waved the man out of the chair once he'd signed in and ordered him to kneel in the corner. He then had him put his hands behind his head and cross his feet, then sit back on them. Bolan kept the muzzle of the pistol steady in the man's direction as he opened a browser from a very familiar-looking icon, then typed a special number into the address bar. A moment later it authenticated and awaited for him to put in his pass code. That would be the tough part. The soldier reached into the breast pocket of his coveralls and withdrew a cellular phone. He dialed a six-digit code into the handset and within less than a minute he had a secure, satellite connection to Stony Man Farm.

"Stony Base, this is Number One," Bolan said, speaking clearly into the recording. "Right now I'm attempting to connect Malik's computer to SpecterNet, but I'm not up on the Arabic keyboards. Go ahead and authenticate for me and get everything downloaded from it. Out, here."

Bolan replaced the phone, then ordered the man to get up and head for the door. As they drew close he could make out frantic footfalls as they moved across the floor beyond the closed door. He could tell it was several men fanning out for an ambush. By the extra effort they had exerted to not make noise, they had simply made more of it. Somehow, the assistant had managed to alert Malik's security force through accessing the computer. Bolan reached out, grabbed the prisoner by the back of his shirt and tossed him aside before diving for his own cover.

The maneuver saved their lives as holes suddenly appeared in the door, rapidly shredding it into splinters under the staccato sound of autofire. Bolan could do little more than keep his head down until the shooters ceased fire and began to shout at one another. Bolan gained a knee and steadied his forearms on the desk before the first enemy gunner came through the door with a vicious kick. The soldier dropped the man immediately with a double-tap from the Beretta. The survivors realized they were up against an armed opponent, and they moved rapidly for cover.

The Executioner knew they outgunned him. There was no way the Model 96 could go against that many armed men in such close quarters, and time wouldn't permit him to bring the Walther SMGs into play. Bolan whirled and took note of a sliding door behind Malik's desk. He got to his feet and raced to it. He fumbled with the latch only a moment before he got it free and the door slid easily aside.

Bolan stepped onto the balcony and looked up to see nothing but open air. That left down as the only choice. As bullets whizzed past him, he tucked the Beretta into the space between his coveralls and blacksuit, then hopped over the railing. It wouldn't be easy negotiating that obstacle toting the sports bag with the heavy guns, but he didn't have time for niceties. He'd known the risks going into this thing. At least he'd managed to get whatever useful information he could to Stony Man, and also a possible location on Malik's residence. On second thought, he hoped Kurtzman had time to download the data before Malik's assistant shut down the computer.

Bolan dropped to the balcony below and shaded his eyes against the window. The office interior appeared empty. He tried the door and found it locked; a single shot from the Model 96 followed by a swift kick rectified that. Bolan ducked inside to prevent being cut by the overhanging shards, and then crunched across the broken glass to the door. The floor plan here seemed identical to Malik's offices, although this one was significantly more conservative and traditional in decor.

Bolan moved quickly to the office door, opened it and peered out onto an empty foyer. He moved through the office and closed the door behind him before proceeding through the greeting area and out frosted glass doors to the hallway. Bolan sprinted to the stairwell and began to descend it rapidly. He needed to get out as quickly as possible. Malik would undoubtedly be alerted to the Executioner's impending arrival at his residence, and Bolan needed every advantage if he expected to succeed.

Yeah, he'd have to hit Malik hard and fast.

JACK GRIMALDI WAS GLAD Bolan had given him the Browning BDA 9 when a knock at the door came.

"That isn't room service," he said quietly to Julian, withdrawing the pistol from his waistband. He waved in the direction of her bedroom. "Go."

"But—"

"No argument," he replied.

She scooped her laptop off the table and headed for the bedroom. She'd barely reached halfway when there was another knock, this one louder, imperative. Grimaldi ensured he had a shell in the chamber, then went for cover. The next minute seemed to go in slow motion, almost as if he were watching the instant replay of a football game. From the corner of his eye, he saw Julian get to the door at the same time as the door flew inward.

Two men, big and swarthy, came through the doorway with wicked-looking Uzi machine pistols in their meaty hands. Grimaldi had found cover behind a sofa.

He took careful aim and squeezed off a shot. The 9 mm Parabellum round perforated one man's ribs and drove him sideways. He collapsed into a cabinet in the kitchenette and slid to the ground. His partner turned and leveled his machine pistol in Grimaldi's direction. He squeezed off a burst. The weapon rose with the recoil and the man rode it one-handed. The muzzle spit 9 mm slugs that ripped through the cheap fabric of the sofa and split the wood of the cheap frame beneath it.

Grimaldi rolled from cover for fear the rounds would find their way past the sofa and into his body. The pilot knew a pistol against Uzi wasn't a great match, and it became even more apparent to him as two more men scrambled into the room. One of them headed directly toward the bedroom where Julian had fled. Grimaldi came out of the roll, landed on one knee and snap-aimed his pistol. He squeezed the trigger twice and scored both hits. The rounds entered the man's spine and drove him into the closed bedroom door. His body bounced off and dropped to the carpeted floor.

The remaining pair of invaders reacquired their target. Grimaldi knew he wouldn't be in time to stop them. Only a heartbeat later did he realize he wouldn't have to. Both of his opponents began to jerk spasmodically as gunfire resounded throughout the room. It didn't come from their weapons. A shadowy figure stepped through the door before either body hit the ground.

Mack Bolan wore a grim expression. "You okay?"

Grimaldi nodded, swallowing hard at the afterthought he'd been at death's door just a moment earlier. "You're a damn welcome sight, Sarge."

"I'm sure," Bolan said with a half grin. "Where's Julian?"

Grimaldi pointed at the bedroom door.

Bolan crossed to it immediately, started to turn the handle, then thought better of it. He shouted a warning that it was him coming through the door. For all he knew, Julian was waiting on the other side and probably ready to clobber whoever came through with any solid object she could get her hands on. Grimaldi smiled at the warrior's caution, knowing it would be hard to explain that Bolan had come through all he had just to end up being beaten to death by a frightened woman.

"I've never been so glad to see anyone in my life," she told Bolan.

"Grab your stuff," he told her.

He turned to Grimaldi. "Things went south at Malik's office. I'll explain on the way."

Both men reacted when they heard the sound of sirens approaching.

"Uh-oh," Grimaldi said. "Locals are on the warpath."

"All the more reason to get the lead out."

Grimaldi took that cue and headed into the bedroom to help Julian gather her things. They had barely survived this encounter and they stood less chance against an entire army of Egyptian police. Those men were quite experienced at handling aggressors with firearms, and Grimaldi was of no more mind to stick around for that game than he knew the Executioner was. Mack Bolan had always maintained the rule about never dropping the hammer on legitimate law-enforcement officeres, and that included those of foreign countries, particularly in light of the fact they were the invaders here.

"Let's go, let's go," Bolan told them.

"Where to?" Grimaldi asked as they left the room amid the gasps of a half-dozen guests whose heads were poked through partially open doors.

"I've got a lead on Malik," Bolan said. "If the information pans out, we'll actually be successful this time."

"That would be a nice change," the Stony Man pilot replied.

CHAPTER TWENTY-TWO

Despite their best efforts, the trio didn't quite manage to get away before Cairo's finest arrived. The cops caught their scent as they were climbing into the sedan, obviously attracted to Bolan's odd mode of dress. He had ditched the coveralls in a garbage bin off the back parking lot of the hotel, and was now attired in full battle gear. Various items of war dangled from his combat harness.

"We've got trouble," Grimaldi said as they reached their rental.

All three looked in the direction of the driveway leading from the back lot as two police vehicles closed in. Both continued on a direct-approach course for their vehicle.

"Keys," Bolan told Grimaldi.

The pilot reached inside his jacket and tossed them over. Bolan caught them one-handed, disengaged the alarm system and locks with the remote, and all three jumped in simultaneously. The Executioner started the large sedan, put it in gear and burned rubber backing out. The overenthusiasm of their pursuers proved to be a mistake in his favor. Had one of the squad cars parked at the entrance, it would have effectively pinned them in, but as they both swung into the parking lot and fanned out, Bolan found an out by driving right between them.

"Nice play, Sarge!" Grimaldi shouted.

Bolan didn't reply, instead keeping his eyes on the road ahead. They were hardly out of the woods. Any celebration to the contrary would have been premature, at best. Bolan had learned from very early in his career that leaving a pursuer behind took no effort if skilled in putting an automobile through its paces, but to outrun a radio was a virtual improbability. The odds were totally in favor of the police on that count.

Bolan tore onto the street and made a hard left, taking the turn on two wheels. He darted through traffic, swung into the oncoming lane at one point in the break, then retook his own once past the block of cars. He checked the rearview mirror and didn't see a sign of his pursuers yet. It didn't matter. He knew they'd get onto his tail eventually. As Bolan blasted through an intersection with the green light, the flash of lights caught his peripheral vision. He checked his rearview mirror and watched as a police cruiser swung into view from a side street, the driver struggling to keep the lightweight vehicle from fishtailing.

Grimaldi had managed to rent a sedan that sported a heavy-duty V8 engine. The attendant had first offered an economy car, but the ace pilot had dissuaded him from the idea, citing just such a situation behind his reasoning. Bolan was now glad he'd listened to his trusted ally. The warrior continued through the next three intersections, all sporting green lights and very light traffic. He'd gone about another mile when a second police car joined the pursuit, and then a third.

"L.A.P.D.'s got nothing on these guys," Grimaldi said, jerking a thumb over his shoulder.

"Don't ever let Ironman hear you say that," Bolan replied.

Bolan kept his hands locked on the steering wheel. It wasn't the movies where the guy outran the cops with ease while he had one arm around the girl, the other holding his beer, and steering with his knees. One small miscalculation would likely land them in an accident, their broken and bleeding bodies merged with the scrap metal.

Julian leaned forward. "I hate to sound like a pessimist, here, but we're not going to get away with this."

"Watch us," Grimaldi replied.

Bolan didn't choose to comment.

He saw a major intersection and instantly formed an alternative to their present quandary. "I'm going to turn left up there and dump you two before they can see it. Get ready."

"What are you going to do?" Julian inquired.

"Give them something to occupy their time," Bolan replied.

The Executioner thought about the two incendiary grenades provided by Donkor. He needed a distraction in a bad way, one that would clog the pipeline and yet not endanger any bystanders. That plan stood a much better chance than continuing a high-speed pursuit, and as he'd already considered the ability to outrun police radios as naiveté, this seemed the most credible option at his disposal. The soldier took the corner on two wheels and slammed on the brakes.

"Go!" he told the passengers.

Grimaldi and Julian bailed, their doors hardly closed before Bolan had the sedan in motion once more. He continued to gain momentum, hoping as he watched the flashing lights round the corner that he was far enough ahead they wouldn't know he'd stopped. Bolan allowed a smile when he saw the pursuing vehicles continue without pause. He looked for another broad intersection but the road he'd turned onto, while not congested, was narrow with few side streets. He finally spotted an alley, nearly spinning out to make the turn, but managing to negotiate it at the last moment.

Bolan stopped midway up the dead-end alley and bailed from the car. He reached into his weaponry bag and withdrew the incendiary grenade, popped the pin and tossed the bomb in the back seat. He pulled a second device from the bag, this one a smoke canister, primed it and tossed it toward the rear of the car. He waited only a moment to ensure it popped and began to issue smoke before spinning on his heel and sprinting for a small door he spotted leading into one of the commercial structures. He found it locked but a good kick took care of the lock. He closed the door behind him, extinguishing the bright sunlight of the day to find himself in a dark, musty-smelling room no larger than a hundred feet square.

Bolan slipped the Beretta Model 96 from its holster and allowed his eyes to adjust. Square shapes began to take form, and Bolan concluded he was in some type of storage room. He found a large, heavy box and with some effort managed to push it into place to serve as a temporary barricade to the outside door. The smoke and fire would create enough of a distraction that by the time the police figured out what had happened he'd be long gone.

The Executioner found a door leading from the storage room and opened it. He poked his head through to find it led onto a deserted hallway. Bolan stepped out, eased the door closed behind him, then went off to find a discreet exit from the building, dismissing any thought of lying low inside until the police had gone. They were probably already throwing a net around this place, and it was small enough they could cordon a very large area in a short span of time. He didn't plan to be anywhere near there by that time.

Bolan had an appointment with Agymah Malik.

GRIMALDI AND JULIAN headed for cover as soon as they went EVA from their ride. The Stony Man pilot had no idea what was in Bolan's mind, but he did understand the dire need for separation. The police had no reason to be searching for their quarry on foot. As long as he and Julian could make a decent appearance as tourist types, just a married couple taking in the sights, they stood a good chance of evading apprehension. That part of Bolan's plan seemed quite solid.

What Grimaldi couldn't understand was the Executioner's choice to take out Malik ahead of Downing, especially considering the threat of the death machines in the hands of a group like the Apparatus. Still, Grimaldi wouldn't second-guess Bolan. His friend had an uncanny sense for these situations and Grimaldi would have trusted Bolan's instincts over those things other declared as facts. But now he had to find a way to get them out of harm's way; it wouldn't take the Cairo police long to figure out what was going on.

The pilot led Julian to a secluded eatery two blocks down from the intersection where they'd bailed. She got them a seat while Grimaldi found a phone and contacted Stony Man. Hal Brognola picked up on the second ring.

"It's me," Grimaldi said. While he knew the call wouldn't be monitored across the international lines given the secure access number, he had no idea who might be listening on the local end. He wasn't about to take chances.

Brognola obviously picked up on Grimaldi's ambiguous identification, an indication that the pilot suspected the line was insecure. "You okay?"

"Yes, the wife and I are having a great time, although cousin Matt's been staying busy and we haven't seen him much."

"That's too bad," Brognola replied.

"Yeah." It was all he could think to say.

"Any way we can help?"

"We may need to find another way home," the pilot replied. "I'm not sure our current tickets will get us home. I'm sure the airlines will charge us a small fortune to switch flights."

"I'll see what I can do about getting you an alternate flight out," Brognola replied.

Grimaldi nodded, not thinking Brognola couldn't actually see him. He didn't know how to express his concern for Bolan. The Sarge had been pushing the envelope of human endurance for the past three days without sleep, and it didn't look as though he'd get a decent break any time soon. It was one thing if Bolan's mission against Malik would have put an end to their mission, but even with the Egyptian out of the way it was clear Downing and the Apparatus posed a significant threat to American security. Especially with an advanced weapon like the *Hadesfire* at their disposal.

Still, he knew there wasn't much Brognola could do at that end. Bolan had always been a loner and he'd continue to operate in that fashion. He'd never been known to request any support he knew might put Stony Man in a compromising position, whether it involved security, politics, or otherwise. Hell, Grimaldi knew Brognola had already offered it and Bolan had turned him down. The best they could do was to provide whatever their support network made available, and Grimaldi would have to take what he could get and use it to give Bolan every advantage.

"You know, I've been wanting to take some flying lessons in a helicopter while I was here. Any possibility you could help make those reservations like you did on my last vacation?"

"You bet," Brognola said. "I'll give it my full attention."

"Outstanding. Well, I'd better get back to the missus. She's waiting to have lunch with me."

"Okay, you take care."

"You, too, Dad." Grimaldi hung up before Brognola could reply.

Julian waited at the table where he'd left her, and had ordered a small pot of Turkish coffee. It was a welcome sight to the pilot. They hadn't caught much of a break since their arrival in Cairo, and Grimaldi figured they would be safe there for the moment. No doubt the police had some semblance of their descriptions and would be looking for them, but for now he felt it was safe enough to take a short rest. And he wasn't sure how much further he could risk pushing Julian. She was a scientist, not a fighter, and probably not resilient to such intense situations.

"I'm impressed by your stamina," Grimaldi said with a slight grin. He took a sip of the coffee and added, "I don't imagine you're too used to this."

"No," she said. "And I'm not overly anxious to get used to it, if you take my meaning."

"I do," Grimaldi replied.

"I don't understand your friend. Just when I think I have him figured out, he goes and does something to surprise me."

"Yeah, he's a unique guy."

"That's one way of saying it, I suppose," she said.

Grimaldi could hear a little ice in her tone. "You don't know him like I do, Doctor."

"I'm not sure I want to," she said over the rim of her cup. After taking a sip of her own, she added, "Although I certainly owe him my life. A couple of times over."

"There are a lot of people I know who could say the

same thing," Grimaldi replied. "Myself included. Those goons that came me through our door had me dead to rights. If Sarge hadn't shown up when he did, well... let's just leave it there."

"So, what do we do now? He's probably on the way to take out this Malik, and we're stuck here without wheels or an escape plan."

"I wouldn't start writing any dirges just yet," Grimaldi said.

"What do you mean by that?"

"I've touched base with our people." Grimaldi flashed her a wicked grin. "They're going to arrange new transportation for us."

"What's wrong with the plane we have?"

"Nothing, it's perfectly fine with all the proper credentials," Grimaldi said. "And that's just the point. They'll throw a net over the city and pin us down."

"But how would they know?"

Grimaldi didn't spare any surprise in his expression. "Are you kidding me, Doctor?"

"You don't have to call me that," she said. "I think we know each other well enough to be so informal."

"Fine...Crystal. And I'm sorry for being a smart-ass. Just tired I guess." Grimaldi took another slug of coffee and then leaned forward, gesturing for her to do the same. To anyone else, they would appear like just another couple having an intimate conversation. "My point is that in this country there probably aren't many secrets. They'll find our plane, and they'll know it belongs to whoever they're looking for. I'm guessing that's Sarge, since he was exposed a lot more in Iran than we were."

"You're right about that," she said. "We didn't even leave the airport."

"Right. Now we're on our own until we can hook up with Sarge, and that means I need to get us whatever support I can from our people back home. They're going to arrange for a chopper and then I'm going in to support Sarge."

"What about me? I assume I'm going to get tucked away safe in some little apartment or hotel?"

Grimaldi shook his head. "No way, lady. You're much safer with me than on your own."

"What makes you think so?" Julian countered. "You just said it's more likely they're looking for Cooper than you or me."

"That's all true," Grimaldi said. "Except one of those goons back at the hotel seemed pretty intent on getting to *you*."

"I thought maybe those were police," Julian replied.

"Those men definitely weren't cops, intelligence or any other authorized crew. I don't know who sent them or how they found out we were there, but they weren't friendly. If they wanted to take us down legitimately, they would have acted entirely different. That little incident was neither well planned nor well executed. It was rushed, spontaneous."

"Sounds like nonprofessionals," Julian said.

"No, I think that's what *someone* would like us to think."

"Well, we haven't been in-country for that long, which tells me somebody is keeping tabs on us."

"I think someone followed us."

"Wouldn't you have been able to detect that?"

Grimaldi shrugged. "Not necessarily. That equipment on that plane isn't as advanced as on the one back in the Philippines."

"Yes, it seemed a little strange that you left it behind."

"It didn't have the range we needed, and a Gulfstream with that kind of equipment on board would certainly have drawn more attention from Middle East authorities than the standard Executive LearJet we're in now."

"And it would now appear we have to abandon that one," Julian said.

"At least for a while," Grimaldi said. "Once the mess dies down some, we—"

Grimaldi noticed flashing lights outside and watched as two Cairo police officers stepped from their car. Their heads and upper torsos appeared over the decorative shadings strung across the lower part of the window, but the sun glinting off the glass would prevent them from spotting the couple immediately. Grimaldi took only a moment to decide how to handle this one, and he couldn't shake feeling like a trapped rat.

"Don't turn around but the cops just pulled up," Grimaldi told Julian. "I don't think we're going to be able to play this one off. Nobody in here will certainly try to protect us."

"Is there a back way?" she asked as they got up and left the table.

Grimaldi reached out and took her hand before turning and heading for the back of the café. "I'm not sure

I noticed one when I made my call before. Let's hope so. From here on out, looks like we'll just have to play this by ear."

"Great," Julian said, some hint of her normal sarcasm having returned. "Just great."

CHAPTER TWENTY-THREE

Alek Stezhnya flicked his cigarette into the cool, desert night and looked at the stars spread across the vast, inky sky. He wasn't sure what had brought him out here—having forgone the company of his men and relative safety of their makeshift desert base—but the peace and solitude seemed to be what he needed at the moment.

The mission in Iran resulted in utter failure and Stezhnya had it on good intelligence the reason for the failure fell, once more, to the interference of Matt Cooper. Despite Garrett Downing's leads inside the NSA, nobody seemed to have any intelligence on Cooper. His name and fingerprints didn't show up in any intelligence database, and he appeared to have no known connections inside the U.S. intelligence committee other than Neely. At first he and Downing had considered Cooper's presence in the Philippines a mission to rescue Neely, but Cooper had remained after Neely was escorted out of the country back to the United States. Then he stole Crystal Julian from them and killed half the men in the Apparatus, not to mention his near destruction of the *Hadesfire*. Downing had taken a contrary view on the subject of Julian during their discussion—cited witnesses who claimed it looked more like she was helping Cooper than a prisoner—but Stezhnya stood by his own version of things. Cooper'd had contact with Peter Hagen, knew of Julian's involvement, and taken her hostage to interrogate her.

"She won't tell them anything," Stezhnya had told Downing.

"What makes you think so? I wouldn't have that much faith in her. She's a scientist, not a field agent or mercenary."

"She is still a very intelligent and resilient woman," Stezhnya argued. "And because of that fact they will be more gentle with her, less likely to commit atrocities to get her to talk."

"So you don't suppose she will do this out of some egotistical misconception of her loyalties to you or me?" Downing asked.

Stezhnya knew a goad when he saw one. "I don't think anything of the kind. I'm deluded with neither ideologies nor thoughts of grandeur. I am simply a soldier, Garrett. I would have thought you knew that about me by now."

"Still, you *did* have a personal relationship with her," Downing pressed. "And I am familiar with matters of the heart."

"Frankly, I don't think she'll talk because she will blame the government for Hagen's death."

"She doesn't know anything about that yet."

Stezhnya's smile lacked warmth. "You don't think Cooper will mention this?"

"I don't know he'll have any reason to," Downing replied. "Very few people know of the connection between them, and even if he did he wouldn't necessarily consider it of importance."

"You really should consider giving your enemies more credit, sir," Stezhnya replied.

"And you should not give advice when it isn't solicited," Downing warned.

That had brought an end to the conversation, and they hadn't discussed it again since. It didn't mean Stezhnya agreed with Downing. In fact, he was beginning to find them seeing eye to eye on issues with lessening frequency. Stezhnya wasn't sure how much more he could take of Downing's deprecating views and grandiosity. For an intelligent man it didn't seem like Downing lived with both feet in the real world at all. Maybe that was the main difference between them. Stezhnya understood his reality, his place in the grand cosmic scheme of it all, and Downing lived…well, someplace else.

Whatever the facts were, Stezhnya knew one thing: he'd become increasingly dissatisfied with the relationship as it stood, and it would soon be time for some radical changes. He would start with engineering Downing's demise and work his way up from there. Too many of his men had been lost already, and not having sacrificed their lives gloriously but instead wasted them due to temporary alliances with their enemies. Stezhnya believed in Downing's original cause, but he didn't see how this would get them there. Yes, something would have to change very soon.

Stezhnya heard the crunch of a foot on gravel, and whirled as he whipped out his sidearm. Downing raised his arms. "Don't shoot *me,* Alek."

"Sorry, sir," Stezhnya said, immediately lowering the pistol. "But it's never wise to walk up behind men like me. We tend to shoot first and ask questions later."

"I have no doubt of your skill," Downing said. More of his damned deprecation through self-aggrandizement. He continued. "What I question of late is your judgment—"

"It wasn't my idea to watch those men walk into a slaughter," Stezhnya cut in, already certain of where Downing was headed with this conversation. "I warned you about Cooper and the threat I thought he posed to our mission. This proves it. And I have watched entirely too many of my men die to stand by anymore while you continue to plot alliances with the very vermin I have pledged to eradicate. No more, Garrett, or I swear I'll pull my remaining men and leave you to your own devices. And I guarantee you don't have what it takes to go up against Cooper."

"A very eloquent response," Downing said. "Albeit the entire thing is based upon a very uninformed and impassioned viewpoint. You knew when taking this job that there would be risks. I didn't hide them from you. And I think your compensation is adequate."

"My *compensation* has nothing to do with it," Stezhnya said through clenched teeth. "Many years of experience have taught me that it's very difficult to get men to follow you into battle when they know you'll sacrifice yourself and them with utter vanity."

"None of your men have died in vain," Downing countered.

"That's not what they tell me," Stezhnya said. "I don't know how much longer I can convince them in the validity of our cause. They have already lost way too many, and they're blaming me solely for it."

"Let's not mince words, Alek," Downing said. "What do you really want out of this?"

Stezhnya took a deep breath. He'd been waiting for just such an opportunity to present itself—he didn't think it ever would—and now that the moment had arrived he wasn't sure how to respond. Still, he had only one chance to make it right or he stood to lose it all. It didn't change his feelings about Downing, but perhaps it would give him a chance to get away and do something constructive instead of just sitting there waiting for something to happen.

"I will take a specific team with me to handle this Cooper. Maybe if we can accomplish this mission without his interference we will achieve the goal in a much shorter time."

"You are still convinced one man is so much of a threat to our operations," Downing replied.

Stezhnya made a sweeping gesture with his arm into the darkness. "You already have the proof. Our one man who survived in Iran claims he nearly wiped out our entire force single-handedly. And *you* saw the kind of destruction he brought to us in the Philippines. He not only infiltrated our base of operations but he came very close to destroying the *Hadesfire.* He is a danger and must be dealt with swiftly and decisively. And I believe that only men of the greatest skill can do that."

"Meaning you," Downing concluded.

"And a few others I have in mind."

Downing sighed. "How many men will it take?"

"Myself and three others," Stezhnya said quickly. "And if you give us one of the ships."

"I need them to finish the mission," Downing said.

"And so you do," Stezhnya said. "But we both know only one is required to actually succeed. And we will be back well before the MEK joins up with Malik's remaining forces here in Oman."

"Very well, Alek," Downing finally replied. "You have stated your case well. I'll give you the leave to complete this activity so we can move onward with our mission objectives. Just make sure you bring down this Cooper once and for all. Is that understood?"

"Yes, sir," Stezhnya said. "Thank you, sir."

Downing turned on his heel and walked away.

At long last, Stezhnya thought. He would finally deal with Cooper on his own terms, and avenge the death of his men both here and back in the U.S. And when that assignment was completed, he would return to Oman and take care of Downing once and for all. Then he would lead the Apparatus against the forces being amassed by Malik and his allies, and he would destroy them once and for all. And with both of the *Hadesfire* weapons at his disposal, he would complete the cleansing process and eradicate his country of the terrorists. Forever!

GARRETT DOWNING PLACED a call on a secure satellite phone upon returning to his quarters.

The lights were dim within the caverns they had procured as their field base of operations. The Oman interior wasn't the most hospitable place in the world, but it wasn't the worst, either. Downing could remember the "worst" places, and it made him uneasy. Not as uneasy as Alek Stezhnya, however. Downing knew the time had come where he couldn't trust the mercenary anymore. Stezhnya might once have sworn allegiance to Downing's cause, but he could see that time had come and gone. There was no idealism left in Stezhnya, no vision for what the future held. He'd taken a blow to both his skills and his reputation as a military leader, and if Downing knew anything he knew that was something Stezhnya's tender ego wouldn't be able to stomach.

The best Downing could do now was to protect his investment and to make sure Stezhnya didn't return from this mission. His special operations unit, the men he knew were personally devoted to him and would obey any command without question, would have to bring the *Hadesfire* back in one piece, too. He would then appoint them to oversee the Apparatus and with his private army he would set out to do exactly as he'd promised his people.

Downing had always prided himself on keeping his word and showing his loyalty, but in this case it was Stezhnya who had betrayed *him*. Downing knew he wouldn't be long for this life as long as Stezhnya remained alive. He could see it in the man's eyes: the plotting and conniving that would eventually lead to betrayal. Stezhnya had become the Judas of this company, and Downing experienced no heartache in ridding himself of such a man.

The voice that answered the line was deep and quiet, but there was no mistaking the menace behind that voice. That voice was the voice of death as far as Downing was concerned. Crossing a man like Stezhnya was one thing but to cross the man who answered was something else entirely.

"It's me."

"I'm listening."

"That liability we discussed has broken his leash," Downing replied. "I'm planning to let him implement this insane plan of his. Did your men find our missing tigress?"

"Yes, sir," the man replied. "But she managed to get away from them. That government operative and his pilot somehow overcame them and got away. But they now have the Cairo police hounding them."

It was of no great surprise Downing didn't know the speaker's name. They had met on only a couple of occasions, and during those times the man hadn't offered his name and Downing hadn't asked. This arrangement suited both of them. There would never be any direct tie between them, and so the fact Downing couldn't compromise the man made their business relationship perfect.

"The police? That's not good. I don't want them drawing the attention of the local authorities," Downing stated. "Otherwise, your men will draw the same attention."

"You don't need to worry about *my* men," the man

snapped. "You appear to have plenty of troubles managing your own."

"Don't lecture me," Downing said. "I've had enough of that. Just get the job done I'm paying you so well to do."

"Don't we always?"

"Yes, that's why you're still on the payroll."

"Cooper won't leave the country," the man added. "You have my personal assurances on that."

"Fine. Now, I want Cooper and his lackeys dead, and I want Dr. Julian returned safely to me here. You can eliminate Stezhnya and his team as a bonus. Do you think Cooper's still in the country?"

"There's no doubt of it," the man said. "I'm sure from what we've seen so far that he won't leave until he finds Malik. We've made all the necessary arrangements."

"That's fine," Downing said. "I'll make sure Stezhnya knows he's still in Cairo. Once you have the good doctor, she'll be able to instruct you in operating the *Hadesfire*. Get her and my equipment back here in one piece and I will pay you more money than you could ever dream of."

"Consider it done."

"I already have," Downing said. "As I've already told you, that's why you and your men are still on the payroll. Now get it done!"

Downing killed the connection. He considered the call and wondered if he'd made the right decision. Something in his gut told him he had. He'd put his money on that team before and it had always paid off, where other times and other places lesser operatives had failed. They would ensure the job got done. And with Cooper and Stezhnya eliminated, and Crystal Julian under his dominance once more, he would emerge victorious—a true American hero and the idol of his people.

BEHROUZ KIYANFAR SOUGHT vengeance. The man he had trusted, with whom he had supped and smoked and called friend, had betrayed him and he wanted that man's head. Agymah Malik was nothing but a whore for the GIA, a former member of the jihad who possessed neither the stomach nor the honor to fight against the enemies of Islam. To make matters worse, the offending son of a dog had fueled the war between the MEK and Tehran police, a war Kiyanfar had thought left far behind.

What had brought it all to clarity was the involvement of the American, Matthew Cooper. More than one witness swore they saw Cooper fighting alongside their MEK brothers, and had pledged on the hem of his garment that he'd killed the others of his kind. According to his information, the American had even attempted to help the Tehran policeman he'd been with. And there were other informants who said he'd gone to visit a known vendor of information and intelligence who had family ties to both Tehran police authorities and devout members of the MEK.

Even more puzzling and complicated was Cooper's message. He had told Kiyanfar's spy that he was on the side of the MEK. That didn't make any sense, and yet his actions seemed to back it up as truth. Kiyanfar had wondered for just a small time if this wasn't simply a tactic, but he dismissed the idea when not only did Cooper let the spy live, but then left Iran in peace. The spy died, of course, for his incompetence and his betrayal of information to Cooper. Kiyanfar would have thought that was the end of the incident, but then his intelligence network indicated the American was headed for Cairo.

Now Kiyanfar faced a dilemma. He could have simply ordered his spies to track the American into Egypt and eliminate him. He also could have warned Malik of the American's interference, but again he couldn't simply act prematurely without knowing exactly where the man fit into all of this. And then he received word from his connections to Malik's arms dealer that the American planned to eliminate Malik for causing a break in the cease-fire between the Iranian government and the MEK.

"So this is how we are treated by our brothers," Kiyanfar told his aide. "*They* betray us but the American, our sworn and most hated enemy, allies himself with us and uncovers the plots of our alleged friends."

"There is no way you could have seen beneath such treachery, sir," his aide replied.

"Perhaps not," Kiyanfar grumbled. "But that is not an excuse. I should have known better than to trust anyone outside of our own people. I nearly cost the lives of my entire family, my brothers within our sect, and betrayed our allegiances to al Qaeda. That is an unforgivable sin."

"But you did not," the man reminded him.

"No, I didn't," Kiyanfar said. "And now I will make sure that something like this never happens again. Send word to all of our contacts that our war against the government is no more. There is to be an immediate cease-fire."

"But they will not like this. Many of them have left families—"

"It's not a request!" Kiyanfar jumped from the table where he'd sat in the back of a small café, and slammed his fist on the tabletop. "After the word has been given, we will gather our best warriors and we will make our way across the borders until we reach the encampment in Oman. And then we shall take Malik's forces by surprise. We shall eliminate them from our sight, and guarantee something like this will never happen again. I will make this right! I will undo the curse on the blood of our people! Now go do as I bid!"

The man nearly fell over himself to escape the ferocity of his master's presence. Kiyanfar hated to speak to him like that—the man had been a faithful ward—but he had to operate with some gravity now if he expected to maintain discipline. He would already lose respect to a good number of the members once word got out of his naiveté in dealing with Malik. If he undid that error quickly enough, he stood a very good chance of earning back the respect of the MEK and restoring the faith of his allies in his ability to guide both the spiritual and personal lives of their sect.

Another of Kiyanfar's aides stepped forward in the absence of the other, obviously ready to do whatever his master requested. He had served faithfully along with the others, and Kiyanfar recalled he possessed an extraordinary talent for military strategies. Kiyanfar waved the aide closer and offered him something to drink. The man hesitated at first but eventually Kiyanfar convinced him it was okay. At last, he recalled the aide's name: Rahami.

"You are a man of some military prowess, as I recall."

"Thank you, sir," Rahami replied with a bow. "I am not worthy of such notice."

"Never be ashamed of possessing talents. Especially when your leader can put those talents to good use."

"How may I be of service to you, sir?"

"I want you to gather thirty of our finest men. Pick from any in the entire complement. You will then take our fastest and sturdiest vehicles across the desert, westward and then southward through the Saudi wilds until you rendezvous with our crew. They have already been ordered to abandon Malik's operations in Oman. You will see to it they come back to us safely. You are all to return alive. Do you understand?"

"It shall be done just as you have ordered," Rahami said with another bow.

"And remember, you shall show no mercy to those who would stand in the way of your safe return. Our warring is done. We will let the ministers of God decide between us and Malik. We have remained true."

And so it would be that one day his ancestors would proclaim Behrouz Kiyanfar as one of the finest religious and military leaders of all. They would sing songs that told stories of his exploits. He would restore the faith of his people and of those who had invested in his skills and leadership. And he would make sure the sands of Oman did not run red with the blood of his loyal brothers. And when his men had returned safely, Kiyanfar would restore peace to his country and his people. There would be another time to make war with America.

For now, he was satisfied to let the Americans war among themselves.

CHAPTER TWENTY-FOUR

The foot chase started less than ten minutes after Julian's and Grimaldi's departure from the café. They managed to evade detection by three road cruisers and lose another pair of policemen on foot patrol in a bazaar, but then they somehow managed to walk smack-dab into a substation of some kind. One look from the officers and the guilt on their faces had to have told it all. Moments later, without even a lick of forethought on direction or a plan to escape, Grimaldi and Julian were racing for their lives.

Or at least that was the story as far as Grimaldi was concerned. He was certain Julian would have her own version of it for Bolan...*if* they got out of this one alive.

They paused only a moment to catch their respective breaths at an alley entrance opposite of where they had crossed a very busy street thronged with cars, trucks and pedestrians.

"Next time...you decide to walk...into a police station while on the lam," she said, nearly wheezing with the exertion, "leave me at the coffee shop."

"I thought you said you kept in shape," Grimaldi shot back with a wry grin.

"Not toting *this,*" she replied, holding up the bag that barely contained her laptop.

"Our friends get their hands on that and we're done for," he told her. "Let's go!"

As they turned and raced up the alley, Grimaldi was conscious of the smattering of voices and the shouts from officers. The citizens were probably pointing the way for the cops quite nicely. Grimaldi could only wish he had that kind of support. Of course, he would probably have done the same thing if the situation were reversed. Still, it would have been nice to catch a break somewhere along the way in this little adventure. Grimaldi couldn't remember the last time he'd felt so tired.

"Any way we could get to this mysterious chopper of yours?" Julian asked him as he helped her onto the roof of a car before turning to an open, darkened window he'd spotted in the building at the far end of the alley.

"Not until we lose them," Grimaldi said. "I don't have any desire to lead them right to our new wings. Now get your tail up in there."

Grimaldi looked wildly in the direction they'd come from, watchful for their pursuers. He knew they couldn't be far behind. He wasn't even sure they could get inside the building before the police spotted them. If that happened his entire idea would be for nothing. As a matter of self-preservation, Grimaldi opted to give

Julian a less-than-gentlemanly boost through the window, and immediately followed up with a gazelle-style leap of his own. The pilot nearly choked on the dust that rose from the hard floor he landed on. He bit back a cry of pain as his left elbow struck the unyielding wood. He had no idea why they called it a funny bone since there wasn't a damn thing funny about hitting it against something. The pilot quickly regained his composure and rubbed away the sting.

The blood from his heart pumping adrenaline had rushed to his ears and made it difficult to hear anything. He couldn't tell if the cops were in proximity, and it didn't help any when Julian began to berate him with something a bit stronger than a forced whisper.

"What's the big idea?"

"Shush!" Grimaldi replied hoarsely. More quietly he asked, "Big idea about what?"

"Putting your hands all over my ass," she snapped.

"Don't flatter yourself. I was just trying to save our necks."

"Well "

"Which you're bound to get stretched if you keep flapping your pie hole," he whispered. "Now shut up or we're both dead."

Less than a minute passed before he could make out footfalls that sounded so deafening he could have sworn they were right next to his ears. His heart thudded relentlessly, and he realized about midway through the second minute lying there as soundlessly as possible he'd been holding his breath. He let it out slowly and willed his body back under control.

As they laid there, just inches from each other, Grimaldi considered his next move. They didn't stand a chance against that many armed men, and the chase had taken them through such a maze of streets and shops he no longer had any concept of direction. One thing for sure: the Executioner wouldn't likely show up this time to save their asses. Not that it mattered anyway, since Bolan would have avoided a confrontation with the police at any costs. No, they'd have to get out of this one on their own.

Another minute passed before it sounded as if the footsteps were moving away from them. Grimaldi felt a tap on his shoulder and turned to see Julian hold up two fingers. Yeah, he could only hear two distinctly different voices, as faint as they were, but they were definitely moving away. Grimaldi nodded, then held up the palm of his hand to indicate they should wait right where they were. He wasn't taking any chances. It could be a ruse to draw them out, or there was even an outside chance the cops would figure there was no way they could have lost their quarry and they'd double back for a more thorough search.

After another five minutes, Grimaldi slowly rose and crawled to the window. He poked his head over the top and looked onto a deserted alley. He didn't hear anything and he didn't see anything. He sunk to the floor, his head propped against the wall below the window, and let out a sigh of relief.

"Now that was too close," he told Julian.

"Let's get the hell out of this roach motel," she replied.

"I'm with you."

MACK BOLAN LAY FLAT against the dense undergrowth of flora that grew along the fertile, green borders of Malik's estate south of Cairo.

The landscaping was verdant and lush, a symbol of substance and wealth in a country literally starved for water. It appeared Malik had done quite well for himself. There was obviously something to be said for the illegal funneling of millions of dollars to further one's own personal cause over using it to support its intended benefactors. So Malik had the power and the financial backing to do anything he wished.

And if that were true, then why had he chosen to ally himself with poverty-stricken freedom fighters in Iran? Bolan had pondered that question for quite some time, and he still didn't have any answers. Malik obviously didn't have the guts to stick it out as a high-ranking protector inside the GIA, so he quit and took on the role of a financier. There was power in money, sure, but it wasn't as if he didn't have plenty of eyes watching his every move. He could have entered significantly less risky ventures and instead he'd chosen to distribute funds on extremely high-profile projects.

And maybe that was exactly the genius in Malik's plan. Perhaps he had gone with the IFC *because* it was under so much scrutiny. Nobody ever would have dared tried to pull the wool over the eyes of investors in a power project for some third world country, so they weren't looking too hard. They would just figure everything continued to be on the up-and-up, and by the time they realized they had lost all their money it would be too late.

That left Bolan wondering if Downing had figured

this scenario through in the exact same way. If he had, then he was more clever than anyone gave him credit for. Downing had obviously seen the potential in this, and like any good chess player he'd thought four, five, even ten moves ahead of his competitors. The Executioner had to admit he hadn't seen anything like this coming. When he considered all the players, the odds for calculating any sort of logical outcome seemed astronomical. But Bolan could appreciate that as he was a man who'd grown quite accustomed to having the odds stacked against him.

He had noticed Malik come out once and have lunch on his veranda, but that angle had never afforded Bolan a decent shot. To move for a better position with half a dozen guards spread across the roof and twice that many at ground level, would have most certainly attracted attention. It had proved a greater risk than it was worth.

Now Bolan would be forced to go up against Malik's force personally. It wasn't his first choice but he knew he was out of options. This was an all-or-nothing situation he'd chosen, and there was no turning back. Too much rode on his successful execution of Malik, and Bolan planned to make sure nothing stood in his way. He wanted it to be over and this was his opportunity to do that very thing.

The soldier pressed his cheek to the stock of the M-16 A-3 with attached M-203 grenade launcher and studied the front door once more. He'd have to hit the place hard and direct. Coming through the front door wouldn't have been his first choice, but he didn't have time for the niceties of a soft probe first. He'd have to go in full-throttle and accomplish his objective as quickly as possible. Come hell or high water, Agymah Malik had an appointment to meet his maker today, and it was the Executioner who'd set it up.

Bolan took a deep breath and let out half, pulled the butt tighter to his shoulder and squeezed off his first shot. The 5.56 mm round left the muzzle at a velocity of 1,760 meters per second, crossed the expansive lawns in under a second, and split apart the skull of one of the armed pair guarding the front door. Bolan could see only a crimson spray, which was followed a moment later by a shout of surprise. He'd already acquired his next target by that time, the second man standing post at the door. The guard dropped from Bolan's sight picture, obviously bent over his friend in concern, and the Executioner adjusted to compensate before squeezing off the second shot. The bullet struck its mark and flipped the guy off his feet.

Bolan rose and sprinted for the front door. He reached his first point marker of cover, a large pile of stones surrounding a decorative, miniature fountain. He flipped up the leaf sight for the M-203, acquired the target of rooftop sentries now bunched up at the close end of the roof and set his estimate at 125 meters. He leaned back on the heavy pull of the M-203 trigger. The weapon popped with the report of a 12-gauge shotgun, followed by the familiar sound of the 40 mm HE round leaving the tube. Seconds later the men on the roof disappeared amid a brilliant orange flash. What flesh and body parts weren't immediately vaporized in the intense, explosive rush of superheated gases and shrapnel ended up spinning off the rooftop in every direction.

Bolan loaded a fresh shell, then pressed forward, reaching the front door unchallenged. It surprised him the other sentries spread throughout the grounds hadn't responded. He had only taken four of at least twelve who he'd counted roving the grounds earlier. They had either gone inside at some point during his observation and reconnaissance, or they had a set rendezvous point and had a plan to trap Bolan by cutting off his escape with a force of sheer numbers.

The soldier thought it high time to spring that trap.

The Executioner went through the front door of the house with a single kick and moved inside quickly, rifle held at the ready. The enemy came through faithfully on the deal and tried to throw a number of attackers from different locations, but Bolan had planned on the tactic. The Executioner dropped to the ground, swung the muzzle upward on the grenade launcher and squeezed the trigger. The report was almost deafening even in the open air of the main foyer, but the grenade arced gracefully before striking the ceiling just above a side hallway. The room exploded into a haze of dust, debris and light as the high explosives did their intended work.

The cloud of dust and man-made combustibles threatened to choke the Executioner, but he held his breath and found cover behind a large metal statue out of the immediate fallout area. There were a few hasty shots sent through but none of them came close to Bolan. He'd provided enough of a diversion and cover in the dust to get out of the immediate kill zone. Bolan crossed the room in a few strides and reached the set of stairs he'd noticed. He took them three at a time until he had a better view of the area below. The dust was clearing through the still-open front door and Bolan could now see several of Malik's guards enter the room in full force and sweep its expanse with the muzzles of assorted handguns and machine pistols. One of the men appeared to be in charge and began to shout at the men who still appeared a bit dazed.

Bolan didn't intend to let them recover enough to gun him down. The Executioner leveled his weapon into the center of the organized chaos and squeezed the trigger on his M-203. He whirled and continued up the steps before waiting to see the results. The blast rocked the walls on either side of the winding stairwell, generating additional dust and causing a couple of molding pieces to drop from the ceiling. The steps rumbled beneath his feet and Bolan wondered for a moment if they would hold. He could hear the sounds of flame crackling as the heat ignited the combustibles below.

There would be no returning that way, and Bolan hoped an alternate exit would present itself in short order. His next task would be to find Malik, since he'd eliminated a good part of the house opposition. Bolan began a room-by-room search but came up empty. Unfortunately there hadn't been time to get a layout of the place; Cairo's finest had seen to that. For an instant, the soldier considered the status of his friends, but that only lead him to wonder if they were still alive.

You can't allow that to distract you, Bolan told himself.

With that, the Executioner pushed it from his consciousness and continued his search.

WITH ONE FOLLOW-UP CALL to Stony Man, Grimaldi and Julian soon found themselves whisked from the Cairo ghettos by a pair of burly CIA agents, and out to a comfortable hangar of a small airfield in the Egyptian interior that the government probably didn't even know about. The hangar included a shower stall and stocked kitchenette. After a warm but quick shower and a quick simple meal, Crystal Julian was feeling about half human again.

"I don't think I'll have anything nice to say about this trip when I get back to the States," she told Grimaldi as she entered the hangar and tried to brush some of the tangles from her hair. She'd found it dried very rapidly in this climate.

"I don't think you should even mention you were here," the pilot retorted as he wiped the grease from his hands. "You'll probably live longer."

Julian nodded and then looked at the chopper. "She doesn't look like much. Certainly no match for the *Hadesfire*."

The pilot looked at the converted bird and grinned. "Don't judge a book by its cover, lady. You're looking at a Hughes 500M our CIA friends have converted for black ops. It's outfitted with not only twin Allison turbines, they've also geared her up for us with a 7.62 mm machine-gun pack and an M-75 grenade launcher."

"I'm so thrilled to be here for it," Julian deadpanned. "You ever heard the old saying about the difference between men and boys?"

"Yes, which means I'm not interested in hearing it again."

"Okay, truce," she said, holding her hands up in time-out fashion. "I'm not hear to make your life miserable, despite what you might think. *And* I've decided to forgive you for putting your paws all over my backside."

"Good," Grimaldi replied, apparently satisfied with that. He turned, reached into the chopper and removed a bulky bundle of dark black material. "Here, put yourself in this."

Julian barely managed to catch the weighty package. She bent over to smell it, certain she wouldn't like what she found. She didn't. "And what, pray tell, is *this?*"

He grinned. "Flight suit."

"Excuse me?"

"Flight suit. I have a mission and you're going along with me. We need to provide some support for Sarge. I can almost guarantee he'll be expecting us."

CHAPTER TWENTY-FIVE

It wasn't long before the Executioner encountered additional resistance.

The attacks were interspersed, coming at odd times and places, and neither well timed nor organized. Bolan could admire the zeal of his attackers, but he couldn't credit them with having much in the way of brains. Four men tried to pin him down in a large room and, in their haste, ended up shooting one another while Bolan lay sheltered beneath a heavy wood table.

A quick search of all the rooms on the second floor left Bolan empty-handed. Malik was nowhere to be found.

Bolan eventually discovered the back door exit. As he crossed the threshold he immediately came under automatic weapons fire.

The soldier sought cover and realized he didn't have much so he dropped to his belly and crawled to a centralized air unit. It wouldn't totally protect him, but it would offer some minimal cover and concealment. They had obviously planned this assault well, and he cursed himself for having underestimated their ingenuity. His enemy had figured Bolan would either find his way to the back or they were covering Malik's escape. Bolan was betting on the latter since there wouldn't have been any other explanation for them to pack such a wallop of resistance at the rear of the house and yet allow him to force his way through the front door.

A hailstorm of lead buzzed just inches above Bolan's head, which kept him focused on keeping it down. He considered putting out some grenades but at this point he thought it would only serve to fix his position for them. He was trapped: they knew it and he knew it. And if the tide didn't turn on his luck real soon it was going to get much worse; the kind of worse where he could end up dead.

There was a minor lull in the shooting and Bolan could hear the voices of his enemy shouting at one another, and then there was silence followed by a new round of autofire. Slugs slapped into the exterior walls of the house behind and around his minimal cover, and others chewed up the earth and concrete around him. If they managed to keep him pinned down, that was most probably all they had to do. They would just have to stall him long enough to allow Malik to escape, and Mack Bolan wasn't entirely sure what he could do about that.

Seconds elapsed, and then he didn't have to wonder. The roar of chopper blades filled his ears like music, followed a moment later by the whoosh of

40 mm grenades as they erupted from the M-75 grenade pod along the starboard side of the chopper. The sleek aircraft swung around for a second pass as several enemy positions erupted into expanding balls of red and orange flames. The second pass saw a pinpoint surgical strike on a new set of positions with a machine-gun pod chattering away along the chopper's port side. The precision with which that aircraft moved told Bolan only Jack Grimaldi could have been behind the stick.

Bolan's suspicions were confirmed less than a minute later when the chopper buzzed the area just above his head, did a 360-degree turn, then quickly dropped to a landing less than twenty-five yards from the house. Bolan broke cover and ran to the chopper, jumping inside as the door slid open to admit him. Bolan experienced just a moment of déjà vu as he thought of a similar scene not that long ago. At that time he'd been coming from another failed mission, and this time he planned to make sure the same hex didn't fall on him.

The soldier nodded a quick acknowledgment to Julian, who was grinning from ear to ear and obviously elated to see him alive. He rushed to the cockpit, slapped his pilot friend warmly on the shoulder and indicated they should get airborne immediately. As Grimaldi complied, the warrior looked backward and quickly found what he sought only because Julian stood there holding the earphones out to him.

Bolan donned the communication device and said, "Thanks, Jack."

"Anytime," Grimaldi replied as they left the ground.

"So maybe this isn't the best time to ask, but what's the big rush?"

"Malik is still close by," Bolan said. "He managed to get out of the house before I could get to him. That means he couldn't have gone far."

"Any idea how he'll try to escape?"

"I'm guessing a car," Bolan replied.

"How about there?" Grimaldi asked.

The Executioner peered in the direction he pointed and saw a shiny black sedan rolling down a road on the far side of a series of outcroppings. It left a dust trail as it continued southward, deeper into the desert. How Malik could have expected to get away in such a conspicuous vehicle seemed almost preposterous, but he had obviously figured Bolan was working on foot with no support.

"That must be him," Bolan said. "See if you can get closer so we can confirm the target. If it isn't Malik, I don't want to alarm whoever's in the vehicle."

Grimaldi pushed the chopper in the direction of the sedan and within minutes he was less than a hundred yards above them, having matched course and speed. From that vantage point Bolan could see that they were actually driving along some kind of makeshift road, maybe used for utility access or simply as a route for locals into the interior. In either case, they didn't stand a chance of escaping the chopper.

Suddenly, men leaned out both rear windows and began shooting at the aircraft. Muzzles winked in near-perfect unison as the attackers laid down a hasty fusillade of autofire.

"Guess that leaves no question about whether we got the right guy," Grimaldi said. "This Malik and his crew are some real sweethearts."

"Just keep on them while I think this through," Bolan said.

"Good to see you alive," she said.

"You, too."

"This is something to write home about if I had anyone there to read the letters," she replied.

Bolan could understand that, actually. He'd suffered enough similar personal tragedies that he could empathize with her.

According to what he'd read, Julian was an only child. Julian's mother succumbed to undiagnosed Alzheimer's at a fairly young age. She had died ten years earlier after burning down their lakeside Minnesota home with herself inside it. Less than ten months after that, doctors diagnosed her father with hepatic cancer. He suffered a lonely existence in a nursing home—the decision of Julian's paternal aunt since she'd been out of the country and unreachable—which took his life after only a year.

"What's the news on the *Hadesfire?*" Bolan asked her.

"I'm afraid it isn't good," she replied in a rather curt tone. "I'm almost one-hundred-percent sure your theory about there being two of them is probably correct. Also, I hooked up as soon as we were airborne and found out one of them is headed directly toward Egypt. I expect it'll be here within the hour."

"That's not good news."

It also didn't seem to fit within any of the parameters of Downing's plan. What was he up to? Bolan had hoped they would come to him, rather than force him to trudge into the Oman Desert, but he hadn't planned on Downing acting quite this soon. Then again, maybe it was strictly a killing mission. That was a possibility, and something Bolan could perhaps turn in their favor.

"No, I didn't think so, either," she said.

"How would they have managed to get past the air defense forces of Saudi Arabia and Egypt?"

"I've already told you that they can go just about anywhere they want. They managed to do it in the same way they were able to touch down in the Iranian desert and take off again without the Iranians ever being the wiser."

"What are we going to do, Cooper?"

"Let's cross that bridge when we come to it," he said. "We still have some time. Right now, we need to bring down Malik. He's my priority and I won't let him get away this time."

Bolan returned his attention to the matter at hand. He had an idea but he knew he'd only get one shot at it, and he risked a few bystanders if he was wrong. Still, it wasn't the time for diplomacy. This was one of those moments where only good old-fashioned firepower would do the trick.

"Jack," Bolan called into the headset, "get me as close as you can to that thing without risking your own tail."

"How close do you need to be?"

"Close enough to take out its tires. You can swing that?"

"Are you kidding?" the pilot replied with a grin. "It'll be just like the good old days."

Grimaldi let out a whoop and then swung in on the sedan's tail, keeping the chopper just back far enough that any shooters from the vehicle would be ineffective. It was definitely difficult to hit a chopper holding position rearward at about thirty degrees from the rear tail-point. And yet it turned out to be a perfect place to line up the Executioner for a clear, safe shot.

The warrior braced the stock of the M-16 A-3/M-203 against his shoulder and waited for the moment the shot would be perfect. He wasn't going to get more than one chance at it, in all likelihood, and even if he disabled the vehicle, that would go a long way toward putting Malik on ice permanently. Bolan ignored all the sounds and distractions and sights around him, keeping his mind on the simple task at hand.

Bolan squeezed the trigger, and the vehicle began to fishtail as its left, rear tire blew out. A cloud of smoke poured from the vehicle to mix with the dust left in its wake, nearly threatening to blind its pursuers. The vehicle eventually slowed and swerved off the makeshift road, coming to a stop just outside an abandoned mosque.

Bolan ordered Grimaldi to take him down, but as the chopper touched the ground a blast of autofire reached their ears. The soldier bailed from the chopper and in moments Grimaldi lifted off.

The Executioner managed to draw the fire away from the aircraft and Grimaldi appeared to get clear without damage. Bolan knew there wasn't much likelihood he'd meet heavy resistance since the ground vehicle clearly didn't hold more than a few passengers. Unless Malik had crammed his men inside like sardines, there would probably be only a few enemy gunners, and they were most likely scarce in the ammunition department.

Bolan approached the mosque in a crouch, weapon up and ready. He might not have had them outnumbered but they were surely outgunned this time. It would be nothing like the firepower he'd faced at Malik's estate, and at the time he didn't have a crack pilot just above him to provide additional fire support.

Autofire from a machine pistol greeted Bolan but he quickly identified the target that had broken the cover of a pile of broken boulders and rock. Bolan made short work of it. He leveled the M-16 and triggered a single, 3-round burst. Two slugs caught the man in the chest and blew out his heart and one lung, and the third neatly cleaved his skull.

Bolan continued up the slight rise toward the mosque.

AGYMAH MALIK SAT huddled in the shadows of the mosque's interior, his bodyguard shielding him with as much of his body as possible, and wondered what had gone so horribly wrong. One minute he'd been enjoying a quiet rest following lunch, and the next there were explosions and shards of glass shrieking through his bedroom. He had implemented an immediate escape plan, drilled with his cadre time and again, but he hadn't counted on Cooper having air support. That wasn't something Donkor had mentioned.

Malik took small comfort from the weight of the pistol in his hand. He would have felt a bit more comfortable with the SMG in the hands of his bodyguard, but he didn't mention it. If the rumors were true about the American's proficiency with weapons, he wasn't going to end up anything but dead anyway. The Egyptian didn't know what vendetta the American had with him, although it didn't really matter at this point. His main goal was to survive the encounter.

So this is where he would make his stand. He had no idea what the American wanted from him, but he didn't plan to die like a dog. He would do whatever he needed to survive, and if that meant facing the American one-on-one he would do that, too. The sound of dirt and rock loosening beneath the footsteps of someone close by caused Malik a sense of panic. His bodyguard was distracted by his reaction and the man stepped directly into a shaft of light streaming from the dilapidated roof of the church. That single miscalculation cost him his life.

BOLAN HEARD HIS OPPONENT before he saw him. A flash of light on metal in his peripheral vision followed the shuffle of feet, and he turned in time to see one of Malik's men standing there with a wicked-looking SMG in his hands. The terrorist tried to bring his weapon to bear, but Bolan shot him through the chest and stomach before his enemy got off a single shot. The soldier dived for cover just in time to avoid being cut down by two pistol rounds fired from shadows very near the man he'd just killed. Bolan caught the approximate locations of the muzzle-flashes before losing his view. The Executioner took a moment to consider his options. Whoever he faced at the other end of this encounter was probably low on ammunition, also, and since he hadn't met any other resistance he wondered if this was his only remaining opponent. That would make his would-be assassin Agymah Malik. The former GIA enforcer would most likely be surprised Bolan wanted to punch his ticket. That was fine. As far Bolan was concerned, it wasn't the stature of individual that marked him to be passed over for judgment, it was his actions.

Bolan shifted positions and two more shots rang out, these high and wide. The Executioner managed to get outside the building and take a flanking position against the exterior wall. He moved slowly along the wall, careful to remain as quiet as possible. When he reached the open window behind where he'd taken down his last target, Bolan slowly rose and risked a glance inside. A man with dark hair sat on the floor beneath the window, a pistol held firmly in his grip.

The soldier considered his options, saw he had none, and with all the force he could muster he threw himself through the open window and onto his quarry. The man's pistol was knocked from his grasp, but Bolan overshot his target by a few feet and couldn't maintain any sort of control hold as a result. The man reached his feet nearly as fast as the Executioner, who shoulder rolled into a standing position.

Bolan recognized Agymah Malik's profile in the sunlight that streamed through the open window. The two men said nothing, simply stared each other down like a pair of titans prepared to clash in immortal combat for the final time. Bolan waited for Malik to make his move but the man stood stock-still, his fists held in a rather awkward position and his legs locked equidistant from each other. Bolan recognized the Egyptian fighting stance.

The Executioner took up a standard military defensive posture of his own and waited for his opponent to attack. He didn't have to wait long. Malik launched himself at Bolan, producing a knife at the last second he seemed to pull from thin air. Bolan sidestepped and tried to strike the brachial nerve running along his opponent's bicep—a pressure point designed to disarm him—but Malik managed to place a kick on the point of Bolan's knee while deflecting the attack with a slash of the knife.

The Executioner managed to maintain his balance, and he ignored the sharp pains that lanced up and down his leg. Malik feinted to the right, then attempted a cross-slash, but Bolan was too experienced to fall for it. The Egyptian's failure took him off balance and the Executioner made his move. He stepped inside the boundaries of the knife's killing zone and latched on to his adversary's forearm with his right hand. He snaked his left hand under Malik's arm and with a quick pull forward displaced his elbow. The terrorist leader screamed and dropped the knife as his upper arm separated from lower. Bolan wrenched the man's shoulder downward and spun on his heel, then wrapped one muscular forearm around Malik's neck. Bolan twisted his body outward and dropped to one knee, bringing the base of his adversary's neck against his shoulder blade. The snapping of vertebrae resounded through the high-ceilinged interior of the mosque as Bolan ended the fight with the technique.

Bolan could feel Malik's body stiffen and then go slack as he release his hold and allowed the body to land on the dusty, earthen floor that had once been decorated with the craftsmanship of a hundred artisans. Malik made a few gasping noises and then lay still. At long last, the Executioner had put an end to the Egyptian's business of financing terror.

CHAPTER TWENTY-SIX

"How long?" Bolan asked Julian as Grimaldi put the chopper on final approach for the CIA's secret desert hangar.

"Fifteen minutes," she said. She didn't take her eyes from the screen of her laptop as she continued, "Twenty, at the outside."

The Executioner nodded. That wouldn't give them much time to prepare, but it would be enough. "You're sure you can control this thing."

"Once it gets into range, I can use my pass codes to hack into the security systems and remotely order it to do just about anything I want, including land, shut down or even self-destruct."

"We're not there quite yet," Bolan replied. "If I had my choice, I'd like to take the thing intact."

"I thought you were more concerned about destroying it, Cooper. What changed your mind?"

"Nothing," Bolan replied flatly. "And if I have a

choice between destroying your beloved machine or letting it fall into enemy hands, I'll choose the first option. But if you really think you can get this thing under your control, I'd prefer to exploit its abilities. The only thing that remains is how you plan to keep Downing from doing the exact same thing you can do."

"Simple," she said with a grin and a wink. "Change the codes and digital signatures."

It made sense to Bolan, what little he understood of it. And while the warrior would never have admitted it openly his attitude had softened toward Julian. She was still as sarcastic as always, but the sarcasm she kept on the surface purposefully. Something in her past had obviously cut her deeply, and she wasn't about to let it happen again. And that was something Bolan could appreciate. He knew the feeling all too well.

The chopper touched down and three weary sojourners unloaded their equipment. Julian began to funnel it inside the camouflaged hangar while Bolan assisted Grimaldi with rolling the chopper into the hangar on portable wheel-sets. Once inside, the Stony Man pilot sealed the outer opening and effectively concealed their makeshift base of operations from outside observers.

The threesome congregated in the kitchen to put the finishing touches on their plan. Actually the Executioner had been comforted by the fact Julian could actually hack into the systems aboard the *Hadesfire* and control it remotely. It was when she'd told him of this that Bolan had come up with the idea to bring the enemy to them. They would fly right into the trap and the Executioner would be ready.

"You have any idea who might be flying this thing?" Grimaldi asked Julian.

"There are maybe a handful actually qualified to do so, and about half again that many intelligent enough to control it," she said. "I know Downing can fly it, as well as Alek. I'm not sure of the others. I wasn't privy to that kind of information."

"If we can get control of it, do you think you can instruct Jack on how to fly it?" Bolan asked.

She laughed. "Are you kidding? This guy's a natural."

"Aw, golly gee whiz and shucks," Grimaldi cracked.

"Don't let it go to your head," Bolan chided, but he did so with a grin. "What about the crew? You said it can hold fifteen?"

"Give or take, depending on the equipment. But I don't think there's that many on board this one."

"Why not?" Grimaldi said.

"Because she wouldn't be able to make her current speed if she were fully loaded."

"So I'm back to my original quandary," Bolan said. "Assuming we take the thing in one piece, can we use it to destroy the other one?"

"Most certainly," she said. "Although you must understand I can't make any guarantees. Peter was a first-rate physicist and aeronautical engineer, not to mention his savvy for maximizing the effect of military weapons."

"You think one might be superior to the other," Grimaldi concluded.

"Yes, I would think we have to consider that a distinct possibility. Look, I never saw any other plans for the *Hadesfire* outside of the technical schematics I worked from, along with some computer-generated images that Downing told me had come from Peter. To the best of my knowledge, they are equal in every way. I just can't give you a total guarantee."

"We'll take what we can get then," Bolan replied.

There was a rap at the door, then one of the CIA operatives who monitored the security of the hangar stepped through the doorway. "Sorry to interrupt you guys, but I was just wondering if you were expecting any company."

"No," Bolan replied. "Why?"

"Well, we've detected about a half dozen heat signatures headed this way. They're approaching in almost tactical fashion. Looks like maybe a breach or hit of some kind."

"Who the hell could have found us here?" Grimaldi asked.

"And why?" Julian added in afterthought.

"Well, unless somebody here ordered a pizza," Bolan said, "we could have some trouble. You two stay here. I'll take care of this."

The Executioner grabbed his combat harness from a nearby rack and shrugged into the shoulder straps. He double-checked the action on the Beretta Model 96, and then grabbed the Walther MP-K and headed for the door. "If I'm not back in ten minutes, Jack, you two proceed on mission."

"Sure," Grimaldi said. "Just make sure you *come* back."

The Executioner didn't reply.

BOLAN CHECKED the luminescent hands of his watch and then donned the night-vision goggles the CIA security analyst had loaned him.

Only seven minutes remained before the *Hadesfire* would touch down just a few yards from where he stood. Seven minutes to identify the five intruders, neutralize them if they posed a threat, and get back in time to handle whatever trouble might be waiting aboard the *Hadesfire*. That meant less than a minute per man. That certainly ruled out any time for useful interrogation.

The Executioner didn't really need to ascertain if the newcomers were a threat; he could already surmise they probably were. Very few people were privy to locations of CIA operations like this one. Mostly it was members of the intelligence community—high-ranking members to be sure. That would include someone like Downing, who had obviously decided to send his goons for one last try.

Mack Bolan planned to give them a reception they wouldn't soon forget. He spotted the first approaching figure as it topped a hill. Bolan went prone and crawled to concealment behind a two-foot-high cactus. As the man got closer, Bolan could see he was also wearing night-vision goggles. The Executioner reached into a concealed pocket of his blacksuit and withdrew a laser penlight he kept stashed for just such occasions. Lasers were murder on eyes using NVDs. Bolan took careful aim, waited until his target was almost close enough to touch him, and then shone the beam directly at the centerpiece. The man's hands went wildly into the air as the bright flash from the laser threatened to blind him permanently. The man reached to his head and ripped the NVDs from his face.

Bolan was on him in a heartbeat. The soldier grabbed the intruder by the throat with his left hand, stuck his left leg behind him and shoved back and then around. The move knocked the guy off his feet and he landed on his back with a grunt as the air erupted from his lungs. Bolan quieted him forever with a crushing punch to the throat. He relieved the man of his weapons and proceeded to the next target.

Bolan spotted the next intruder as he approached from the south end of the hangar. He waited until the man had moved past his cover position behind a craggy stand of rocks, then took him from behind. The soldier drove the blade of his Ka-bar fighting knife into the man's kidney while clamping a viselike grip over his mouth and jaw and hyper-flexing the neck to one side. The man slumped to the ground without a sound.

Bolan checked the time. That made two down in just over two minutes. He'd have to move more quickly if he expected to be on time for the grand entrance of Downing's machine. The Executioner soon found another pair of attackers as they crawled toward the hangar. He grabbed the closer one by the foot, forcing the man to look backward. Bolan continued lifting the foot, bending it at the knee and pinning it there with his weight. The maneuver prevented the man from doing much of anything, immobilizing him long enough for Bolan to drive one of his boots into his opponent's crotch. Before the guy could utter more than a moan Bolan fell against the leg with all his weight and drove the Ka-bar into the man's chest, sinking it to the hilt. The Executioner realized as he rose that the man's counterpart hadn't heard the disturbance.

Bolan dropped to the sand and crawled until he got parallel to his next opponent. He whipped out the Model 96, pointed it at the man's head point-blank, and squeezed the trigger. The report cracked through the night air like a whip, and the man's head exploded.

The sudden shot generated the desired effect by flushing Bolan's final target. The man ran toward his position. It wasn't until the man got close that he realized his critical mistake, but by that time Bolan had the Model 96 leveled. The soldier put two shots through the man's chest. The guy's body stiffened just slightly before it collapsed to the sand.

Bolan waited another minute to make sure the CIA guys hadn't miscounted. A soldier didn't survive long by taking such things for granted, and as it stood he had a little time to spare. The Executioner had regained his feet by the time he heard it, approaching on a direct course for the hangar, or at least as near as he could tell. He searched the star-peppered skies but he didn't see a thing. And yet the whine-hiss continued to grow in strength and intensity. It was nearly on top of Bolan before he could actually make out its distinctive markings.

The *Hadesfire* had arrived right on schedule, and in very good condition Julian had promised it would. Bolan found himself at almost a loss for words. She'd actually done it; she had actually brought that machine under her control and in one piece. She really was some kind of lady, and Bolan found himself admiring her more by the minute.

The Executioner raced toward the dark bird, the Beretta Model 96 in one hand the MP-K in another. It was time to make his contributions as prime member on the welcoming committee. Whoever was aboard that ominous bird was about to get a taste of the Bolan blitz.

AT FIRST, ALEK STEZHNYA couldn't be sure what was happening. One moment he was in complete control of the craft and the next thing he knew none of the controls responded to his commands. The computer systems aboard the *Hadesfire* were complex, at best, but suddenly the entire thing acted like it had gone haywire. It simply had a mind of its own. If Stezhnya told it to climb it would instead lose altitude, apparently oblivious to his presence.

"If it were me, I'd take a hammer to the thing," Kofi Jamo said.

Stezhnya fired an angry look in Jamo's direction but then just as quickly he dismissed his irritation. There was no point in taking his frustrations out on the best soldier he had. Jamo had been the only survivor of the original group in Atlanta. That was part of why this mission to find Cooper was so important to him. It wasn't just Cooper's meddling in the affairs of Downing or the Apparatus, neither was it the fact that he'd taken Crystal forcefully from them. Sure, those things left him angry, but not nearly as much as when he thought about how Cooper had gunned down Tufino, Prichard, and Galeton in cold blood. He *had* to have killed them blindly because Stezhnya wouldn't believe for a second Cooper was skilled enough to take all of them clean.

"We can't bust up the controls," Stezhnya told his colleague. "We damage this thing and Downing will have our asses, not to mention we risk stranding ourselves in the godforsaken pit, and I for one don't have much desire to let my flesh rot in the middle of the Egyptian desert. The Oman interior's bad enough."

So Stezhnya, Jamo and the two other troops accompanying them could only stand by and watch helplessly as the *Hadesfire* continued to lose altitude until it finally settled gently on solid ground. Well, whoever had control of the craft at least wasn't interested in killing them or crashing it. And there was only one person Stezhnya could think of that would take loving care of such a deadly and advance war machine as this one. Its chief architect: Crystal Julian.

Stezhnya jumped to his feet and started to turn when Jamo stopped him short by grabbing his arm and pointing out the window. A shadowy form approached the craft at a full sprint, and Stezhnya could see a second shape following. Stezhnya didn't need to be a clairvoyant to see what was coming. They were setting him up for an ambush. Well, they might have been able to control the *Hadesfire*, even land it, but it would take a bit more than that to get to them. They would have to cut through pretty thick homogenous armor or blow the hatch, neither of which would prove easy.

Stezhnya moved forward to the cockpit controls to see if any of the onboard weapons were active, but the entire panel went dark before he could even check a battery level. That meant all systems were now inert, including the security hatch. Then again, that wasn't just controlled by the computer system. It also had a manual fail-safe, and Stezhnya planned to make sure nobody could get inside. He barely got the thought firmly planted in his head when he heard a familiar hiss and a moment later the sound of the hatch opening automatically, as if some unseen force had simply opened it.

"We've been boarded!" Stezhnya shouted, but it didn't do him any good.

The grim visage and dark hair of the first man aboard was only secondarily imposing to the man's height and muscular build, both obvious attributes against the stark blacksuit he wore. Weapons of war dangled from the various belts and harnesses he wore over the skintight suit. He stood there for less than a moment as their eyes locked, and in that moment Stezhnya thought he'd looked into the face of some avenging angel.

And for the first time in more years than he could count, Alek Stezhnya experienced fear.

Stezhnya knew, without any question that he was looking at Matt Cooper. He was looking upon the man who had taken so much from him. He could feel his anger build, babbling like a springtime brook as it spilled over rocks and tree branches and other natural obstacles in its path. The most important thing this man had taken from Stezhnya was his pride and dignity. And as far as he was concerned, this was the moment he would get it back.

Even as he watched Jamo become the first to fall

under the assault, Stezhnya reached down and drew his side arm. He wouldn't go without a fight. Cooper had to understand that his luck wouldn't hold out forever. Stezhnya raised his pistol and triggered one round after another, hopeful his bullets would find their mark.

Alek Stezhnya experienced just a brief moment of pain, but then the pain stopped and it seemed as if the entire world had closed around his body to leave him with the sensation he was walking through a tunnel. And at the end of the tunnel was light. But as Stezhnya drew nearer to it, he realized the light didn't represent the peace he had sought. Instead, it became quite apparent that all he'd done was trade one hell for another.

CHAPTER TWENTY-SEVEN

Crystal Julian preened under Bolan's acknowledgment of her skill in taking the *Hadesfire*.

The Executioner let her bask in the glory while he occupied his mind with more important matters. She'd estimated their flight time to the Oman Desert at just under four hours, which gave Bolan a chance to grab a couple hours of overdue sleep. With that under his belt, Bolan began planning his assault against Garrett Downing. He used Julian more as a sounding board than anything else, especially since Grimaldi had plenty to keep his hands full at the moment, and it was only during one point when she didn't answer his question that he looked up and found her sleeping.

It was just as well—he preferred to be left alone in these undertakings. After familiarizing himself with all the statistics and capabilities he could on the *Hadesfire*, Bolan began to map the satellite imagery from Stony Man against the data collected from the other prototype's signal. With that information Bolan could estimate the size and approximate layout of Downing's makeshift quarters in the Oman interior.

Bolan had hoped, slim though it was, that perhaps one of those aboard the *Hadesfire* would surrender. But they resisted him all the way and that left him with no information about what he was actually walking into. Julian had confirmed Stezhnya was one of the dead.

So this would be one of those times where he'd have to play it by ear and see where the numbers fell. For now, he could go off what he'd logically concluded based on the limited intelligence. Julian had said the estimated strength of the Apparatus was about one hundred men, give or take. He had eradicated more than half their numbers, and that didn't even account for how many of them were field units. Their numbers wouldn't likely prove much of a problem, especially with Grimaldi at the stick of the *Hadesfire.* They had agreed that during Bolan's campaign Grimaldi would run interference against any other craft attempting to escape, or in the event they were hiding some heavy armor or artillery and couldn't wait to use it.

With the air cover and enemy troop strength logistics behind him, Bolan turned to Garrett Downing. Where had the guy gone so wrong? Here was a man who had served his country's intelligence and national security communities for more than fifty years, and then one day found himself on the other side of the law. Downing was deluded, to be sure. There was no way a normal personal of his intelligence would have believed the U.S. government was prepared to sanction global vigilantism against the terrorist network. Somehow, that wasn't a reality Downing could perceive. The guy was intelligent, sure, but he was living in his own world and that made him a severe liability to American security.

It seemed almost a waste to Bolan, since deep down he knew they weren't all that dissimilar. Downing just wanted peace and justice for a secure America; he wanted to be free from the threat of terrorism. Those were the exact same things Bolan wanted; in fact, the very things he put his life on the line for every day. It wasn't in his nature to stand idly by and ignore the problems of the world. In many respects, that's why Bolan had chosen his lifestyle and called it his sworn duty. But Downing had lost sight of the true goal: to protect the innocent. And now it was more important than ever he stop a sadly twisted and deluded man from inflicting any worse damage on the innocent. Then again, Bolan didn't figure he'd be walking among any of the innocent this time around. No, this was strictly a hard mission. He'd get in, do the job, and get out before attracting the attention of the Oman authorities.

It was time to start returning some of that friendly fire.

GRIMALDI BROUGHT the *Hadesfire* in as low as he could, and touched down less than twenty meters from the entrance to Downing's Oman base of operations.

They had sent a prearranged signal to Downing, hoping they would assume it was Stezhnya on the return. Their hunch proved right. Only a couple of sentries stood between Bolan and the makeshift operations center, and the soldier took them both out with clean head shots courtesy of the Beretta Model 96.

The entrance to the base was anything but glamorous, and Bolan immediately realized it was by design. It wasn't as if they were going to put out neon signs and have a recruitment drive. Bolan had one Army buddy that called that kind of setup "security by ignorance." Most people weren't observant enough to recognize something quite often right in front of their noses, and especially in war time the enemy could lose or gain an advantage over such a seemingly trivial thing. Bolan wasn't one of them.

The Executioner met resistance as he came around the corner, two men obviously on a break and about as enthused about their accommodations as they were the food they'd been served. Looks of horror splashed across their faces and they tried to reach for their weapons, but their timing wasn't fast enough to save them from the battle-hardened readiness of their opponent. Bolan leveled the muzzle of his Walther submachine gun and blew both Apparatus sentries away.

Bolan heard shouts coming from deeper inside the rocky caves. He reached to his webbing and extracted his last grenade as the shouting and footfalls drew closer. It sounded like a quartet of men approaching.

The soldier yanked the pin on the frag grenade and let it cook off for a couple of seconds, then tossed the bomb underhand around the corner. He dropped to one knee, opened his mouth and rode the shock wave of an explosion. The cavern walls vibrated, but as the initial fallout of the blast subsided Bolan felt the rock at his back continue to pulse. And he knew he'd triggered a cave-in!

The Executioner clutched his subgun tightly as he regained his feet and sprinted for the nondescript entrance. He could hear footfalls behind him, which told him a few of the enemy gunners were savvy enough to know what was occurring. It seemed to Bolan at first that maybe he was mistaken, but he quickly drove the idea from his mind. There was no mistake. He would listen to his intuition. As he reached the summit of the rise and burst from the cave, he was glad he had. The shock wave was actually audible from where he stood.

Bolan could hear the tremors as they began to do their damage to the operations center. He whirled with a nod of satisfaction. If the Apparatus gunners were smart, they would all get out of there. There wasn't any point in going on—the Executioner had done his job. All that remained was apprehending Garrett Downing.

The Executioner's earpiece crackled. "Sarge, you better get back here. The engines were just fired on the other *Hadesfire*."

Bolan nodded grimly and then turned and sprinted for their craft. Downing was trying to flee, and whatever it cost, the Executioner had to make sure that didn't happen. They couldn't let someone like Downing get away. He would just keeping returning with some new plot or a new army of mercenary killers, and he would continue with the bloodletting. The time had come to bring Downing to his knees once and for all.

GARRETT DOWNING WASN'T sure where it had all gone wrong, but he did know that it had gone wrong.

His men were scrambling in every direction, and a couple even pounded on the exterior of the hull as he fired the engines on the *Hadesfire*. They were fools if they thought he was going to risk saving his own neck to open up his prized possession. He would get much better speed and range without passengers. The cowards should have been able to counter against Cooper instead of letting it come to this.

When he was at full power, Downing keyed a signal to clear the runway for launch. He watched as the caverns seemed to melt away, and then the lift brought him through the reinforced base frame of the launch pad and at last to the surface. The *Hadesfire* took off like any aircraft except that it had a hover capability very similar to a Harrier jet's. In short order, Downing had the engines to full power. He felt the *Hadesfire* rise, slowly leaving the ground as the engines lifted him away from the sand and broken rock of the desert. When he reached sufficient height, he rotated the engines and shot into the early morning sky.

Daylight had just barely broken on the horizon, and the predawn light of the morning cast pale tinges of pink and yellow across the eastern horizon. It was a good day to die for one's beliefs. Downing had sacrificed more for his country than anyone had a right to ask of a man, and she had betrayed his loyalty to serve her own purposes. When he needed her most, America had let him down. Downing couldn't understand it; he sure as hell would *not* accept it. He'd been true to his ideals and values and he planned to remain that way.

An alarm began hooting through the cabin, and Downing noted a second blip on the radar screen. It was a signal identical to his, and Downing now realized what had transpired. His insurance plan had failed him, too. He knew it wasn't Stezhnya piloting the other *Hadesfire*, and nobody alive at the base he'd left behind knew how to pilot such a craft. There was only one explanation: Matt Cooper.

So Cooper had managed to thwart his plans to kill Stezhnya and get his rightful property back, his machine and the woman who created it. Downing decided to have a little fun with his pursuers. The two craft were identical in every way except that Hagen had perfected rear-firing weapons in this one, an effective new tool that could either blow a tailing craft out of the sky, or act as an effective countermeasure against missiles. Downing had never considered this before, though. The two greatest vessels on Earth were about to go toe to toe. And Downing would go down in history as a part of it. Maybe his plans were salvageable.

Downing keyed up the transmitter that would give him private channel access to the other *Hadesfire*.

"Attention pursuers…" he began.

"…ATTENTION!"

Downing's voice came clearly through the headsets worn by the all three crew members aboard the *Hadesfire*.

"Downing," Julian whispered.

"You are guilty of espionage, high treason and theft of government property," Downing said. "You are ordered to land your craft immediately and surrender your weapons, or I will be forced to shoot you down."

"Is he kidding me?" Grimaldi said, his voice rising with sheer disbelief. "This guy couldn't fly his way out of a wet paper bag with a machete in his hand."

"Well," Julian replied, "that's not exactly true."

"You want to try that again?" Grimaldi asked.

"She's right," Bolan said. "Downing served as a pilot in the Air National Guard. He flew quite a number of covert missions for them, some so secret it's possible even we don't know about them."

"Just another case of left hand doesn't know what the right hand's doing, Sarge," Grimaldi replied. "That's no great surprise. I just wish someone had told me before now."

"What, you don't like surprises?" Julian asked.

It was the first time Bolan could remember hearing nothing more than what sounded like good-natured kidding in her tone. She was entirely absent of her usual sarcasm.

"Not those kind," Grimaldi retorted.

"In either case, we have a twofold advantage," Bolan pointed out. "We have Jack *and* we have the designer of this thing on board. Downing's probably operating that thing on his own and he isn't nearly as familiar with its systems."

"I see," Downing's voice said over the speakers, "that you're not going to heed my warnings. That's too bad because I don't plan on issuing it twice. You can consider yourself at risk for instant destruction." There was a pause, then, "Ah, I see you're trying to hack into my systems and shut them down. Too bad, I have already altered them with a 164-bit encryption algorithm. You'll never be able to crack it."

Bolan looked at Julian who nodded her confirmation. The Executioner turned his attention to Grimaldi. "Well, Jack, looks like it's up to you. Think you can work your magic with this thing?"

"Strap yourselves in," Grimaldi replied with a whoop. "We are going to the show!"

The pilot whipped the craft onto its side, almost knocking Bolan from his chair. He had to appreciate the crack pilot's enthusiasm. He was at the stick of the most advanced multipurpose vehicle ever built, and he had its designer along on his maiden voyage. There was something to be said for the inventions of humankind, and this was a moment the Executioner wouldn't soon forget. Mostly that's because of how long it would take his stomach to settle with Grimaldi's various gyrations and aerial acrobats.

The pilot flipped a switch and the targeting system came on. The heads-up-display showed the other *Hadesfire* in perfect silhouette. Its squared, illuminated numbers in green, red and blue across the front visor looked like something out of a science-fiction movie.

"This is definitely state-of-the-art," Grimaldi told his passengers.

"Do you think you can beat Downing?" Julian asked, and when she saw the look Bolan gave her she added quickly, "I had to ask."

"Lady, this is going to be like taking candy from a baby. I've got tone!"

The soft warble went through their headsets and Grimaldi pressed a button on his console. There wasn't even so much as a shudder from the ship as the first missile was away. The missile tone continued, and beneath it a second tone that increased in frequency as it moved closer and closer to the target. When that second tone was nearly one steady pulse, it suddenly ceased and was followed by a brilliant flash of light.

"Got him!"

"Nice shooting, Jack," Bolan said.

"No, you didn't," Julian cut in. "Look at your screen."

The ship hadn't, in fact, been destroyed. Grimaldi double-checked the instruments and a bit of increased nervousness showed in his body language.

"I'll be damned, Peter," Julian muttered under her breath. "You did it. CPFT."

"C-P *what?*" Grimaldi asked. "Something else you forget to tell me?"

Julian shook herself from her moment of fascination and said, "CPFT. It stands for Countermeasures Paradox Fail-safe Theory. I know, Cooper, in English. Look, it's the idea that the plans of every new invention might fall into the wrong hands. It was a concept Peter developed in all of his work for military weapons. He felt there were some things you didn't write down about a new weapon, such as a plane or a ship. Peter believed those things should be the countermeasures of the weapon."

Bolan nodded. "That way if the enemy designs a weapon of equal abilities, you still have the advantage over them. Makes good sense."

"He *was* a genius."

"That's all fine," Grimaldi said, "but what do we do now?"

"We countermeasure the countermeasures," Julian announced. "Get a lock on him again, but then when you have it, reach to the panel near your right elbow and slide that panel aside." When he'd done so, Julian said, "See that yellow switch? Flip it to the down position. Okay now…take your shot."

Grimaldi brought the *Hadesfire* into a shallow arc and fired the forward GAU-12/U guns. Rounds burned through the air, coming within just a few yards of the ship. Grimaldi aligned his sights once more and waited until he had tone lock. He steadied the *Hadesfire*, intending to get the shot right this time, and then trigger the second missile. The ATA-1700 Newsome missile raced to its target and just as it reached the aircraft there was another explosion much like the first.

Bolan started to get a sinking feeling then heard Julian's voice, soft and steady, in his ears. "Wait."

Two seconds later there was a major explosion that lit up the early morning sky. Flaming wreckage expanded and dispersed and then began to rain toward the ground like the remnants of a hundred million fireworks set off at one time. Bolan and Grimaldi sat in complete silence, unable to put into words their fascination by what they had just witnessed.

It was Grimaldi who finally broke the silence. "Now *that's* what I call a countermeasure."

"We aim to please," Julian said with a laugh.

"Your country owes you," Bolan told her. "And I definitely owe you."

"Well, then, maybe I'll have to look you up one day and collect."

And maybe she would. Yeah.

NEUTRON FORCE

The ultimate stealth weapon is in the hands
of an unknown enemy...

A grim presidential directive comes down to
Stony Man: an unknown entity is in possession of
one of the deadliest weapons known to man, and the
death toll across the globe is mounting. It's a silent
murdering machine, killing with no heat, no noise,
no radiation—just silent, invisible slaughter from
ultrafast, subatomic particles. With no nation able
to defend against it, Stony Man's only option is to
destroy it. But first, they must find it....

STONY® MAN

*Available
June 2007
wherever
you buy books.*

James Axler
Outlanders®

SKULL THRONE

RADIANT EVIL

Buried deep in the Mayan jungle amidst a civilization of lost survivors and emissaries of the dead, lies a relic that hides secrets to the prize— planet Earth. In sinister hands, it guarantees complete and absolute power. Kane and the rebels have just one chance to stop a rogue overlord from seizing glory, but must face an old enemy to stop him.

Available May 2007, wherever you buy books.